The Duke Gets Even

A splash snapped him out of his dark thoughts. Saint's teeth, she was beautiful. In truth, he'd never seen a more captivating woman. The sight of her slim limbs, high breasts and incredible hair wound through him like vines, expanding and twisting, strangling him until he had no choice but to dive under the cool water.

When he resurfaced, she was there, directly behind him.

Long arms twined around his neck and she wrapped her legs around his hips. Bare flesh pressed soft and cool against his back. "About time you arrived," her husky voice said in his ear, like a whisper of silk over his soul.

He shivered. The right thing to do would be to let her go. To put his hands up and acknowledge the mistake. His title as a gentleman demanded it.

But he was tired of always doing the right thing.

Also by Joanna Shupe

The Duke Gets Even

The Fifth Avenue Rebels

JOANNA SHUPE

AVONBOOKS

An Imprint of HarperCollinsPublishers

THE DUKE GETS EVEN. Copyright © 2023 by Joanna Shupe. All rights reserved. Printed in the United States of America. No part of this book may be used or reproduced in any manner whatsoever without written permission except in the case of brief quotations embodied in critical articles and reviews. For information, address HarperCollins Publishers, 195 Broadway, New York, NY 10007.

First Avon Books mass market printing: January 2023

Print Edition ISBN: 978-0-06-304507-1
Digital Edition ISBN: 978-0-06-304409-8

Cover design by Guido Caroti
Cover illustration by Anna Kmet

Avon, Avon & logo, and Avon Books & logo are registered trademarks of HarperCollins Publishers in the United States of America and other countries.

HarperCollins is a registered trademark of HarperCollins Publishers in the United States of America and other countries.

FIRST EDITION

23 24 25 26 27 BVGM 10 9 8 7 6 5 4 3 2 1

For my two girls, Sally and Claire,
because they keep bugging me
to dedicate another book to them.
You're welcome.

Chapter One

❦

"The sea, once it casts its spell, holds one in its net of wonder forever."
—*Jacques-Yves Cousteau*

Off the coast of Newport, Rhode Island
June 1895

Mermaids existed.

At least Andrew Talbot, the eighth Duke of Lockwood, was fairly certain of it. At the moment a creature with long limbs and red hair was most definitely splashing in the frothy waves near the beach. If not a mermaid then a naiad, perhaps.

Though he hated the ocean, he'd come out after dark to swim in the chilly, murky water of the Atlantic, his body requiring the bloody exercise. He hadn't expected to see anyone else. Who was out frolicking at this time of night, if not a mythical creature?

Bare legs flashed in the surf. A shapely arm followed. He continued to tread water, unable to look away. Then a form rose up in the foam, and long red hair flipped backward. A woman. A *naked* woman. He was entranced.

As if the moon pulled him toward her, he soon found himself in the surf, too. The water reached his waist, and he watched her tumble and roll in the waves, like a small child who'd been cooped up all day and finally had a taste of freedom.

What did it feel like, such freedom?

Lockwood had never experienced it, not truly. His life had been shaped and molded since birth. He was a line drawn on a family tree to future generations of the same. The weight of it all fell on his shoulders—the crumbling estates, the empty bank accounts, the judgment of long-dead ancestors—and there were days when he feared for his sanity. Not a soul would remember him, unless he was the one who failed.

A terrible legacy, that.

A splash snapped him out of his dark thoughts. Saint's teeth, she was beautiful. In truth, he'd never seen a more captivating woman. The sight of her slim limbs, high breasts and incredible hair wound through him like vines, expanding and twisting, strangling him until he had no choice but to dive under the cool water.

When he resurfaced, she was there, directly behind him.

Long arms twined around his neck and she wrapped her legs around his hips. Bare flesh pressed soft and cool against his back. "About time you arrived," her husky voice said in his ear, like a whisper of silk over his soul.

He shivered. The right thing to do would be to let her go. To put his hands up and acknowledge the mistake. His title as a gentleman demanded it.

But he was tired of always doing the right thing.

Couldn't he act instead of think? Feel for once instead of strategize?

Heavy breasts rubbed on his shoulder blades, and despite the cold water his cock responded, thickening and rising against her calf. His problematic heart thumped behind his ribs, the beat echoing between his legs. He couldn't seem to move or speak. Frozen by sensation.

Perhaps a shark would swim by and eat him. All his problems would be solved, then.

Sadly, his third cousin would inherit the title. Tooter, as he preferred to be called, was a complete nincompoop. Lockwood would wrestle the bloody shark with his bare hands to prevent that travesty from coming to pass.

"I thought you had forgotten about me," she said, nibbling his earlobe.

Say something. Tell her she's mistaken you for someone else.

Christ, she felt good.

When her bare quim met his lower back, his mouth went dry, and he began contemplating the practicalities of naked depravity on a beach. Better if she remained on her hands and knees so that no one would find sand in unfortunate places . . .

Now is the time to speak, before this goes too far.

Keeping his hands at his sides, he cleared his

throat. "Madam, I believe you have mistaken me for someone else." He winced. Even to his own ears, he sounded stuffy and ridiculous.

She eased back to study him, her expression solemn. "Turn to your right. I cannot see your face."

He moved as instructed—and she gasped, releasing him as if he were engulfed in flames. "Damn and hell! Why did you not say something?"

He could see her then, but he almost wished he hadn't. No matter what else happened in his lifetime, he would never forget this face.

She was simply stunning. Flawless skin and delicate features, with green eyes that glittered nearly gold in the moonlight. Her lips were full and lush, with a small bow in the center of the top one, and the lines surrounding her mouth meant she smiled a lot. "I couldn't be certain you were real."

"What?" She bent her knees to hide her nakedness in the dark water. "Are you some sort of masher?"

"I beg your pardon, but you accosted me. I was swimming and minding my own business when you wrapped around me like a limpet."

She splashed him with her hand. "I thought you were someone else."

"Obviously."

Her gaze traveled over his chest and shoulders encased in the thin bathing costume. He resisted the urge to flex his muscles. For some inane reason he wanted her to like what she saw. "You must swim a lot," she finally said.

"I do." He hated every second of it, but he hadn't a choice. Like so many other things in his life.

"Why this late at night, though? What if you drowned?"

That would be Tooter's good fortune, then. "I don't sleep well. I also prefer the quiet."

"Yes, I understand that. It's peaceful out here at this time, before high tide rushes in."

"The perfect time for midnight trysts," he teased.

"Stop. I feel ridiculous enough as it is. Incidentally, I'm sorry for throwing myself at you."

"I didn't mind."

"I suppose most men don't mind when a naked woman swims up and clings to his very fit body."

Very fit? "I cannot speak for most men, only me, and I liked it. A lot."

"I noticed." She smirked. "The water must not be all that cold."

He choked on a laugh. "My apologies. I wish I could control it, but alas."

"I'm quite fond of the organ myself. It's temperamental but has a mind of its own. Sort of like a woman."

"I like that comparison."

"Well, fair warning, I can make it because I am a woman. You cannot."

He moved to his knees, so their faces were on a more even level. "Is that how it works?"

"Yes. I love women and we have to band together as much as we can. Men are good for only one thing."

"Midnight trysts?"

She grinned, showing him even, white teeth. "Precisely." Then her grin fell as her gaze darted to the cliffs. "Though I suppose I've been stood up tonight."

"My good fortune, then."

"Don't get ahead of yourself, Poseidon. I don't even know your name, only that you're English."

Poseidon? He felt his lips twitch. In any other circumstance, he would introduce himself. Yet, he hesitated. The urge to remain anonymous with her, to forgo any and all reminders of his life on dry land, won out. Which meant he could not ask her name, either.

He hooked a thumb in the direction of the open water. "Perhaps I fell over from one of Her Majesty's ships out there and swam to shore."

"With that upper-crust accent?"

"I might be an officer."

"That would explain the lack of scurvy."

He smiled. He wasn't normally one to banter with women, but this was proving enjoyable. Indeed, when in recent memory had he felt this light, this happy? She was quick-witted and clearly no innocent, so a servant from one of the houses? Or perhaps the daughter of a local shopkeeper. "Would you believe I've been months at sea with other men, no contact from a woman in all that time?" It was partially true, anyway. He'd given up his mistress a year ago, unable to afford anything for himself beyond a basic necessity.

"I might believe it, based on—oh, shit!" She threw herself at him, but not in lust. Her eyes were wide with terror.

He caught her and stood up, cradling her close

and definitely not thinking about her nudity. "What is it? Is something wrong?"

"Something bumped against my leg. Something big. And do not tell me it was a plant because this was not a plant." She tried to climb up his body, doing all she could to lift her legs out of the water.

"There is nothing in this water but harmless fish and turtles," he said, rubbing his hand down her back soothingly. "Furthermore, I am a much bigger target. If something decided to take a bite out of one of us, it would definitely be me."

"You can't say for certain." She stared down at the water as if expecting a shark to jump up and attack her.

"I am absolutely confident you will not die out here. How about that?"

"You're laughing at me, but I don't care. I might look foolish, but I'll still be alive."

"You don't look foolish," he said with all due seriousness. "Indeed, you are the most beautiful creature I've ever seen."

She leaned to see his face. It occurred then that he had an armful of naked, wet and lush woman, one who wasn't mistaking him for anyone else. One who didn't know he was a duke, but simply a man. When was the last time that had happened?

He tightened his hold slightly, wanting to protect her. Wanting to keep her close and warm, and drive away anything that dared to scare her. He didn't want to let her go.

When she trembled, he eased her back under the water but stayed close. They floated together, bobbing up and down in the gentle waves. Was it his imagination or had her breathing picked up? "Have we ever met before?" she asked. "I feel as though I know you."

"We have not been introduced. I definitely would have remembered a woman like you."

"A woman like me?" She stiffened and floated away, and he had to hurry to keep up. "Loud and brazen, I suppose. Scandalous." She drew out the word, as if she heard it quite a bit.

"Absolutely not. I was thinking clever and unafraid."

"Hmm. That is a very good answer, but I cannot tell if you're genuine or not."

He slowly moved in closer, back to where they'd been a moment ago. "Why would I lie? We hardly know each other. There are no repercussions if I insult you."

She bobbed on the surface, letting him hold her hand, maintaining their connection. "You, sir, are very good for my confidence. Pray, continue."

"More compliments, then? Let's see, you are gorgeous, but you likely know that. You curse like a sailor, which I find endearing. You have excellent taste in organs and possess the most remarkable laugh."

Moonlight sparkled across the surface of the water, illuminating her shocked expression. Then she dragged her fingertips along his collarbone. "Beauty, charm *and* brains. The female population must absolutely adore you."

"I could say the same about you and the male population."

"I do my best. I plan on sampling as many of them as possible before I'm done, after all."

"Before you marry, you mean."

"No, before I die. I will never marry."

She said this so casually, but with a note of finality in her voice, and he couldn't help but say, "That's a bloody shame. You should belong to someone. A lucky man who worships the ground beneath your feet." Not him, unfortunately. The plans for his future had already been set. The ring was in his luggage, in fact.

"I'd rather not belong to anyone. Novel idea, I know, but I'd like to retain my name, my worldly possessions and my control over my body."

"When you put it that way, I suppose the only appeal is children and regular bed sport."

"Both of which do not require marriage."

"What of disease?"

"Shields."

He glanced around dramatically. "Have I traveled to the future, to a place where women have progressive ideas and independence?"

"Perhaps you are stuck in the past." She pulled her hand out of his and pushed off his stomach to swim away. Legs kicking, she dove beneath the water, then resurfaced and shook water off her face.

"I thought you were afraid of the water."

"Not with you here to protect me. Though I suppose you'll have to catch me first." She angled away from him and began swimming, water churning around her as she performed a very competent breaststroke.

She was no match for him, however.

Lockwood dove in, kept his face in the water and started a hand-over stroke. It required a flutter kick as his arms rolled up and through the water, like a windmill. Every few strokes he rolled to the side and took a breath.

In seconds, he caught her.

She laughed and fell into his arms like she'd always been there. "That is hardly fair. You swim like a god."

"I am a god, remember?"

"How could I forget?" She pressed close and wrapped her arms around his neck. He could feel her warm breath on his cheek. There was no one else around for miles, as far as he was concerned. The water was their safe haven, the moon their only witness.

It was magical, a world away from responsibilities and marriages.

"Are you married?" she asked. "I sincerely hope the answer is no, that your wife isn't staying at one of the cottages here."

"No wife. I am staying at the inn near the train station." Real life began tomorrow. This was fantasy, a few stolen moments in the water with a beautiful stranger. So he made the offer without stopping to think of all the ways it would complicate his plans. "Would you like to come back to my room?"

She sighed near his ear. "I can't. My absence would be noticed."

Disappointment burned in his throat, but at least she hadn't refused on the basis of being uninterested. "I see."

"It probably sounds silly but I've made a promise and must abide by it, even if it does ruin all my fun."

"And mine." He cupped her face and dragged his thumb over her jaw. They were drifting away from the beach and into deeper water, but he didn't care. He felt untethered by this woman, cast about from his moorings. Fitting they should make it literal, then. "This is quite probably wildly inappropriate," he whispered, "especially as you have already refused my offer, but I should very much like to kiss you right now."

"And here I was waiting for you to ask," she murmured and moved to gently place her mouth on his.

Oh, thank Christ. Relieved, he let her control the kiss, her lips soft and pliant as she explored him. It was a kiss full of curiosity and anticipation, a slow slide into the depths rather than tumbling in. He followed, content to let their breath mingle as the water rocked them into the deep. After a minute or two she shifted to wrap her arms and legs around him, and he held them above the surface, his body moving and straining to tread water as they continued to kiss.

Suddenly, she broke off and swam backward toward the shore. When she crooked her finger at him, he was lost. Diving, he grabbed her and towed her closer to dry land, just until he could stand on the sandy bottom. This time he captured her mouth in a brutal kiss. He held nothing back, letting her feel how much he wanted her, and she returned the kiss with abandon. When he flicked at her lips with his tongue, she opened and he thrust inside that warm haven. Their mouths and tongues worked in tandem, the lapping of water against their sides, and she held on, lightly digging her nails into his scalp.

"Harder," he said into her mouth, and her nails found purchase in his skin. The rush of pain made him feel alive, like he was sparkling inside, tiny crackles of energy and light in every vein. His balls were heavy and his cock throbbed. He bit her lip, sharing a bit of that dark energy, hoping she liked it even a fraction as much as he did.

She gasped and clutched him tighter.

Suddenly, he was ravenous, his mouth slanting over hers at a frenetic pace. She kept up, her hands pulling at him while little whimpers escaped her throat. He let his lips wander over her cheek, along her jaw. Down her neck and across her collarbone.

He wanted to eat her alive.

"Are you certain you won't come back to my room?" He panted onto her wet skin and tried to regain a bit of his reasoning ability. He should not be asking, considering his pending commitments, but the words tumbled out before he could hold them back. One night. That was all he needed. One night with this woman before he settled into responsibility.

"I can't. I could meet you there tomorrow afternoon, however."

"I'll have relocated by then. What about here on the beach?"

"What time?"

"Midnight. I swim every night when I can. Will you meet me?" His stomach clenched. He wasn't certain what he would do if she said no.

Looking up at him through her lashes, she

whispered, "Another midnight tryst. I can hardly wait."

Then his mysterious redheaded siren hurried up the rocks, where she stopped to collect her things before blending into the darkness. It had only been minutes but he already craved her again.

How was he going to survive the next twenty-four hours until he could have her?

Chapter Two

❦

The lemonade sparkled in Nellie's glass, bright and shiny, pure like the debutantes crowding the tent. She contemplated spiking the drink with something strong. Bourbon, maybe. How else to make it through the day with her sanity complete?

"Why are you frowning into your lemonade?" Maddie Webster, one of Nellie's only two friends, arrived at Nellie's side. "Has it offended you somehow?"

"Yes," Nellie said. "By being boring. Remind me why I'm here again?"

"Because I need you. I'm hosting this house party to help match Harrison with one of these debutantes. You're here to help keep things interesting."

"Interesting for whom, exactly? Because we all know Harrison is in love with you. This weekend is a waste of time."

"You know that isn't true—and I hope to marry the duke." Maddie moved away to talk to the other guests in a not-so-subtle ploy to avoid the conversation.

It was a waste of time. Everyone could see that Maddie wasn't meant to marry an English aristocrat. Nellie hadn't met the Duke of Lockwood, Maddie's matrimonial target for the past three months, but she knew the type. Stuffy and full of self-importance. Boring. Maddie deserved better.

Nellie's midnight friend certainly hadn't been boring. Even now, merely recalling the encounter had her tingling. The meeting in the ocean had been unexpected, fierce and—dared she say it?—romantic. Yes, the scandalous Nellie Young had allowed a man to sweep her away with sweet words and fiery kisses. In fact, the giddiness had stayed with her since she awoke.

You are the most beautiful creature I've ever seen.

She held the cool glass to her forehead and took a few deep breaths. Katherine Delafield, Nellie's other friend, sidled up. "Don't you dare claim a fever," Katie said. "You cannot abandon me today."

"This is a farce," Nellie muttered. "And it's too dashed hot for whatever Maddie has planned."

"My, someone is grumpy this morning. Were you up late with Robbie?"

Katie knew about Nellie's intended rendezvous with Robbie Chesterton, a nineteen-year-old polo player she'd flirted with two months ago. Thank God he hadn't shown up last night.

Her mystery man was leagues away from young men like Robbie, the kind who couldn't find a clitoris even with a detailed map. Poseidon, with his talented mouth and tongue, would assuredly know how to pleasure a woman the correct way. Meaning, orally.

"You have the weirdest look on your face right now," Katie said. "What are you thinking about?"

"Later." Nellie tipped her head toward Maddie, who was currently talking to Harrison near the refreshment table. "Has she said what's planned for this morning?"

"An egg hunt."

Nellie groaned. "My God. I must really love you both an awful lot to suffer through this nonsense."

Katie slipped her arm through Nellie's. "And we love you back, Eleanor Lucinda Young."

Nellie squeezed her friend closer, not about to let go just yet. "Besides, this party is a waste of time. She's going to marry Harrison."

"I don't know," Katie said. "Maddie's been chasing Lockwood all spring. She seems determined."

"Do we know if the duke returns her interest?" Shocking absolutely no one, Nellie's invitations to society events had long dried up, so she knew little to nothing about Maddie's intended beau.

"I think so. He's paid her quite a bit of attention, and they like all the same things. Sports and whatnot."

"Foxes and hounds and shooting, I suppose. How dreadful."

"I think more like golf and tennis." Katie drank her lemonade. "Croquet, that sort of thing. For some reason I recall he also swims."

That reminded Nellie of Poseidon, and she took a sip of her drink to moisten her suddenly dry mouth. Though he was English, Poseidon was no prig. He liked *pain*, after all. Had even asked for it. Nellie hadn't stopped to think why because it didn't matter.

People liked what they liked in the bedroom. She'd heard tales over the years, such as men who asked ladies to walk on their backs while wearing heeled boots. Or others who liked to play with feathers, whips and paddles. Ice and melted wax. So her English stranger liked a bite of pain. She did, too, sometimes. A well-timed swat on her bottom during intimacies was not unappreciated now and again. Live and let live, she always said.

The nape of Nellie's neck suddenly crawled, disapproval hanging in the air like stale perfume. Glancing toward the chaperone table, she noticed two of the older women whispering back and forth while casting gazes full of condemnation her way.

That's right. I am unmarried and have no chaperone. Get over it.

Nellie's father hadn't insisted on a chaperone in ages, not since Nellie's first season. He didn't like society any more than Nellie did, not after the Fifth Avenue matrons turned their backs on Nellie's Irish mother. Cornelius Young hadn't forgiven or forgotten the snub in all these years. And thank goodness, too, because his ambivalence for their rules allowed Nellie to do exactly as she pleased.

She turned away from the sour chaperones and came face-to-face with Kit Ward, another guest and friend of Maddie's. "Hello, Ward."

He eased between Katie and Nellie, as if trying to hide. "You two have the right idea. I think I'm better off over here."

"Were the heiresses eyeing you like a bowl of ice cream on a hot day?" Katie asked.

He grimaced. "Yes, if I'm being honest."

Nellie put a heap of fake sympathy into her voice. "Poor Kit. It must feel truly awful to be ogled like that. But who knows? Harrison may not be the only man who finds a wife here this weekend."

"Bite your tongue," he snapped, the horror in his voice making Katherine and Nellie chuckle. "And I'm not sure he's all that interested in these debutantes."

"I knew it!" Nellie pointed at Katie. "Harrison wants Maddie."

"Good afternoon," a clipped English voice said.

"Oh, my goodness, Your Grace!" Maddie exclaimed. "I had no idea you were coming. Welcome to Newport."

Everyone looked in the direction of Maddie's gaze. A tall, broad-chested man stood at the edge of the tent. He removed his hat and stepped in, giving Nellie a good gander at him.

A jolt of recognition rooted her to the spot. Those shoulders . . . that jaw. That thick mess of golden-brown hair, now tamed with oil. Bright blue eyes that pierced your soul, made you feel important and seen. She *knew* him. Had kissed him. Had clung to him and dug her fingernails into his scalp.

Jaysus, Mary and Joseph.

It was Poseidon, here at the house party.

Except he was now kissing Maddie's cheek, looking down at Nellie's friend as if she hung the moon. And she'd called him *Your Grace*.

What on earth?

"Oh, shit," Kit muttered.

Katie chuckled. "I hope Harrison is ready for some competition."

A sinking feeling came over Nellie, a portentous dread that had her bracing for bad news. "Wait, who is that man?"

"That is the Duke of Lockwood," Katie answered. "Maddie's would-be fiancé."

The information felt like a blow right to Nellie's heart. No, her stomach. She actually put a hand on it, hoping the eggs she'd ingested earlier wouldn't make a sudden reappearance.

Poseidon was the duke.

The duke was Poseidon.

No wonder he hadn't introduced himself.

Are you certain you won't come back to my room?

She had considered it—oh, how she'd considered it. And what a fool she'd been. The man was about to propose marriage to her best friend, for God's sake. How could Nellie live with herself knowing she'd shared a kiss with her best friend's husband? That she knew the size of his cock, even in cold water? That she knew he liked it when a woman dug her fingernails into his skin?

Dizzy, she put a hand out to steady herself using one of the tent poles. This was a disaster. She would have to tell Maddie, of course. It was the right thing to do. Unfortunately, this would leave Nellie with just one remaining friend, not two, because Maddie would never forgive her. How on earth was this fair?

And what the hell kind of man kissed strangers in the ocean when he was nearly engaged?

Before she could wrangle her emotions into some semblance of order, Kit said, "Look out. She's bringing him over here."

"Oh, shit," Nellie echoed.

THE RED-HAIRED MERMAID was here.

Except she was not a mermaid but one of Madeline Webster's friends, apparently. Lockwood could not believe his terrible luck. How had he erred this badly?

He was normally so careful. Encounters with strangers were a terrible idea, one he resolutely avoided. Except that red hair had drawn him in like a beacon, while her smile and wit charmed him into staying. Now he was being introduced to her as if they'd never met.

Maddie gestured. "And this is my best friend, Miss Young. Nellie, may I present the Duke of Lockwood?"

Nellie. The name didn't really suit her. He'd expected something worthy of a warrior queen. Elizabeth or Boudicca, perhaps. Nellie sounded too frivolous for this woman.

Do something, you fool.

From years of practice, Lockwood pushed his emotions deep, intent on staying polite and letting nothing slip. He inclined his head. "Miss Young. How do you do?"

Eyes devoid of last night's sparkling mischief, she merely nodded once.

Had she recognized him? It seemed unlikely she wouldn't, considering their proximity last evening, but it had been dark, after all. The introductions continued and he made all the correct responses by rote. He'd been doing this for as long as he could remember and was able to shut off that part of his brain with ease. *How do you do? A pleasure to meet you. Yes, I am quite enjoying my stay in America.* The outside of him appeared perfectly calm.

The inside, however, was a different matter altogether. There he was tied up in knots, his stomach hollowed out like a rotten tree. Christ, he'd seen her naked. He'd kissed her, invited her to his rooms. She'd felt his cock, albeit unintentionally.

Worse, he'd begged her to dig her nails into his scalp, then bit her in return. He winced, unable to prevent the outward reaction.

Maddie noticed, lightly touching his arm. "Are you hurt, Your Grace? You haven't twisted your ankle in the grass, have you?"

"No, I'm perfectly well." He shoved it all down, down, down. "What fun have you planned for this afternoon, Miss Webster?"

She began explaining the activity to the group and he listened with half an ear. A distraction in the form of a redheaded vixen was nearby, and he could feel his skin prickling and heating. Even if he considered pursuing her, her thoughts on marriage had been made quite clear last night. Unfortunately, thanks to his father's poor business sense, only one path remained open to Lockwood, and that was to marry an American heiress with all due haste.

Madeline Webster was a fine choice. They got on well together, as well as could be expected in these situations, and there were no scandals attached to her name. He planned to propose during his visit here in Newport and a wedding would follow this autumn. After a few children, they would each live separate lives and carry on the Lockwood title for future generations. It was the very best outcome a man in his position could hope for.

Furthermore, he was running out of time. For many reasons this marriage needed to happen quickly.

The brim of a hat hit the middle of his chest and Maddie grinned up at him. "Your Grace must play. I insist."

"And so I shall." It was impossible to resist the request, considering he was going to marry her. He selected a slip of paper and forced his most charming smile.

She moved on and he tried not to think about last night. Tried not to watch Nellie out of the corner of his eye as she nibbled on a fingernail. Why hadn't he kept on swimming? Why had he gone in search of her, like Odysseus, full of hubris and longing?

I plan on sampling as many of them as possible before I'm done, after all.

He shook his head. This was absurd. The encounter would've meant nothing to her, a diversion from a boring house party. Why was he worrying over it? She'd mistaken him for another man, after all. Today he would get her alone, beg her forgiveness and ask for her discretion. Then he could propose to Maddie as planned and this secret would never, ever be revealed to his future wife.

"Everyone, please look at your slips of paper,"

Maddie instructed. "Your partner is the person with the same number. Form teams, please, then we shall begin hunting eggs!"

Lockwood inwardly sighed. Was this what he has been reduced to? An egg hunt like a child to secure a rich wife? He checked his paper and saw a number four. For some reason he instantly glanced over at Nellie. She was staring at the slip in his hand, a matching number on the paper dangling in her fingers.

Excitement hummed beneath his skin before he could think better of it. Then he remembered the awkward conversation they needed to have, and he supposed now was as good a time as any.

That man you were swimming with last night, the one who invited you to his rooms? That was me. We mustn't ever tell anyone, especially your best friend, who will be my duchess. Have a nice life and all that.

God, that sounded awful.

The guests began filtering out of the tent and Nellie headed straight toward him, her eyes flat and chin set. She wore a straw hat atop her glorious red hair, and the cream-and-blue striped dress hugged her curves. He definitely did not glance in the direction of her bodice.

When she was upon him, he bowed. "Miss Young, it appears—"

"Stuff it," she hissed under her breath. "Follow me."

Without waiting, she breezed out into the sunshine. So much for thinking she hadn't recognized him.

Throat dry, he followed slowly, his hands thrust deep into his pockets. He found her around the side, close to the house. Everyone else seemed to be going in the opposite direction. "This way," she said, and led him away from the house, as if headed toward the street.

"Are there eggs over here?"

Her expression was full of exasperation. "We are not hunting eggs, you idiot. We need to talk and I'd rather not be overheard."

He wasn't certain about returning to the tent empty-handed. Wouldn't that appear suspicious?

She darted into a copse of trees. After checking no one else was around, he dodged a branch and went in after her. "Should we be in here? Someone may happen upon us."

"I know where all the eggs are hidden and there aren't any even close to here. And we have bigger worries than eggs, *Your Grace*." She folded her arms over her chest. "Why didn't you tell me you were a duke? And worse, a duke who is thinking of marrying my best friend?"

"I generally do not present myself as a duke when I'm half-naked and swimming in the middle of the night."

"I was *fully* naked and swimming in the middle of the night. What are you so embarrassed about?"

Quite a lot, actually. Dukes were expected to be perfect. They were not expected to have defective hearts that required regular exercise. "You didn't introduce yourself, either."

"I'm an unmarried woman having a tryst on a beach in the middle of the night. Of course I would not introduce myself."

That made sense. He waved his hand. "All of

this is immaterial. We've now been introduced and must pretend last night never happened."

He expected agreement, a pact to take the encounter with them to their graves. What he got, however, was a deep frown.

"I don't like lying to my friends, scant as they are, about men. Especially about men they might marry."

"Well, I should hope you'll make an exception in this case, considering."

"For you? Not bloody likely."

A knot began to tighten between his shoulder blades. "Whatever is that supposed to mean?"

"It means that you are courting my friend while kissing strangers in the middle of the night. I plan to tell her exactly what kind of man you really are."

"You absolutely mustn't do something so foolish."

"Why? Worried it'll ruin your chances at getting your hands on all that cold American cash?"

Her green eyes were something to behold. He'd never seen anything like them, emerald rings with a sliver of gold just near the pupil. They were even more mesmerizing in the daytime.

"Lockwood!" She clapped her hands in front of his face. "This is serious. Pay attention."

He had been paying attention to her—just not to her words. "You cannot tell her. Ever."

"Why not? She deserves to know."

"That we were attracted to each other? That we kissed while I held your naked body against my mostly naked body? That I asked you back to my rooms?" He scoffed. "Are you mad?"

"Maybe, but she also deserves to know you were planning to meet me again tonight on the beach. You were going to sneak out of her home to meet with another woman, a complete stranger."

Everything Nellie said was true. He had no defense, other than a temporary lapse in judgment brought on by red hair and green eyes. But this stopped here and now. "Hardly sneaking out. I swim every night. If you happen along, too, then I cannot prevent it."

"Oh, so it's my fault?"

"Don't be a fool. She'll hate us both if she finds out."

"You are underestimating Maddie," she said, but he could see the doubt creep into her expression.

He had to make her see reason. "Miss Young, I wish to marry Miss Webster. She is the perfect woman to become my duchess. Athletic and pretty, outgoing and kind. Most important, she is absolutely scandal free."

The words were out of his mouth before he realized how they sounded, yet he couldn't take them back. They were true.

Her jaw snapped closed. A bird fluttered nearby, its wings beating in a useless, steady rhythm, while Nellie stared up at him. Finally, she said, "I suppose that was a dig at me. Intended to put me in my place, just in case I was considering having a go at you myself."

Was that why he'd said it? Perhaps. Last evening had been fun, more fun than he'd experienced in quite some time. Maybe he was trying to remind himself of her unsuitability before he made a fool of himself. Again. "While I did not intend you any harm, I won't deny that I must marry a woman who is beyond reproach. It's how things are done."

She gave a dry laugh containing no amusement. "You needn't worry about me, Your Grace. I've no interest in becoming a duchess—or even a wife, for that matter."

"So that is settled." The knot in his gut eased ever so slightly. "We'll never speak of last night and I will propose to Maddie once the house party concludes."

"What makes you so certain she'll accept?"

Hadn't she heard? Maddie had chased him around Manhattan for three months. Yes, he needed money, but America was crawling with heiresses. Every mother with a daughter of marriageable age had vied for his attention, desperate to have their daughter become a duchess. There had been *a lot* of them, too. He'd selected Maddie from that group because he believed they would best suit. "A man knows these things."

The side of her mouth twitched, as if she held a secret. "Oh, he does, does he? Indeed, then. I wish you luck in getting Maddie to marry you." She started for the edge of the trees, her delicate shoulder blades shifting through the thin fabric of her shirtwaist.

"Are you going to tell her?"

She paused but didn't turn around. "No, but not as a favor to you. I don't want to hurt her. She will misunderstand last night's encounter and wrongfully conclude that I like you."

"You liked me last night," he stupidly said.

Why was he making this harder? The woman had just agreed to keep their meeting a secret. He should be thanking the heavens, not baiting her for a reaction.

"Yes, but everything appears so much clearer in the daylight, doesn't it? Good day, Your Grace."

He stood there a moment, the sting of her rejection like sour candy in his mouth. Why wasn't he relieved?

Chapter Three

❧

The duke proposed."

Maddie's words caused Nellie's head to snap up. The rest of the guests were still outside on the lawn, playing croquet. Nellie left the game early, unable to take one minute more of Lockwood's broad shoulders and chiseled jaw. She'd retired inside with a glass of lemonade laced with gin.

Now she was staring at the Duke of Lockwood's engagement ring sitting on Maddie's finger. Her mouth tasted like that time she'd smoked four cigarettes right in a row. "I see. Congratulations, then." Rising, she went to the sideboard for a refill. No way could she survive the afternoon without more alcohol.

"Thank you." Maddie stared at the ring. "I can't believe it. I feel as if I've been working toward this goal all spring. Now that it's happened . . ."

"You're realizing what it actually means?"

"Yes, I suppose so."

Tell her, Nellie's inner voice urged. *Tell her now. You'll have a good laugh over it and then she'll forgive you.*

Nellie added more gin to her lemonade and stirred, thinking of how to actually say the words. Would Maddie forgive her? It seemed unlikely. Nellie had kissed and groped Maddie's fiancé, for God's sake.

When Nellie debuted, she'd gone into the gardens during a ball with Charlie Appleton, completely unaware that Charlie had an "understanding" with Mary Bishop. Though it had been an unintentional slight, the other girls branded Nellie a loose woman trying to steal all the men for herself.

Which was ludicrous. She and Charlie hadn't even kissed. When she complained of boredom, he'd offered a cocaine tablet to try. While Nellie didn't care to repeat the experience, the buzz had helped her survive that awful ball, like when Mary and two of her friends cornered her in the women's receiving room. *You're a whore, Nellie Young. Just like your Irish mother.*

She gulped gin and lemonade, trying to wash the taste of those horrible words from her brain.

"You think this is a mistake," Maddie said, misreading Nellie's silence.

"I think all marriage is a mistake," she hedged, guilt sitting in her chest like a rock. "The question is what do *you* want?"

"To be a duchess, obviously. And Lockwood is perfect. Beyond perfect, really. I mean, he's utterly perfect."

"We get it," Nellie snapped. "He's perfect. But is he perfect *for you*?"

"Yes, of course. Why wouldn't he be?"

Because he likes to swim at midnight and kiss strange women in the ocean.

Because he can be rough during intimacies.

Because I actually liked him.

Was she trying to poach a man from another woman? No, she would never. No man was worth losing a friend over. Therefore, she had to keep her mouth shut and let Maddie do as she pleased. If the marriage never happened, it wouldn't be Nellie's fault.

She forced a smile. "Stop overthinking it, Maddie. Relax and have a drink with me."

Maddie's brows rose as she eyed the glass in Nellie's hand. "This isn't like you, to drink so early in the day. And you acted very strangely yesterday. What's going on?"

A lump formed in Nellie's throat, the truth burning to get out. It was awful, this feeling. She wished she'd never gone out to the beach that night. Once again, her recklessness had landed her in trouble. "Just tired," she lied, and hated herself for it. Absolutely loathed herself.

Tell her.

Maddie had stuck by Nellie despite the snubs and scandals. Perhaps this one confession would not negatively affect their friendship.

Now you are delusional.

Still, she hated dishonesty. It went against everything in her nature.

She said, "You should know—"

The French doors flew open and the guests began streaming inside. Nellie closed her mouth with a snap, her eyes closing in misery. Shit, why hadn't she told the truth earlier and gotten it over with?

When her lids opened a second later, she saw the duke edge around the furniture and head into the house. He hadn't even greeted his fiancée, the ass. Maddie didn't seem to notice, as she was quickly removing the engagement ring and shoving it in her pocket before anyone—namely, Harrison Archer—saw it.

What a dashed mess.

Nellie's ears began ringing, the tips tingling. All of this was Lockwood's fault. Every bit of it. Actually, he should be the one to tell Maddie everything. Why should Nellie suffer as the bearer of bad news?

She threw back the rest of her gin and lemonade, then set the glass on the low table. "I'll see you at dinner," she said to Maddie, who was now watching Harrison from underneath her lashes. Her friend didn't respond, so Nellie slipped from the room and went up the main stairs.

The higher she climbed, the angrier she became. Lockwood never should have proposed. He should've confessed to Maddie, then found another heiress to marry. One who wasn't Nellie's best friend.

The men were staying in the opposite wing from the ladies and chaperones, and it was deserted at the moment. She knocked on his door. More like pounded, actually.

The wood flew open and Lockwood's handsome face frowned down at her. "What on earth?" he asked.

She pushed her way inside his bedchamber. "I need to talk to you."

He closed the door. "This isn't a good idea. If we're caught—"

"We won't be caught, and you have bigger problems on your hands right now."

"Bigger than causing a scandal with you at my fiancée's house party?"

He'd removed his sweater and was covered in just a lightweight linen shirt that did little to hide the ropes of muscle on his torso. It annoyed her that she noticed those muscles. "You need to tell her. You're the one who acted dishonorably. Therefore, you should be the one to confess. I did nothing wrong."

"I did nothing dishonorable. I was not engaged at the time." He folded his arms over his chest and braced his legs. "We shared a brief kiss in the moonlight. There is no need to make such a to-do out of something so trivial."

Trivial.

The word dropped between them, echoing in her brain and piercing her pride. Fuck, that hurt. Why did that hurt?

Nellie rubbed her forehead, cursing the gin for making her more emotional than usual. Normally, insults glanced right off her heart without a nick. Yet, he'd wounded her. Repeatedly. She hated him for it.

"Trivial or not," she gritted out, "Maddie deserves to know before she marries you."

"I won't cause her unnecessary harm," he said nobly, full of self-sacrifice. What a joke, when they both knew he was merely trying to save his own hide.

"Does no one else see you for the monster you

truly are?" She marched up to him and though he towered over her, she stared him down, unafraid. "Does that ducal charm and easy polite smile really fool everyone?"

A flash of something uncertain moved through his bright blue eyes, but he masked it quickly. "It does, actually."

They stood there, not even an arm's length apart, and she imagined she could feel the heat from his big body. What a fool she'd been over this man, one who was undeserving of a kind and vivacious girl like Maddie. After they married, he would tuck her away in some Mayfair town house and visit his mistress every Tuesday afternoon like clockwork.

Nellie would not allow it.

"I loathe you," she whispered. "And I will do everything in my power to see that she doesn't marry you."

His right eye twitched, the lines of his face tightening into an almost sinister expression. "Too late. She's already agreed."

"It's only too late if you've repeated the vows. So prepare yourself, Poseidon, because I will not go down without a fight."

THE ROOM WAS deathly quiet. Lockwood and Mr. Webster were seated at the ornate desk, while Harrison Archer stood at the window, staring out at the lawn. The clock ticked ominously as they waited, and it was all Lockwood could do not to stand up and push Archer right through the glass.

If what they'd just been told was true, everything had been ruined—and it was all Archer's fault.

Finally, the door creaked open and Lockwood's fiancée appeared. He tried to see the truth of it on her face, but she merely seemed nervous. Understandable, considering the circumstances. But was she guilty? He couldn't tell.

Webster waved his daughter inside. "Madeline, close the door."

She did so, then asked, "What is this about?"

"Mrs. Lusk asked to speak with Lockwood and me this morning," her father said. "Apparently, she was up late last night and noted some inappropriate activities in the house."

"Oh?" Maddie glanced over at Lockwood, probably to gauge his reaction, but his face remained impassive.

Webster cleared his throat. "Yes, she claims you and Mr. Archer came through the terrace doors together well after midnight, soaked to the bone. She also said that Mr. Archer returned your engagement ring and kissed you."

Maddie licked her lips. "That is certainly a tale. Are we sure she hadn't been drinking?"

"Madeline Jane." Her father's voice was sharp with disapproval. "Were you outside with Mr. Archer last night?"

She peeked at Lockwood again, and he braced himself for the worst. He could see the truth in her eyes, the regret burning in her gaze. "Yes," she whispered.

Lockwood's stomach plummeted toward the ground and he let out the breath he'd been holding. There it was, his utter humiliation. Everyone would soon learn of it and he'd be a laughing-stock in this godforsaken country. *Christ.* He wanted to hit something. Or rather, some*one*.

Webster sighed and nodded at Lockwood. "I'll write you a check with enough zeroes that perhaps we might keep this quiet for a bit."

The money would help, but it didn't solve all his problems. In fact, things were considerably worse, as he was now a jilted duke instead of a duke.

He forced a polite nod. "Of course, Webster. I am sorry this didn't work out."

"I feel the same. You have my deepest apologies."

Maddie edged forward, brow creasing as if trying to solve a puzzle. "What do you plan—?"

"Not another word, young lady," her father said, his voice low and harsh. "Sit and do not speak until I am ready for you."

Her mouth fell open, but Webster swiveled his chair toward the window and addressed the other party in the matter. "Well, Archer. Are you prepared to do the right thing?"

With a head full of dark thoughts, Lockwood no longer cared about this conversation. His involvement had ended the moment his fiancée admitted to a rendezvous with another man. How had he chosen so poorly? Maddie had seemed a fine choice up until just now. She wasn't reckless or improper, but rather had a good head on her shoulders. Or so he'd thought.

How had he misjudged her so egregiously?

She flew to her feet and put her palms out, as if

to bring order to the room. "I haven't been compromised. I went for a walk last night and Mr. Archer found me and assisted me inside."

Lockwood nearly snorted. Not a soul alive would believe that tale. He kept quiet, however. His part in this little drama was over. She was Archer's problem now.

Lockwood had much bigger problems.

Mr. Webster frowned at his daughter. "Mrs. Lusk saw you both and remarked—quite loudly, I might say—about the intimacy of what she observed. Not to mention you had taken off your engagement ring and given it to Mr. Archer at some point."

Ah, yes. That needed to be dealt with. "Speaking of the ring," Lockwood said. "If you don't mind, Miss Webster." It had belonged to his grandmother, after all, and if Lockwood couldn't find another heiress to marry, he might need to sell the piece.

Slowly, Maddie removed her glove, slipped the heavy ring off her finger and placed it carefully on the desk. Lockwood picked it up and dropped it into his coat pocket.

That was that, then. He'd lost his fiancée to that . . . arrogant American nobody with appalling manners. It was sickening. Lockwood needed to escape this house party as soon as possible, before the news broke. Before he punched Archer's teeth out for humiliating him like this.

Except dukes never lost control. Instead of getting angry, he put on a polite expression and extended a hand toward Maddie's father. "Good luck, Webster."

The older man stood and shook the duke's hand. "You, as well, Your Grace. Thank you for your discretion."

He gave his former fiancée a polite smile. "Miss Webster, I wish you the very best."

Though she seemed dazed, she managed to say, "The best to you, as well, Your Grace."

He spun on his heel and quit the room, his chest burning with rage and humiliation as he entered the corridor. He'd lost. Maddie had chosen Archer over him, a duke. It was inconceivable.

Now Lockwood had to start all over again with the stain of failure hanging over him like bad perfume. Bloody hell.

In the corridor a figure stepped out of the shadows, and by the way his skin prickled he knew exactly who was there. He didn't stop to speak to her. Instead, he climbed the stairs.

She followed, because of course she did.

"You must be loving this," he said, not bothering to disguise the venom in his voice.

"Oh, yes. I love seeing my best friend sad and terrified."

Now at the landing, he started for his chambers. "Go and gloat elsewhere."

"Why, what's happened?"

"Wilkins!" he bellowed as he turned the corner. Where was that blasted valet?

"Will you stop and tell me what happened in there?"

Lockwood didn't break stride. Under no circumstances would he let this woman see into his mind. She'd already seen far too much.

Does no one else see you for the monster you truly are?

He hadn't done anything to warrant this level of disgrace. Once, he'd fallen under the spell of a beautiful creature in the moonlight and kissed her while courting another woman. Was that so terrible? Was it such a terrible transgression that the universe would punish him with a public humiliation as this? All of Fifth Avenue would learn of this scandal before the week was out.

His heart skittered, and he knew that erratic beat all too well. It would soon make him light-headed, if he wasn't careful. He needed to calm down and breathe, but she was here and he'd be damned if he revealed any weakness in front of this particular woman.

He threw open the door to his bedchamber. "Get out," he said and jerked on the bellpull.

Without waiting on Wilkins, he began clearing out the armoire, tossing his things onto the bed.

She walked into his room, as bold as brass. "You're leaving?"

"Obviously."

"She's marrying Harrison."

Her tone held no surprise, like she had expected this outcome all along, and a fine sweat broke out on his forehead. Jesus Christ. How would he ever find a decent heiress now?

Every day his debt mounted by four hundred pounds, six pence and two farthings. The estate was too far gone, thanks to his father's mismanagement. The former duke had believed in the status quo, never looking ahead, so fields were left untended, equipment unmaintained. Repairs hadn't been made and investments placed in all the wrong markets. There was no way out of the hole without an heiress, not for Lockwood.

Yet, he'd hoped to find a wife he actually *liked*.

That would prove nigh impossible now.

"Yes," he growled. "They'll be married by the end of the day. I hope you're happy. Your efforts to sabotage my marriage to her obviously worked."

She closed the distance between them and stood by the bed. "I did very little sabotaging, actually. Harrison managed most of the work all by himself."

"Encouraged by you, no doubt."

She lifted a dainty shoulder, her creamy skin flawless in the morning light. Why was she so bloody beautiful?

He'd heard the rumors about Nellie during the house party, tales of drinking and wild antics. The ménage à trois with Alfie Vanderbilt and James Hyde. Baring her bosom in protest at a police officer and subsequent arrest. Apparently, her father was richer than God and for some unknown reason tolerated his daughter's appalling behavior.

There'd been enough impropriety in Lockwood's family to last a lifetime. He wouldn't take on more. Besides, he needed a quiet, well-behaved wife who would not cause him or his heart any more stress.

He drew in a deep breath and let it out slowly.

"Are you all right?"

"I'm fine. Or rather, I will be as soon as you leave."

A brief hint of pain flashed in her green depths, but he didn't take it back. He needed to leave this house immediately, before he passed out, and she was distracting him.

"There is that Lockwood charm," she said brightly. Too brightly, perhaps? Spinning on her heel, she sauntered to the door, her hips swinging under her skirts. When she turned, she caught him staring at her bottom and he could feel his cheeks heat.

Their gazes locked but neither of them spoke. There were countless things he wanted to tell her, a multitude of confessions burning his tongue. Such as his inexplicable lust for her, his fear over the future. The stupid heart that ensured he'd never grow old. But he shoved it all down, hid everything he was thinking and hoping, and buried it under mounds of duty and honor.

Her auburn brows lowered and she swallowed hard. Then she opened her mouth. "Lockwood, I—"

"Your Grace. I beg your pardon," Wilkins panted, arriving through the adjoining door. "Oh," he said when he noticed Nellie standing there. "Excuse me, miss."

"No, don't go," Lockwood ordered his valet and gestured to the bed. "We're leaving, so pack everything."

"Of course, Your Grace. Shall I have a carriage sent for?"

"Yes. We'll go directly to the train station."

Wilkins nodded and left. When Lockwood looked back at the spot where Nellie had been standing, it was empty.

He told himself it was for the best.

Chapter Four

❦

Six months later

"Hoping the fourth time is the charm?"

Lockwood clenched his jaw and didn't bother looking at the woman who'd sidled up next to him. The smug satisfaction in her voice was plain enough. He didn't need to see it on her gorgeous face, as well. "I haven't any idea what you mean."

Of course he knew what she meant.

Over the past year he'd courted two of her friends—became friends with a third—only to lose them all to other men. He wasn't convinced Nellie was entirely innocent in those outcomes, either. He returned to England for business for a short while, but was once again circulating through New York society to find a wealthy bride.

God knew it was bloody humiliating enough without her here to rub his nose in it.

"Though I suppose, if we wanted to be precise about it," she continued, "you and Katherine never were engaged. It was more of a friendship, one she used to restore your reputation and rub in Preston's face." She sipped from her coupe and studied him above the rim. "Did it work?"

"I was invited to this dinner party, so I think we may assume it did." He suddenly frowned at her. "Speaking of reputations, how did you wrangle an invitation?"

Her lip curled slightly. "Hard to believe, I know, but see that gray-haired man talking to Mrs. Astor? That's my father. He and Lina are old friends."

Lockwood smothered a sigh. It had been foolish to think he could avoid her forever. He'd last seen her months ago at the French Ball, a scandalous annual bacchanal where the demi-monde rubbed shoulders with society men and Wall Street types. He'd been there to try and forget about society, his responsibilities and disastrous reputation. Dressed provocatively, Nellie had been hanging on the arm of some man, and though she wore a costume, Lockwood had known her instantly. It was as if his skin sizzled every time she was in the vicinity.

Including now.

He shifted on his feet and wiped any hint of emotion off his face. He'd been doing it for years and could treat her with banal civility when required. "And how have you been? Enjoying the unseasonably mild temperatures?"

"Oh, my God," she said through a chuckle. "The weather? Is that the best you can manage?"

Irritation prickled across the nape of his neck and into the roots of his hair. "Shall we discuss the French Ball instead?"

Christ. Why had he said that? Thankfully, none of the other guests in the drawing room were paying them any attention.

She tapped a gloved finger on the side of her glass, a *thump thump thump* that matched the erratic pounding in his chest. "Yes, by all means. Let's discuss the French Ball. I hadn't expected you to lower yourself and attend such an outrageous spectacle. Did you enjoy her? The woman I saw you slavering over, I mean."

Though he planned to, he hadn't taken the actress back to his hotel. Seeing Nellie there with another man had ruined the evening for him. It had ruined a lot of evenings for him, actually.

But he'd done nothing wrong in attending. She would not make him feel guilty. "I did. What about that man you were with?" he asked. "Did you enjoy him?"

"Oh, you mean Adrian. That gorgeous creature. My former fencing instructor. He's gone back to France, I'm afraid. But yes, I enjoyed him. Many, many times."

Something uncoiled in Lockwood's belly, a darkness he usually kept firmly in check. It caused the fingers of his free hand to curl into a fist. He finished his champagne in one gulp. "How nice for you."

"It was, indeed. He could do this thing with his tongue—"

His head snapped over as his gaze shot to hers. The second their eyes locked, a jolt passed through him. It was like an electric charge, a swift shock that stiffened every part of him— including his cock, which was beginning to thicken in his trousers. Horrified, he glanced away and tried to compose himself.

This was why he avoided her.

That, and she absolutely loathed him.

"Incidentally," she started, "how is the search for an innocent, scandal-free bride going? I do apologize that I haven't any more friends to throw your way."

"I'll manage," he muttered. "I have three young ladies in mind." All impeccable, all wealthy. All boring.

"Anyone I know?"

She sounded skeptical, like he wasn't capable of finding a decent bride. Like his recent blunders had labeled him unmarriageable. Something perverse inside him wanted to prove her wrong, prove that even a scandal-ridden penniless duke like him still had options.

He tilted his chin toward the fireplace. "The Lanier girl, for one."

"Who, Clarissa?"

The amusement in her voice had him turning toward her. "And what is wrong with her?"

Nellie's plump lips twisted into a sly smile. "Absolutely nothing. The two of you will be perfectly bland together, like vanilla crème."

"I like vanilla crème," he said.

"No, you don't."

The certainty in her voice killed any denial he might have tried. She *knew*. All because he'd revealed too much during their moonlit encounter, and now he had to live with the fact that this outrageous creature was privy to one of his darkest secrets.

"I can appreciate it from time to time," he allowed and shifted his attention to another part of the room. Anything but on *her*.

"I should hope so, with all those ducal heirs to breed."

That word on her lips . . .

Now he was picturing her creamy thighs wrapped around his hips, red hair spilling over her shoulders as his cock drove into her cunt, the slick walls milking his seed from him over and over. Christ, he wanted that.

He swallowed and sent up a prayer that his thoughts were not visible on his face.

"Eleanor, my dear." The older gentleman she'd pointed out as her father came up and put his arm around her waist. "Are you having a nice time thus far?"

"Of course I am, Papa. You needn't worry about me." She kissed his cheek. "Have you met His Grace, the Duke of Lockwood?"

"No, can't say that I have." The man stuck out his hand. "Cornelius Young, Your Grace. A pleasure."

"Mr. Young," Lockwood said as they shook hands. "How do you do?"

"And how do you know my little girl?"

Lockwood's tongue tangled with the truth for the briefest instant. *I nearly fucked her in the ocean off the coast of Newport, sir.*

She quickly stepped in. "We met at Maddie's house party, Papa. Back in June, remember?"

"Right." Young's eyes suddenly went wide. "You were the fiancé."

Forthrightness clearly ran in the Young family. "Yes, I was the fiancé."

"But it worked out for the best," Nellie added. "Maddie and the duke were a terrible match. Everyone thought so."

Lockwood didn't know of a single person who'd expressed such a thought, and he wondered why she was bothering to paint a less humiliating picture.

"I don't doubt it, then," Young said. "My daughter has an eye for these things, Your Grace. Has the same intuition as her mother, God rest her soul."

Nellie smiled softly, her pleasure at the comparison obvious. "There is no such thing as Irish intuition."

"I'll never believe it." Young shook his head. "Never known two women who saw the future more clearly."

Her embarrassment was adorable. Lockwood hadn't thought Nellie capable of experiencing the emotion, yet she now buried her flushed face in her hands. He added this to the list of things he liked about her, a catalogue that was becoming shockingly long.

Young continued, his attention on Lockwood. "It's why I said she can choose her own husband. My girl knows what she wants and anyone who tries to force her will live to regret it."

No wonder she hadn't married. Cornelius Young obviously indulged her, which was how she ran wild over the island of Manhattan.

"You know I don't wish to marry," she told him and threaded their arms together. "I'm going to live with you until I'm a boring old spinster."

Lockwood couldn't help it. A bark of laughter escaped his throat.

Both Nellie and her father looked over at him—one in warning and one with unbridled curiosity—so Lockwood coughed into his hand. "I beg your pardon. There was"—*another cough*—"something stuck in my throat."

Nellie didn't appear to buy it for a minute, but Young looked down at his drink. "My throat's a bit dry, as well. I think I'll get another drink before dinner. Can I bring Your Grace a refill?"

"Just Lockwood is fine, and no, thank you, Mr. Young."

"Cornelius to my friends." He kissed his daughter's cheek. "I'll see you inside at dinner."

After he wandered away, Lockwood smirked at her. "I like your father." He paused. "Eleanor."

"Most people do—and do not call me that."

"Why not? I think it suits you. Far better than Nellie, in fact."

"No doubt I'll regret asking, but why?"

He couldn't explain it, not without sounding like an unmitigated fool. "Is he aware that you run hurdy-gurdy over the island?"

"My father is too busy with his railroads to worry about whether I'm kept under lock and key, thank God. And he's never been fond of society's rules, especially after the way everyone treated my mother."

"Oh?"

She sipped her drink then licked her lips, a gesture Lockwood noticed far more than he should. "She was Irish," she said. "A barmaid when she met my father."

"Ah."

"I can hear the horror in your voice, duke, but not all of us come from a long line of over-privileged aristocrats who made their money off the backs of others."

"And I suppose your father built all those railroads by offering fair wages and safe working conditions. I wonder, then, why the workers are trying to unionize?"

Her mouth flattened into almost a sneer. "I could not hate you any more right now."

Thankfully, the moment was broken as their hostess announced it was time for dinner. As the honored guest, it was Lockwood's responsibility to escort the older woman to the dining room. "Try not to miss me, will you?" he murmured to Nellie before he strode away.

"Rest assured that I won't," he heard her say behind him.

GOD, HE WAS so handsome and charming that Nellie felt ill. Deep-in-her-stomach sick, the kind that had nothing to do with food or a fever. He'd been placed on the hostess's right, with the Lanier girl on his other side, and Nellie watched him through her lashes as he interacted with both women, his smile polite, attention firmly on the conversation around him.

She had the insane urge to lower the bodice of her dress ever so slightly, just to see if she could grab his attention.

Why did she hate it so intensely when he ignored her?

She was not a child. She knew what these

feelings meant—and they were intolerable. Absolutely not to be tolerated. Not for this man. He was repressed, not at all like the young American men she'd fancied over the past three years. They were loud and fun, always up for a good time. Just like her.

Though she'd had a glimpse of the real Lockwood that night in the ocean, the man beneath the stiff ducal exterior. The one who swam like a fish, with muscles to make a prizefighter envious. That man was far more interesting, far more memorable. If only she could purge him from her memory . . .

Papa was seated near Mrs. Astor and the two of them chatted like old friends. Nellie, on the other hand, was at the end near their host and some other gentlemen she didn't know. Papa had begged her to attend tonight, saying he was tired of seeing her hang about the house. The comment stung, but he wasn't wrong. She *had* been hanging around the house, at odds with what to do. Her friends were either married or on their way to the altar, which left Nellie feeling . . . lonely.

She hated feeling this way. Normally, she would go out to a club or a saloon. Spend a night at Alice and Kit's supper club or Florence Greene's ladies-only casino. Those outings usually chased away any blues. But this time was different. A shadow had passed over her heart, like a dark cloud had settled in her chest, and she couldn't shake it. Worse, she didn't *want* to shake it.

In the past few months her friends had all found love. Papa had his longtime mistress,

Mrs. Paulson. Most of the women her age were married with families of their own. Nellie certainly didn't want a husband or a family, but there was something appealing about companionship. Akin to the devotion Harrison had for Maddie, or the adoration in Kit's eyes whenever Alice entered the room. The way Preston softened just for Katie.

It made her own existence seem . . . lacking.

So she stayed home and worked with her plants. The conservatory hadn't looked this good since her mother's death, according to the staff. That brought her enough joy for now. Maybe she needed another lover . . .

The man on her left leaned in. "You seem lost in thought." Mr. Randolph Perry, a wealthy banker, was similar in age to her father and had a tidy brown mustache just starting to silver. "A girl as pretty as you shouldn't frown."

She bit the inside of her cheek to keep from snapping at him. Embarrassing her father in public was something she devoutly avoided these days. "We all have something to frown over occasionally, wouldn't you say?"

"And what is distressing you, Miss Young? Is it boredom? These dinner parties can be dreadfully dull."

"I'm having a perfectly lovely time," she lied.

"It can be difficult for a young girl, I imagine, in a room full of strangers. How many years has it been since your debut? Four?"

Warning whispered across her skin, a cold rush that had her sitting taller. She hoped she was wrong. "Seems like yesterday, though."

"You know, I keep expecting to hear of your engagement, but your father said you haven't chosen anyone yet." Mr. Perry shifted to straighten his dessert spoon. To anyone else's eye, it would have seemed like nothing. Nellie knew better. The move caused his forearm to lightly skim hers. Even through layers of fabric, his touch sent ripples of revulsion through her. He continued, "Having a hard time settling on just one?"

Meaning, she had sampled many. Nellie contemplated her seafood fork and the satisfaction she'd feel upon shoving the sharp tines into Perry's thigh.

She wished she could say this was the first time an older man made a disparaging or crude remark to her, but it wasn't. In their eyes, any unmarried young lady was fair game, and Nellie's reputation meant they didn't even try to conceal their intent. It was like they thought they had a right to proposition and touch her.

Papa laughed and smiled at the end of the table, and she swallowed the setdown she'd been about to deliver. She couldn't cause a scene. Instead, she reached for her wine, hoping he would take the hint if she ignored him.

He did not take the hint.

Instead, he leaned in and lowered his voice. "Perhaps you need someone older to offer a guiding hand. Lend an ear whenever necessary."

His knee pressed to hers, far more invasive than the light touch a moment ago.

This was too much. After putting down her wine, she carefully slid her butter knife into her hand, concealing it as best she could. "Move your leg," she hissed under her breath.

He didn't budge. "Now, there's no reason we can't be friendly."

Other than his age, his wife and the fact that she didn't like him.

When he reached beneath the table and boldly grabbed her knee, she jabbed the butter knife into his thigh, hard. Perry started, the glass of wine in his other hand upending and spilling all over the two of them. Dark red spread over her favorite cream silk evening gown.

Damn it.

Gasps erupted and footmen rushed forward. Quickly pushing back from the table, Nellie stood and looked at her father, whose brows were now lowered in concern. "I do apologize," she told the room, avoiding the duke's eye. "Please, everyone, continue enjoying your dinner. Excuse me."

She left the table and walked out of the dining room, her head high. If they wished to talk about her, fine. She'd done nothing wrong. Perry, that snake, was entirely to blame.

Though she tried her best to clean up in the washroom, there was no help for the stain. The silk was ruined. Hopefully, her father wouldn't mind if she left. The idea of sitting next to Perry in a soiled gown for the next two hours made her want to stab him all over again.

When she left the washroom, a man was leaning against the wall, waiting on her.

Her stomach sank. Perfect. Just bloody perfect.

"It wasn't my fault," she told Lockwood.

"I am aware. I saw him brush his arm against

yours then reach under the table. A butter knife in the thigh is probably the least of what he deserves. Are you all right?"

He'd noticed that?

She warmed, lured in by the concern she read in his expression. He seemed truly worried about her. "I'm fine. I've encountered his ilk before."

Brow pulling low, he stepped forward and searched her face. "What does that mean? What exactly happened?"

His intense scrutiny both thrilled and annoyed her. Best to focus on the less disastrous reaction. "It's nothing to worry your pretty little head over. Run along, before your future duchess wonders where you've gone."

"Don't do that," he said quietly, his mouth stern and unhappy.

"Do what?"

"Patronize and dismiss me. I realize we've been at odds, but I shouldn't wish to see you hurt."

Her insides began to run riot with all sorts of fluttering and tingling, an absolute embarrassment for a woman of her experience. She'd been alone with plenty of men, some more handsome than Lockwood. Why must it be this one in particular to affect her like this?

Because I liked him once. He made me feel . . . more.

Well, there was no dwelling on that now. She wasn't one to waste time with what-ifs. She tried to take a step back but ended up against the wall. "I'm fine," she repeated, unsure what else to say.

"He said something awful to you, something inappropriate."

"I can defend myself."

The edge of his mouth kicked up. "Indeed you can, Eleanor."

Why was he amused by that? Confounding duke. "I should go. I smell like a winery."

"Merely tell everyone it's a new perfume you're trying out. If anyone can pull it off, it's you."

Now, what did that mean?

She had to escape him before she did something irrevocable and stupid. "I think I'll go home instead. Would you mind telling my father so he doesn't worry?"

"Of course. Come, I'll see you off in a hansom."

"That isn't necessary—"

He took her arm and began leading her down the hall. "I know. You don't require my help. Still, I'd prefer to do it."

They walked in silence toward the front door, his stride purposeful yet graceful. An aristocrat down to his bones. She wasn't sure what to do with him if they weren't sniping at one another. They weren't friends or potential lovers. Their one night as strangers was a mistake, brought on by moonlight and magic. Trivial, he'd called it.

So why was he helping her? Out of pity?

Her shoulders straightened as her spine lifted. She didn't need anyone's pity. Nellie had been taking care of herself for a long time—and looking after her father, too. She wasn't helpless or pathetic, and she certainly didn't need a man to make everything better.

"Relax," he said as they arrived at the front door. "I can feel you bristling. Just humor me, please."

The butler arrived, ready to assist, but Lockwood waved the servant away. "I have this," he told the older man. Then the duke opened the door for her and she stepped out into the night.

"I am not a damsel in distress," she informed him.

"I never considered that you were."

Now on the walk, he stripped off his glove, put two fingers into his mouth and let out a piercing whistle. She tried not to stare at his lips or his broad chest. They were in the middle of Fifth Avenue, grand houses each way one turned, and her own home wasn't far. Truthfully, she'd planned to walk, to clear her head of Perry and his advances. But standing here gave her a few extra seconds with Lockwood, a small window of time in which to pretend they weren't ill-suited. To pretend they actually liked each other.

The silence wrapped around them, soft gas lamps flickering in the darkness, the yellow light bouncing off the chiseled planes of his face. The cold temperature meant she could see every breath he took. The question burst out of her mouth before she could stop it. "Are you still swimming every night?"

He tugged at the cuff of his jacket. "The floating pools have closed, so no. I've not been able to swim recently."

"We have a pool," she blurted. "A heated one at my home. You're welcome to use it." Good Lord, what evil spirit had taken hold of her tongue? She hurried to repair the damage. "Or not. It's probably too far north to be of any convenience to you."

Disbelief hung in the air between them. She'd weakened in the face of his care after her incident with Perry and softened slightly toward him, but this was madness. Seconds ticked by and she dared not meet his eye, and instead stared up the street to watch a cab turn the corner. The wheels slowed as it approached until the vehicle finally stopped at the end of the walk. Lockwood took her elbow and guided her toward the street. Her skin prickled where he touched, even through their gloves, and she was certain he could hear her heart pounding like a drum behind her ribs.

In an effort to keep from issuing any other humiliating invitations, she pressed her lips together and climbed up. Lockwood didn't move, just stood in the open door and regarded her. What on earth was he waiting for?

"Lockwood," she said stiffly, gesturing toward the door.

That seemed to shake him out of his thoughts. "Good evening, Eleanor," he said in his steady deep voice as he carefully closed the carriage door.

The vehicle pulled away and she glanced back. He stood there, stalwart and true, hands deep in his trouser pockets, and watched her depart. Then she faced forward, and put him exactly where he belonged. In her past.

Chapter Five

〜❦〜

Morning sun streaked the conservatory as Nellie debated whether to replant the arbor vitae tree. The sapling was doing well in its current pot, but for how much longer? This was part of what appealed to her about gardening: the caring of living things and helping them flourish.

"Eleanor, my dear," her father called from somewhere in the cavernous space.

"Here!" she called. "Back by the lemon trees."

"Is that right or left of the pond? I can never remember."

"Left."

Minutes later her father appeared, looking dapper in his double-breasted brown suit. He leaned in to kiss her cheek. "Hello, sweet pea. You're certainly at it early."

"I couldn't sleep. How are you, Papa?"

"Fine. I hope you weren't bothered by last night."

The dinner party. The memory of Perry and his wandering limbs caused a cold shiver to work down her spine. "I had a nice time."

"Good, I'm glad to hear it. I was worried the wine incident would've upset you."

"It was nothing. An accident." She tried to brush it off.

"That was what I assumed. Though that duke had strong words with Perry after dinner." He shook his head. "I thought the two would come to blows."

Blows? Lockwood? She pulled at the collar of her shirtwaist, suddenly very warm. "He did?"

"He's a decent chap, Lockwood." Her father checked his pocket watch. "He said something about using our swimming pool. You issued an invitation, apparently?"

Stupid runaway mouth. "You don't mind, do you? Because I'm happy to tell him no." More than happy, in fact.

"Nonsense. Neither of us ever uses it. Blasted thing just sits there, empty. I'm happy if he comes by and swims whenever he likes. I told him as much, too."

Nellie could have kicked herself. Why had she opened her mouth and issued that invitation to Lockwood? Now he would be in her home. Under her roof. In their *swimming pool*. She'd seen him in his bathing costume, so she knew what he would look like, wet muscles straining, glistening in the water. It was a goddamn crime, a body like that on such an insufferable man.

I didn't always think him insufferable.

Yes, well.

"Did he mention when he would come by to swim?"

"Late at night. Said we'd likely be in bed."

That conjured images of moonlight glinting off dark water. Ravenous kisses and wandering hands in the gentle waves. The memory sat like a stone in her chest. She snapped, "Shall we give him a key, then?"

Papa finished winding his pocket watch and slipped it into his vest pocket. "That's a good idea. Then he won't bother the staff at odd hours. Will you take care of it?"

She gaped at him. "I was joking, Papa."

His lips quirked as he gazed at her affectionately. "I know. You like having your space, like your mother, but he won't abuse the privilege. I'm sure you won't even realize he is here."

She certainly hoped so.

"Fine," she said, "but when we are robbed by a gang of thieves, we'll know who's responsible."

Papa chuckled. "If the man were going to result to petty larceny to repair his family's finances, I think it would have happened before now." He pulled her into an embrace and kissed her temple. "I must go to the office and I have a dinner engagement tonight. I'm afraid I won't be around."

She was used to this. She patted his lapel. "I understand. Tell Mrs. Paulson I said hello."

His cheeks were pink when they parted. He still wasn't comfortable with Nellie's affinity for his mistress, but Mrs. Paulson was a lovely older widow who cared deeply about him. They had been together for years and, at Nellie's insistence, Mrs. Paulson spent this past Christmas with them.

"I will," he said. "Try to get out today. I realize

last night was disappointing, but I don't like the thought of you sulking around the house. It's not like you."

"That's a good idea. I'll see if someone is free." Alice would be working at the supper club, and Maddie was away at one of her tennis tournaments. That left Katie, who was hard to pry from Preston's grip these days.

Papa was right, though. Nellie had been reclusive lately, which was absolutely not her nature. She liked fun and parties, mayhem and danger. Maybe she'd go visit the Irish cousins on the West Side. It had been weeks since she'd last seen her mother's people.

Then she remembered. "Oh, I have Katie's art show tonight." The idea of it hardly brightened her day. Champagne and small talk, while trying to ignore the whispers behind her back. At least she would see Katie for a moment or two.

"That's right. Which painting did we lend her for that one?"

"The John Martin. The show is highlighting English landscapes."

"Ah, that's one of my favorites. Reminds me of a trip I took with your mother to Leeds."

A familiar pang resounded in her chest, the one that occurred any time he mentioned her mother. They both missed her terribly. "Was that the trip when the carriage wheel popped off and you stayed the night in that lice-infested inn?"

"One and the same." He smiled and chuckled. "She told me not to worry, that lice only liked people with sweet dispositions."

Her parents had been wildly in love, and

Nellie wished she could have seen more of them together. Unfortunately, her mother died when Nellie was eight years old. "I think you're sweet."

"That is because you are my favorite person in the whole world."

Warmth wrapped around her heart. How could she ever think of moving out and leaving him alone? "Even when I am causing trouble?"

Papa shook his head as he walked away. "Yes, even when you are causing trouble. Love you."

"Love you, too, Papa."

Then the conservatory was quiet, with the plants, flowers and insects her only companions. The thought used to offer solace but now brought on that dark cloud again, the one that followed her about more and more lately. She was only twenty-two years old, much too young to feel sorry for herself like this.

Perhaps she needed a cause. She could join one of those women's groups where they distributed fliers and marched in the streets with fabric banners. Or she could sit on the board of some charity, like a hospital or an orphanage. Better, she could use her trust fund to buy a hospital or orphanage. Then she could run it any way she saw fit.

Except all that sounded terribly boring. Nellie hated boring. She wanted excitement and thrills, something that made her heart race. Something like—

No, she wasn't going to think about that midnight swim. Or the man she'd kissed.

There were plenty of other men. Scads, actually.

That was what she really needed—another man to distract her from those memories. Indeed, that fit the bill quite perfectly.

If only Adrian hadn't gone back to Paris. He'd served as a lovely distraction last autumn. She hadn't cared much for fencing but afterward, when they stripped off their thick costumes and he whispered naughty French in her ear? That had been quite nice.

Tonight she would look for a new lover. One who wanted *her*, who didn't care about her past or her scandals. And definitely one who was not tall and athletic and English.

Decision made, she dug the small trowel in the dirt and got back to her plants.

New York's elite had packed into the gallery for Katherine Delafield's latest art exhibition. Lockwood surveyed the crowd, hoping to find her before he wandered the collection. He considered the two of them friends, having grown close this past autumn.

A dark-haired man towered above the rest of the room, so Lockwood headed in that direction. No doubt Preston Clarke was hovering near his fiancée. Lockwood would say hello to Katherine, circulate the room once or twice, then go and find a stiff drink.

He maneuvered through the crush, offering polite greetings when prompted, but moved with purpose. There was plenty of time for conversation later, after he'd found his friend.

Preston frowned when Lockwood stepped into their little circle, but Katherine's face broke into a wide smile. "Your Grace! I was hoping you would come."

He took her hand and kissed it. "I wouldn't have missed it. From the looks of the room, I'd say it's a smashing success. Congratulations."

"Thank you, but it's only a success if we sell paintings. There are many struggling artists hoping to make a name for themselves."

He shifted toward the glowering man at her side and held out a hand. "Clarke."

"Lockwood."

They shook hands. No animosity existed between them, but they weren't chums, either. Lockwood suspected courting the wives of two of Clarke's good friends had something to do with winning the man's enmity.

"Come, let's get you a glass of champagne." Katherine took Lockwood's arm and began leading him toward the side of the room. "Preston, I'll find you in a bit," she said over her shoulder.

"And how are things with your fiancé?" Lockwood asked when they moved away.

"Very well, actually. He looks stern and grumpy, but don't let that fool you. He's a hopeless romantic under all that gruff exterior."

Lockwood didn't believe it for a moment but wisely kept his mouth shut.

"Here." She plucked two glasses off a tray and handed him one. "Cheers."

"Congratulations, Miss Delafield. You are quickly becoming your country's most influential art patron."

A flush brightened her cheeks. "Hardly, but

you're very kind. Tell me how you've been. How goes the search for a duchess?"

"There are three young ladies who seem suitable. I've spent the most time with the Lanier girl."

The two of you will be perfectly bland together, like vanilla crème.

Indeed, and what was wrong with it? Duchesses were required to be respectable and proper, which was why every duke Lockwood knew kept a flamboyant mistress. It was the way these things were done. Nellie couldn't possibly understand that, being an American and all.

"Oh, Clarissa is sweet," Katherine was saying. "I've met her a number of times."

"That is reassuring to hear, though I am proceeding cautiously."

"Understandable, considering. Except Maddie and Alice really were unusual circumstances."

It hadn't felt unusual at the time. More like bloody embarrassing. Mr. Webster's financial compensation over the broken engagement to his daughter had lessened the sting a bit, allowing Lockwood to appease the worst of the creditors for a few months.

Four hundred pounds, six pence and two farthings.

He tried not to think about his mounting debts, at least not tonight.

Katherine's attention suddenly shifted to something over Lockwood's shoulder. "Nellie!"

His muscles clenched, the single word burning through him like a match had been struck in his veins. It was suddenly impossible to breathe.

I like vanilla crème.

No, you don't.

He hated that she knew his secret. Absolutely hated it. Served him right for trusting a stranger.

"Katie, hello." Nellie arrived in a cloud of cream silk that set off her fiery hair. The low-cut bodice made for some daring cleavage, and he actually considered slipping away before Nellie noticed him.

Instead, he forced his feet to remain rooted to the pine floor. When had he turned into such a coward? His family was one of the most prestigious in England, having been given their title in 1574 by Queen Elizabeth. His grandfather served as Captain of the Yeomen of the Guard under Peel, for God's sake. One gorgeous redheaded mermaid would not send him skulking off like some Seven Dials thief.

"Glad to see the place is crammed with Knickerbockers." Nellie's eyes cut to him. "Lockwood."

The word held no warmth or interest, as if she were greeting a wall. "Miss Young." He inclined his head but didn't stare directly at her. She was the sun, bright and dangerous, and if he looked too long she was liable to scorch his insides.

"Oh, Nellie," Katherine said. "Thank you for lending me the John Martin. I've had three patrons ask if it is for sale."

"I'm afraid not," Nellie answered. "It's one of my father's favorites. Something about reminding him of Leeds and my mother."

Katherine's face softened as if this was the most romantic tidbit she'd ever heard. Considering that her fiancé was Preston Clarke, it very well might've been. "That is so sweet," Katherine said.

"I absolutely adore your father. I shall be pleased to tell everyone it is spoken for. Goodness, there's Abby. I must speak with her." She started to leave, then stopped abruptly. "You two will get along, won't you? I can't have any more fisticuffs at my art shows."

"Of course," he replied, while Nellie said, "No promises," at the same time.

Katherine grimaced, but squeezed Nellie's hand before disappearing into the crowd. He clasped his hands behind his back. "Tempted to plant a facer on me, are you?"

"Most definitely, but I'll refrain for Katie's sake."

"Much appreciated."

"Here." She thrust a key at him.

He took the heavy piece of brass. "What's this?"

"That opens the door directly to the swimming pool from the outside. My father thought you should have it."

After slipping the key into his coat pocket, he snagged a coupe of champagne from a passing waiter and handed it to her. "I will remind you it was your offer in the first place."

"Believe me, I'm aware. At least this way, if you have your own key, you may come and go without the rest of us knowing."

Did the idea of him in her home bother her so much? "I won't use it, if you prefer."

"Why would I mind? Swim as much as you like. I'm rarely in that wing of the house."

The crowd swelled and edged them toward the wall, more on the fringes of the room. He took her arm and angled her away from the wayward elbows and boisterous conversation. While he did wish to look at the collection, he wasn't ready to leave her side quite yet. Never mind why.

"You like to swim," he said. "Surprising, then, you don't use the pool."

"I like the ocean." She lifted a shoulder and took a sip of her champagne. "It's unpredictable and wild, a challenge."

"Except when there are sharks in the water," he murmured.

"The benefit of a pool, I suppose. One never needs to worry about becoming dinner." She cocked a brow at him. "Swimming seems awfully un-ducal. It's wet and messy, and you're practically naked. I would think you'd prefer a more boring activity, like falconry."

Standing and watching a bird flap about would not help strengthen his heart. "I generally like more rigorous activity." Low and deep, the words were out of his mouth before he realized how they sounded. Intimate and sexual. Like he was flirting with her.

Perhaps he was.

Nellie hadn't missed it, either. She rolled her lips together and pressed them tight, as if fighting to keep quiet.

He didn't want her quiet. He wanted to hear every outrageous thought in her head, even if it was taking him to task for being inappropriate. Smiling ruefully, he said, "You might as well say it. We both know you are thinking it."

She relaxed but continued to evade his gaze, her eyes searching the crowd instead. "You haven't any idea what I'm thinking—and we should definitely keep it that way." Her brows rose as she seemed to spot someone on the other side of the room. "If you'll excuse me."

Lockwood wasn't the only guest who watched her thread through the crush. Several heads turned to track Nellie as she progressed, her red hair standing out like a flash of brightness in a sea of banal. For a moment he let himself wonder what might have happened that night if she had said yes, if she'd come back to his room with him. If he'd been able to take his time exploring her, before they learned the truth.

Something told him he never would've recovered.

"Your Grace."

The greeting ripped his attention away from Nellie's back. The Laniers were now in front of him, expectant smiles on their faces. He buried the inappropriate thoughts and pointless longing, stuffed it deep inside and remembered who and where he was. "Good evening," he said with a polite bow. Then he lifted Clarissa's delicate hand and pressed a kiss to it. "Miss Lanier."

She curtsied. "Good evening, Your Grace."

Despite what some other people thought, there was nothing wrong with Miss Lanier. She looked like almost every other woman in the room, with brown hair piled atop her head and a tasteful gown not cut too low. Perfectly polite, an impeccable reputation. A fine candidate for a duchess.

For a few moments they engaged in conversation he'd never remember. Then he held out his arm. "Miss Lanier, would you care to take a turn around the room with me to see the collection?"

She bit her lip and nodded. "I would very much like that, Your Grace."

With a nod to her parents, he led her toward the paintings and didn't look back.

Chapter Six

❧

Without looking, Nellie motioned for a passing waiter to stop. "Here," she said, swapping out her empty coupe for a full glass. "Thank you."

"You're welcome. Remember me?"

She glanced at his face. "Wait, you're . . ."

"Pete," he supplied. "I know your cousin."

Then it clicked. She recalled him from Finn's saloon over in Hell's Kitchen. "What are you doing here?"

"Earning a few extra bucks. My aunt's helping in the kitchen."

"Good for you. It's nice to see a friendly face here. This party is a bore."

"Well, gorgeous, I'm more than happy to come around as often as you like."

Normally, these words and the manner in which they'd been spoken would've enticed her to flirt back, engage in some witty repartee. Pete was handsome, probably her age or slightly older, with a hint of downtown in his rough voice. All the things she liked. At the moment, however, she was distracted.

"I'll keep it in mind," she murmured. "You'd best get back to it before I land you in trouble."

"I'll see you around, then." Pete drifted off to serve other guests.

Her mood darkened. This was all Lockwood's fault.

If he weren't here, Nellie would have dragged Pete off to a secluded spot, then talked and laughed for a few minutes. Perhaps more. Instead, she was standing on the edge of the room, alone, watching as Lockwood escorted Clarissa Lanier around the collection like some gallant knight with his lady love. Envy and resentment crawled through Nellie's chest . . . and she didn't like it. Not one bit.

She certainly didn't wish to trade places with Clarissa, so why was she jittery, like ants were crawling all over her skin?

I generally like more rigorous activity.

Her thighs clenched in excitement and she could strangle him for that. Just when their night together had started to fade from her memory, he had to go and say something like *that*. Jaysus, Mary and Joseph. Why had he blurted such blatant sexual innuendo in her presence?

She wasn't the only one who watched him, either. Nearly every woman in the room was covertly—and not so covertly—studying his broad shoulders and chiseled jaw as he moved through the room. A handsome duke under forty was like a unicorn, and the ladies of New York were once again obsessed with Lockwood. He didn't seem to notice as he bent to hear whatever Clarissa was saying, his golden-brown hair gleaming in the electric light.

"Do you think he is good in bed?"

Nellie started at the sound of Katie's voice. Her friend was now drinking champagne at Nellie's side, but her gaze remained on Lockwood. Nellie frowned. "Is who good in bed?"

"Lockwood. I saw you staring at him." Katie took a sip from her coupe. "I've always wondered."

"You are nearly married. You shouldn't be fantasizing about Lockwood, for God's sake."

"Oh, come on." Katie elbowed Nellie. "You know I'm not fantasizing about the duke. Preston is . . ." Her lips twisted like she had a secret. "Well, let's just say that Preston is more than enough."

Nellie made a face. "Stop. I would prefer to keep my dinner down, if you don't mind."

Katie just laughed. "I'm serious. What do you think about Lockwood? He's handsome. Probably has had a lot of practice with women. I bet he's quite good."

"Handsome men make the worst lovers. They don't try as hard."

"Not in my experience. Preston likes to—"

"Nope and no. My dinner, remember?"

A strangled sound of amusement and frustration erupted from Katie's throat. "Someday you must get over your general dislike of my fiancé. He's a wonderful man."

"Hmm, if you say so. All that matters is that he makes you happy."

"He does. So you needn't play mama bear any longer."

The words lanced through Nellie's chest to

nick her heart. Right. Her friends didn't need her to look after them any longer. They had husbands and fiancés for that. Nellie was the past, and these men were their futures. Soon they would all have children and busy lives . . . She would be that poor spinster friend always seated next to the widower or elderly aunt at dinner parties.

Or perhaps there would come a time when she was no longer invited at all.

Any one of their husbands could prevent it, and wives had very little recourse in a marriage. How long before Preston decided Nellie was too wild, too scandalous, to associate with his wife? Or before Kit told Alice that Nellie was no longer welcome at the supper club?

Such a precarious world in which women lived, one that was utterly and wholly controlled by men. And yet, so many women were willing to perpetuate it. They weren't interested in changing things for the better, only maintaining the status quo. Couldn't they see the damage being inflicted on them?

She shoved down her worry and hurt, locked it away with all the rest, and toasted Katie with her glass. "Consider my mama bear duties officially relinquished to your fiancé, then. If you'll excuse me, there's a waiter I have my eye on." It was a lie, but this was as good a reason as any to disappear into the crowd.

"Not my waiters!" Katie groaned. "Nellie! You're incorrigible."

"Which is much better than dull." She blew a kiss to her friend and moved away, letting the bodies swallow her up.

These society events were tedious, anyway. Without one of her friends, she generally stood alone, lurking in the shadows, while ignoring the snubs and whispers. It was exhausting. Tolerable, but exhausting.

However, watching Lockwood court his boring debutantes? That was much, much worse. She couldn't stand a moment more of it.

On her way to the other side of the room, she swept by a group of married women with whom she'd debuted. One was Rosemary Whitney, a nasty chocolate heiress who hated Nellie. Rosemary had vomited after Nellie spiked the punch bowl at a debutante ball, and the woman hadn't forgiven or forgotten in all the years since. Instead, Rosemary took every opportunity to dig at Nellie.

The group laughed and talked animatedly. Nellie averted her gaze, not ashamed but unwilling to let anyone see the emotion roiling inside her at the moment. Rosemary had a knack for picking at just the right scab at the right time, and Nellie was not in the mood.

She thought she'd made it through safely when Rosemary's voice cut through the chatter. "Oh, look. There's poor Nellie Young, alone. Still unmarried. Must be hard to watch everyone find love but you."

Nellie's chest grew tight, like her sternum might split open at any moment, and she longed to snap at Rosemary. Yet, she held her tongue.

Women should not turn on other women, even when they deserved it.

Another member of their group piped up.

"Doubtful. She's far more interested in the husbands, the jezebel."

"Goodness, remember the stories about her and Robert George?" Chuckles erupted, but Nellie didn't stop.

The voices faded from her ears but not from her mind. Instead, they remained there, stacked up like trunks, the hurtful words stored for years and years. In the dark those trunks liked to open up and spill out, all her worst thoughts and insecurities on bare display.

She blinked, that damn darkness sitting in her throat once more.

Never mind that Robert George hadn't been married at the time of their affair. Never mind that Robert George had pursued Nellie relentlessly until she gave in. Never mind that it had been consensual and quite lovely. No one knew the rest, that there had been a consequence to the affair, one that Nellie had handled and endured alone with absolutely no regrets.

Why were people so cruel?

This was not like her, to wallow and grow melancholy. It had to be Lockwood's fault. She'd been perfectly fine until he washed up on the beach in June.

A silver tray caught her eye. There went Pete, a handsome and friendly face in this sea of vipers. Yes, that seemed a perfect idea at the moment. A distraction in the form of big hands and broad shoulders, hungry lips and rough whiskers.

After all, it's what everyone expected of her, wasn't it?

To them, she was a harlot, unlovable by anyone

decent. And perhaps they were right. A good thing because decent men were boring.

She changed direction slightly and trailed Pete to the far end of the space. He continued to serve champagne, oblivious to the woman dogging his steps, so Nellie waited until he turned. When his gaze locked on hers, she lifted a brow in question. The side of his mouth hitched in a knowing, flirtatious manner, so she tilted her head toward the door before slipping through it.

It was as easy as that.

Not even a minute later she heard Pete's voice. "Where are you?" he whispered.

"Over here," she said, slightly louder. She hadn't switched on the light in the empty room, so the gloom would conceal them should anyone walk by.

"Hello, gorgeous," he said, moving in close. They were nearly touching now, and she could smell the starch on his coat. He kept his hands at his sides, however, letting her control the situation, which she appreciated.

She drew her palms up over his chest. Very nice. "Can you take a break or will you lose your position?"

His hands found her waist. "I've got a few minutes to spare. What did you have in mind?"

HE SAW THE sly smile she gave the waiter, the moment she slipped through the door. Was she . . . ? *Here?*

Something terrible and ugly rolled through Lockwood's belly and into his chest. Had she no shame? No sense of propriety at all? The city's most important and influential people were in this room, a gathering organized by her closest friend. Was she trying to cause a scandal? Ruin Katherine's event?

The waiter followed a beat later, and Lockwood could scarcely breathe through the fury squeezing his insides. He lost the thread of the conversation around him, and the room tunneled to that door and the woman who'd disappeared behind it.

Bloody hell.

He took a step in that direction, but a strange hand landed on his arm. "Your Grace, I wanted to ask you—"

"Not now," he said, shaking the fingers off. "Excuse me."

Ignoring the stares and those who tried to engage him in conversation, Lockwood crossed the floor, a gnawing sense of urgency propelling him forward. He had to stop whatever was about to happen. That boy did not deserve her, and she . . . She should be more discriminate, damn it.

As a friend of Katherine's, Lockwood was honor bound to look after her friend. Wasn't he?

After nearly tearing the door off the hinges, he went into the corridor to find his quarry. His heart pumped madly, a riot of arrhythmic thumps that echoed in his ears, but he could still make out soft voices off to his right.

"I've got a few minutes to spare," the waiter responded in a low rumble, flirtatious, eager. Lockwood hurried toward the sound. The man continued, asking, "What did you have in mind?"

"I'm not sure." Nellie's voice, almost like a soft purr. "But I'd rather be here with you than inside with them."

"I can't blame you, gorgeous. That's a dull bunch of snobs. Want a smoke?"

"Maybe. What else could we do to pass the time?"

Christ.

Lockwood came into the room just in time to see the young man lower his head. "I'm sure we could think of something," the waiter said.

Lockwood didn't think. He lunged for the waiter's collar and pulled, all the while contemplating bloody murder. Nellie stumbled forward to catch her balance, but Lockwood didn't take his glare off this unworthy piece of rubbish, dangling in his grasp. He lifted the young man up until their faces were close. "Go away before I make you regret it."

"What the hell?" the waiter snapped. "Who are you?"

"Never mind that." Lockwood tossed him toward the door. "One more word and I'll wipe the goddamn floor with you."

The waiter straightened and pulled his coat. "You all right, Red?"

"I'm fine, Pete. Sorry about this."

"You need me, I'll be close." The waiter cast a furious look in Lockwood's direction, then left.

Lockwood tugged on his cuffs and tried to put himself back to rights, while his heart struggled to catch up. He needed to calm down, immediately.

Nellie folded her arms and glared up at him. "Have you lost your mind?"

She had the nerve to be angry with him? Incredulous, he hissed, "I should like to ask you the same thing. In the middle of Katherine's art show?"

"I'm not hurting anyone. Katie won't mind if I distract one of her waiters for a few moments."

"A waiter? Are you mad? That boy—" He clamped his jaw shut to keep the words inside. *That boy doesn't deserve you.*

"I don't see how it's any of your affair, Lockwood. I never asked you to watch over me."

"Someone should," he snapped, moving in until they were barely an arm's length apart. "What you were doing was dangerous and reckless and infuriating. He could be a murderer for all you know."

"Except he's not. He's a friend of my cousin's." She searched his face, her lips parted as those gorgeous eyes narrowed on him. "You sound jealous."

He could just make out her delicate features in the darkness, the slim slope of her superb nose. The delicate chin and high cheekbones. Long lashes and auburn brows, which were currently pinched in displeasure. But he couldn't stop staring at her lips. They were full and splendid, an absolute masterpiece of craftsmanship. A sculptor could not have done better. He was dying to taste them again . . . and she was about to gift them to that boy?

It was intolerable.

Something wicked and perverse unfurled in his chest, the need to push her rising like a wave, and he advanced. "Do you need to be kissed,

Eleanor? Do you need a man to take your mouth? To press you up against the wall and ravish you?"

Though she backed away, he didn't miss how the tip of her pink tongue emerged to lick her lips.

He kept closing in, unable to help himself. But he understood her, probably better than anyone else. She was everything out loud that he tried to keep hidden away. Bold colors compared to his muted existence. He lowered his voice as he prowled toward her. "Do you need a rough encounter in the dark to make you feel alive?"

Now he could see her panting, the heft of her breasts heaving against her bodice. When she reached the wall, she didn't move, merely waited and watched, equally trapped by this strange connection between them.

Moving in, he stood close enough for his shoes to brush the edges of her skirts. Heat skated along his veins, shimmering under his skin, and his cock began to lengthen in his trousers. Bracing his hands on the wall above her head, he dragged his nose over her cheek, breathing her in. Nuzzling her. She was soft and perfect and everything he wanted in that moment.

Bending, he whispered near her ear, "Do you *need*, Eleanor?"

"Yes," she said on a quiet sigh. "God, yes."

A myriad of unfamiliar emotions roiled through him—anger, lust, jealousy. A feast of deadly sins that only this woman could inspire inside him. "Then what were you doing, flaunting that waiter in my face instead of asking me to do it properly?"

"Can you?" Her voice was a husky whisper. "Do it properly, I mean?"

A taunt, or a legitimate question? Either way, pride demanded he prove it to her. "Have you forgotten? Rough encounters in the dark are my specialty."

Instead of kissing her, he scraped his teeth over the smooth skin of her throat, then bit down where her neck met her shoulder. She gasped and sagged against him, her hips jerking, seeking, so he shifted to let her feel the erection she'd caused, the proof of his desire for her.

A moan rumbled out of her chest, followed by the sweetest word he'd ever heard. "Please."

Before he could think better of it, he grabbed her hands from where they rested on his chest and pressed them to the wall, trapping her. And the way she melted into his hold made him forget where they were, forget that a room full of New York's most judgmental people stood a few feet away.

Guided by instinct, he captured both her wrists in one of his hands and used the other to snatch her skirts, yanking them higher—

Jesus.

He instantly released the fabric and her wrists, then took a step back. What was he doing? He'd charged in here like a jilted lover and was about to now, what? Screw her against a wall?

This was not like him *at all.*

Moreover, he couldn't involve himself with this woman or her trail of recklessness. It jeopardized everything he was doing in America, his entire future. The title.

He held up his palms. "I beg your pardon."

She straightened off the wall, her gaze now wary. "For what, exactly?"

"For following you in here. It shouldn't have happened."

"And yet it did. Why?"

He scrambled to string a sentence together, one that might make enough sense to be believable. "I didn't wish to see Katherine's event tarnished by a scandal."

Something passed over her expression, something like hurt, and he considered taking the words back.

Do not tell her the truth. You are here to find a bride, nothing more.

She tried to undo the damage to her hair caused by his fingers. "God, you are the worst."

He knew this. Something about her brought out a side of him he hadn't even known existed. It was better she hated him, that they stayed away from one another. So he swallowed the apology, determined to keep this woman at a distance. He clasped his hands tightly to keep from touching her. "I will see you into a hansom."

Instead of agreeing, she laughed, the maddening female. "What? No. I am perfectly capable of finding a cab myself."

"Even still, I would feel better—"

"My evening doesn't revolve around making you feel better. Besides, your Miss Lanier will undoubtedly wonder where you've gone off to all of a sudden."

She'd seen him with Clarissa, had she? Had it bothered her? He cleared his throat, hoping to clear his thoughts, as well. "I don't like the idea of you on the street alone."

She lifted her skirts and moved around him. "I'll be fine. I don't need you."

Except he was quicker, shifting to block her path. "Why do you refuse to accept any kindness from me? Why are you so determined to be at odds?"

"Because your chivalry and polite smiles don't fool me. As we've just witnessed, you are not a kind man, Lockwood."

Does no one else see you for the monster you truly are?

She was wrong. He'd spent his entire life living up to the standards of his title, his legacy, doing as he must for Queen and country. Any dark cravings were released infrequently, carefully—except for tonight. He was a duke, constrained by responsibility and honor, and this woman, with her indiscretions and mayhem, would never understand what that meant.

However, there was no use in explaining it to her. Instead, he said, "You almost sound disappointed."

"On the contrary. Your mean side—the honest side—is the only thing I find interesting about you."

"Therefore, you poke at it? Is that it?"

"Something like that," she said with a flick of her wrist. "Now, move out of my way."

"Are you going home?"

"That is none of your concern. Run along, duke. Go and woo your heiress."

They stared at one another intently, challengingly, as if it were a contest to see who would break first. His fingers itched with the need to grab her, to hold on to her again and finish what they had started a moment ago. She was ephemeral, a shooting star, and he worried he might lose this opportunity if he did not seize it.

But an opportunity for what, exactly?

She could never be his.

Shoving all his longing and need down, he stepped to the side. "I apologize. Enjoy your evening, Miss Young."

She didn't hesitate in shifting around him and striding toward the door. Instead of going through, however, she paused. "You should send her flowers. Clarissa is quite fond of them, especially pink chrysanthemums."

He blinked, confused by the swift change in topic. "Why are you telling me this?"

"Because I like women and I hate you. The sooner you are married and gone from New York, the better. Good night."

After she left, he stood there, feet rooted to the floor. The room felt emptier without her in it, a wide cavern of nothingness made up of darkness and gloom. Suddenly, it felt a lot like his future.

He drew in a deep breath and let it out slowly. There was time for wishful thinking later. Right now he needed to return to the gallery and his responsibilities.

Chapter Seven

❦

Still feeling at odds, Nellie couldn't bring herself to go home, not after the night she'd endured. She needed people and excitement, a shoulder to lean on. A stiff drink.

Seeing Pete tonight reminded her of just the place.

Directing the driver to Hell's Kitchen, she sat back and breathed in the cool night air. Winter was here, and in a month's time the entire city would be a frozen expanse. The social season would be in full swing, with another herd of poor young girls forced into miserable marriages.

I didn't wish to see Katherine's event tarnished by a scandal.

Lockwood's words resurfaced to sit in her chest like a stone. For an instant she'd hoped he was jealous and he'd charged into the room to lay a claim on her. She should've known better.

The duke was not interested in her, not in the ways that mattered. Nellie had been a convenience, a naked woman in the ocean with whom to dally. Men like him, powerful and entitled, believed women were disposable, a lark available for when it suited them.

That wasn't how Nellie intended to live her life. She disposed of men, not the other way around. They were larks for *her* amusement. And really, she didn't want Lockwood's attention or jealousy. She didn't want anything from him at all. Certainly not his bites or his kisses, or the way he'd trapped her up against the wall.

Do you need, *Eleanor?*

She shoved it away and deliberately cleared her mind as the carriage headed west.

King's Saloon sat on the corner of West Forty-Eighth Street and Eighth Avenue, in the midst of Irish gang territory. Mama's relatives, the O'Callaghans, ran the Saints, a band of thugs and thieves. But they weren't the only gang here. Groups like the Gophers and the Parlor Mob ruled this part of town, but her being related to the O'Callaghans meant she was safe.

After she paid the driver, she lifted the hem of her silk evening gown off the ground and crossed to the saloon. A piano belted out an Irish drinking song, but most of the patrons were talking and laughing amongst themselves. The mood was surprisingly jovial for this early in the night. It was exactly what she needed to shake off that society event.

She closed the door behind her and approached the bar. A voice cheered, "There she is, boy-os! The Fifth Avenue princess."

It was her first cousin Finn sitting at a table with a large beer in his hand. Six years older than she was, he was the leader of the Saints and also her favorite cousin. He had coal-black hair that was always in need of a trim. "I'm surprised to find you not off causing trouble tonight," she called over to him.

"Trouble done been caused. Can't you see we're celebrating?" He rose to his great height and bent to kiss her cheek. "It's good to see you, caethrair."

"And you, cousin. What are we celebrating?"

A black brow arched. "Do you really want to know?"

"No, actually. I don't. I'm here for fun, not to be arrested as an accomplice."

"If it's fun you want, Red, then fun you shall have!" He slapped his palm on the bar twice. "Peg, I need a beer for my cousin."

"Whiskey, if you don't mind," Nellie corrected.

"That bad of a night, eh, love?" Peg reached for a bottle under the bar. "I'll give you the good stuff, then."

"Thanks, Peg."

"What's got your fancy drawers in a twist?" Finn leaned on the bar, setting his glass down. "Someone I need to rough up for you?"

Nellie picked up the glass that Peg slid over. "Not yet, but I will definitely keep you informed should it become necessary."

"You say the word, Red. I don't care if he's a fancy gent or not. I'll give him a proper Saints greeting."

She imagined Finn, who was big and mean, taking on Lockwood and his impressive muscles. Hard to say who would come out on top. It would be fun to see Lockwood try, though.

Smothering a smile, she took a sip. The rich

burn of the whiskey warmed her throat and stomach. "Thank you. I'll keep that in mind."

They turned toward the crowd, their backs against the bar. Several of her cousins were playing pool, while others drank at a small table nearby. "How have you been?" she asked him.

"Good. We're growing, pushing some of the other gangs farther out. Increasing our territory."

"And Catherine?" She was Finn's girl, though he thought no one knew about her. Nellie took every opportunity to needle him about it.

"Not that it's any of your business, but she's not speaking to me at the moment." He downed a mouthful of beer. "I'll bring her around, though."

"I bet."

"And you? Found a fancy husband yet?"

"That is the last thing I want, as you well know."

"Can't see why not? Women need a man to take care of them. You should have babies and a normal life, Red. Love and all that shite."

"Please cease speaking." She finished her whiskey and put the empty glass on the bar. "Your opinions about women are appalling. I think I'll go and find Aunt Riona."

"She's in the back," Finn said of his mother, tilting his chin toward the rear of the bar. "Working."

Of course. Nellie meandered to the office her aunt kept here for Saints business. While Finn might be the muscle, Riona O'Callaghan was the brains. As the matriarch, she oversaw the finances and kept the family in line. Everyone in Hell's

Kitchen knew of her wicked tongue and mean right hook, and even the most hardened criminals were terrified of getting on her bad side. The tip of her left pinkie finger was missing and her only explanation of the injury was, "Too much whiskey and cigarettes."

Nellie wanted to be just like Aunt Riona when she grew up.

She knocked on the door to the office and waited to hear her aunt's voice. "Who's there?"

"It's Nellie, Aunt Ri."

"Get in here, love!"

Nellie went in and closed the door behind her. Her mother's sister was already on her feet and moving toward the door. "Well, aren't you a sight for sore eyes?"

Her aunt gathered Nellie close for a big hug, and Nellie clung to the other woman, the closest thing she had to a mother in this world.

"Ho, now. What's this? Let me get a peek at you." Aunt Riona pulled back to look at Nellie's face. "What's wrong?"

"Nothing. Just wanted to come over and be with family tonight."

"I suppose Finn's responsible for the whiskey I smell on your breath."

"Peg, actually. Finn tried to give me beer."

Aunt Riona let her go and went back to her chair. "Oh, that piss he drinks? You might as well go over to the North River and fill up your glass there."

"Can I help?" Nellie tilted her chin toward the money on the desk.

"And get those pretty hands dirty with the

Saints' money? Your mother would have a fit, were she still alive. God rest her soul."

"Except she's not." Nellie lowered herself into a chair and reached for a stack. "Am I just counting?"

"Let's get them sorted first. See my piles here?"

Nodding, Nellie began putting the money into the proper stack based on denomination. They worked silently for a few minutes, until Aunt Riona asked, "How was your fancy party tonight?"

Knowing her aunt didn't care about the quality of the food or champagne, she said, "I made a mistake."

"Oh?"

"I let these horrible women get to me and then I tried to make a man jealous by seducing another man . . ." The admission came out easily—too easily. She sighed. "It didn't work and now I just feel worse."

"You know those society bitches aren't worth a lick of your time. Let me hear about the man."

"I'm almost afraid to tell you."

"Because you think I'll judge? Heavens, child. You know me better than that."

"No, because it makes it too real. I can't have him."

"Why not?"

"Because he's looking for a bride, an heiress. One without a scandalous past."

"And how do you know this man?"

The entire story tumbled from Nellie's mouth, the only person to whom she'd ever confessed the tale. From the night in the ocean to tonight's encounter in a dark room, she told her aunt everything.

"I'm confused," Aunt Riona said. "You want this duke, not as a husband but as a lover, which is not a problem at all in my eyes."

"He doesn't want me."

"Bollocks. He came to check on you at the dinner party. He's chasing after you and Pete. His cock's nearly busting out of his trousers every time you're around, it sounds like. Put the poor man out of his misery and sleep with him already."

As if it were that simple. "He tried to marry two of my friends, Aunt Ri."

"People in your world don't marry for love, and your friends are married to others now. Besides, you don't need to tell anyone if you decide to sleep with him."

The door flew open and a man poked his head in. Before he could speak, Aunt Riona picked up a paperweight off her desk and threw it at the door. It barely missed the man's head. "Get out, you trealaich!"

The door slammed shut. "Can I come in, Riona, my love?"

"No! Come back later, James. And you should knock first!" She rolled her eyes. "You fuck them and they think they own you. Never forget it, Nellie."

"Is that why you never remarried after Uncle Colin died?"

Her aunt was in her early forties, beautiful with reddish-brown hair and the famous Flanagan green eyes. Skin like cream and a gorgeous smile. No doubt she'd had many offers over the years. "What would I need another husband for?" Aunt Riona asked. "I have my three boys, the work we oversee. Why do I want a man taking control of all that?"

Excellent point.

Aunt Riona finished the last of her stack and folded her arms. "So what will you do about your duke?"

"I don't know."

"You like him."

"Definitely not."

"You know what happens to liars, love." She pointed to the floor. "They go right down to the eternal furnace."

"Fine, I like him. Or rather, I could have liked him once."

Her aunt leaned back in her chair and fished around in the desk drawer. "If you don't want to marry him, then I can't see why there's a problem. But if you want to marry him, then you're setting yourself up for heartbreak. Men like that put duty before everything else." She held up two cigarettes. "Smoke?"

Nellie chewed the inside of her lip. She shouldn't smoke, but that word rattled around in her head. *Heartbreak.* No, not her—and definitely not with Lockwood. She knew better.

You are the most beautiful creature I've ever seen.

"Yes," she said suddenly, reaching to take the cigarette. "Why not?"

THE GALLERY SHOW was just ending when a young woman stopped in front of Lockwood.

He tried to place her, as he was certain they'd been introduced at some point, but all of these bloody heiresses were beginning to blend into one another.

"Your Grace," she said with an elegant curtsy, lifting her hand for him.

"Good evening, madam." He bowed over her hand and released her.

When he stared, waiting for some hint of recognition, she finally said, "Oh, it's Mrs. Pierce Whitney. We've met a few times during Your Grace's stay here in New York."

That didn't help his memory, but he nodded once. "Of course. Have you enjoyed the art this evening?"

"Most definitely. My husband and I donated the Édouard Joseph Dantan painting. It's one of the largest on display here."

Was she under the impression this made it the best? He forced a smile. "That was generous of you. I know Miss Delafield has worked quite hard on the collection."

"Yes, I forgot the two of you are friends," Mrs. Whitney said. "Generous of Mr. Clarke to allow it, after he and Miss Delafield arrived at an understanding."

Lockwood and Katherine had never been serious, but he wasn't about to tell this woman as much. Also, it was less generosity on Clarke's part than knowing he could not stop Katherine if she made up her mind on something. "Yes, I suppose," he hedged, not knowing what else to say.

Her eyes swept over his shoulders and chest

in an unseemly fashion, one that set Lockwood's teeth on edge. "My husband is generous, too," she said. "Though he's much older, so he's more set in his ways."

"Is that so?" It was clear where this conversation was headed, but Lockwood had no interest in getting there.

"Yes. Does Your Grace know him?"

"I cannot say I've had the pleasure, Mrs. Whitney."

"Please, call me Rosemary." She moved closer, the edges of her skirts brushing his shoes. "Speaking of friends, did I see you with Miss Young earlier?"

Trepidation crawled along the nape of his neck like spiders. He shifted away half a step. "I believe I saw her here at one point, yes."

"Well, Your Grace probably isn't aware of her reputation, but it would be wise of you to stay clear of that one. She's nothing but a troublemaker. Not invited anywhere, really."

Mrs. Whitney wasn't saying anything Lockwood didn't already know, but he still didn't care to hear it. Not now, while he was smarting from discovering Nellie and the waiter, the boy's hands all over her like he had the right. If Lockwood hadn't arrived, what would she have done in that dark room?

I plan on sampling as many of them as possible before I'm done, after all.

And he'd acted like a jealous fool, bursting in and breaking them apart. When would he learn? He needed to stop chasing after her.

The other woman watched him carefully,

awaiting his reaction. Why was she so determined to keep him away from Nellie? Whatever
the history between these two women, he
would not step in the middle of it. Nor would
he disparage Nellie. "I appreciate the warning,
though I must admit I find Miss Young's spirit
and progressiveness refreshing."

That was not the response Mrs. Whitney expected.

Her face pinched, lines forming between her
brows and around her mouth. "I can assure you,
most of New York does not. She is not someone
with whom Your Grace should associate if you
intend—"

"His Grace should not associate with who?"
Katherine Delafield asked, now joining them.

Mrs. Whitney didn't answer and instead set
her chin. Lockwood said, "Mrs. Whitney is
kindly warning me away from Miss Young and
her troublesome reputation."

Katherine glared at the other woman. "Oh,
Rosemary. Stop holding a grudge against Nellie.
You've been jealous of her since you debuted to-
gether."

"Jealous!" Mrs. Whitney acted as if this were
the most ridiculous thing she'd heard. "You had
best be careful, Miss Delafield. It would be a
shame if no one came to your art shows because
of the guest list."

"It would, wouldn't it? And I know of at least
one person I'll be cutting from such future lists."

With a huff, Mrs. Whitney departed. Katherine
made a face. "Lord, I despise that woman. I hope
you didn't listen to her."

"No, definitely not."

"Good." She searched his eyes. "You and Nellie, you are so prickly about one another."

"Prickly?" He tried to keep it light by adding a small chuckle. "I have nothing against her whatsoever."

"I am relieved to hear it, though I cannot understand why the two of you don't get along. You're both outdoorsy sorts of people."

The night in the ocean flashed in his mind, her wet skin and salt-coated lips. He pulled at his necktie to loosen the knot lodged in his throat. "I think she holds my past with Mrs. Archer and Mrs. Ward against me. Not to mention you."

"That's absurd. These things happen all the time in our world, though perhaps not when a duke is involved. Not many would be brave enough to let you slip through their fingers, but all three examples were extenuating circumstances."

That was a nice way of putting it. "Indeed, while that's true, I cannot waste time winning over Miss Young. I have to find a bride and return home as quickly as possible."

"How are things back in England?"

Grim—failing crops, a leaky roof, a sagging foundation—but he would not burden her by complaining. His problems were his own and no one else's. "Fine."

"Is that an English *fine* or an American *fine*?"

"I am almost afraid to ask, but what is the difference?"

"Americans like to complain and we're honest to a fault. We'll happily tell our woes to anyone who'll listen."

"Then it's the other type," he said dryly.

"I knew it. You may tell me, you know. We're friends and that means always having a shoulder on which to cry."

"You had better not cry on my fiancée's shoulder, Lockwood." Preston Clarke joined them and stood closer to Katherine than politeness dictated.

"Oh, for heaven's sake," Lockwood muttered. "I am not crying and even if I were, it certainly would not be on Miss Delafield's shoulder."

"See that it stays that way."

"Stop," Katherine said to Preston. "You know I meant metaphorically, and anyway you cannot dictate to my friends, Preston Clarke."

Before this could get heated, Lockwood said his goodbyes. Katherine made him promise to take her to lunch—a request that caused Clarke to frown, the possessive arse—and Lockwood readily agreed. By the time he settled into a hansom, he was exhausted. His heart thumped erratically and he realized with horror it had been quite some time since he last exercised. Riding and walking were all fine, but he needed serious physical exertion to keep his heart strong, according to the doctors.

The key to the Young swimming pool burned in his pocket. *If you have your own key, you may come and go without the rest of us knowing.* Would he appear too eager if he went tonight?

I just want to see her again.

God, he didn't want that to be true, but he was terribly frightened that it was.

The Fifth Avenue Hotel bustled at this late

hour, guests returning from their various evening plans around the city. Lockwood paid his driver and bounded up the steps, tipping his hat at the attendants. He started for the elevator, ready for a drink and then bed.

"Stoker!"

The nickname in a clipped deep voice caught Lockwood by surprise. Turning, he found Potter Pierce, Earl of Harkness, striding toward him. "Potsie?" The two shook hands. "Christ, man. What are you doing here?"

Lockwood had gone to school with Potter, though the other boy had been a year younger. It had been ages since they'd seen one another, probably three years ago or more at Boodle's. The one thing he remembered about Potsie? The man was a terrible gossip.

"I'm here same as you." Potsie leaned in and lowered his voice. "Need to find a wealthy heiress. The coffers ain't what they used to be, you know."

Lockwood folded his arms over his chest. "Ah. How long have you been in New York?"

"Just arrived two days ago. Say, why don't we go to the bar and fetch a drink together? Catch up on old times."

The idea of it sounded awful. For one, Lockwood hadn't much liked the old times. For another, he didn't much care for Potter Pierce. But a duke was expected to be polite, so he shoved down his weariness, the thoughts of Nellie and his desire to be alone. "Of course. Lead the way."

They ended up in the bar with a bottle of Kentucky bourbon. "I love this stuff," Potsie said, pointing to the bottle. "There is nothing like it in England."

"It is nice. How is your family?"

Potsie droned on as they sipped their drinks, going into far more detail than necessary, and Lockwood experienced a sudden and violent urge to tell the man to shut up. Loudly. He longed to cease this civility, drop his polite mask and show how he truly felt for once.

Does no one else see you for the monster you truly are?

Only Nellie, apparently. For some reason he found it impossible to conceal his true thoughts and feelings around her, which made her extremely dangerous. She caused him to have inappropriate, dark thoughts that were unacceptable for a man such as himself.

"Where did you go, Stoker?"

"Hmm?" Lockwood refocused his gaze and found Potsie frowning at him from across the table. "I beg your pardon. I must be more tired than I realized. How about we do this again another time?"

They both stood and Lockwood threw money on the table. Potsie stretched out a hand. "I'd like that. I daresay we'll be seeing quite a bit of each other at these society tiddle-taddles, wooing our American dollar princesses together."

Lockwood smothered a groan and forced a smile instead. "It will be nice to have a reminder of home around."

"Indeed—and I can help find your duchess. I've heard about your recent troubles, but don't worry, I've a nose for these things." He touched his nose meaningfully. "I helped both Basing-stoke twins and Rummy Rumshire find their brides."

Those idiots? Oh, bloody hell. And did Potsie honestly believe Lockwood needed *help* in finding a woman? For God's sake, the nickname "Stoker" came from Lockwood's reputation for making older women hot and bothered, like the men who stoked the coal furnaces. So no. Despite his recent setbacks with Maddie and Alice, Lockwood did not require anyone's assistance with women.

Before he could say anything he might regret, he smiled tightly and walked away.

Chapter Eight

❦

$\mathcal{N}$ellie strode in the front door three nights later—and stopped short. Their butler was rushing toward her, a concerned look on his face. She'd been at Alice's supper club all evening, sitting in the kitchen and watching the dinner rush, after which she and Alice drank several glasses of wine together.

"Is something wrong?" Nellie asked, a hand flying up to cover her heart. The staff never stayed up this late, knowing she would use her key to get in, which meant something had happened. "Is it my father?" Her biggest fear was losing Papa, that the anxiety and long hours of his company would catch up with him.

"No, miss." The butler stopped and relaxed. "Nothing like that. I apologize if I gave you a fright."

She blew out a breath and began removing her coat. "Phew. For a moment there, I thought you might need to fetch the smelling salts. What is it, Crocker?"

He took the coat from her and hung it up in the

closet. "There is a man down in the swimming pool. No one seems to know who he is."

Nellie paused in the midst of removing her hat. Ah, so he was here. Tingles swept along the backs of her thighs, though she did her best to ignore them. "That is the Duke of Lockwood. My father has offered up the use of the swimming pool. The duke has a key to the door."

"Oh, forgive me." The tips of Crocker's ears flushed. "We were not informed and the kitchen staff became concerned. I told them a burglar wouldn't bother swimming back and forth across a pool, but they wouldn't believe me. I'll go down and reassure them now."

"Don't bother. I'll go myself and speak with them. I feel like stealing a few cookies, anyway." The lie fell so easily from her tongue. She had no interest in cookies or any other treat at this hour. The only temptation was the man in the pool. "And apologies for not warning you of His Grace's visits. Feel free to ignore him."

If only she could, as well.

The cook and kitchen maids were relieved at the news. After accepting a few pistachio macarons (her favorites), she decided to go upstairs to her room and try to fall asleep.

Except she ended up at the swimming pool instead.

The lone swimmer cut swift, decisive strokes across the glassy surface of the water, arm muscles straining as he propelled himself forward. It was like nothing Nellie had ever seen, as if he were a machine. Only the quick breath every few strokes gave any hint that he was a man. At the edge of the pool, he touched and quickly dove back the way he came, not stopping to rest even once.

He swam as if he had to, like the hounds of hell were nipping at his heels, chasing him. What drove this need of his? Was he so vain over his physique?

An ache twinged in her leg and she realized she'd been standing in the doorway, watching him, for almost twenty minutes. This was ridiculous. He was in her home, for God's sake. She wasn't intruding.

Lifting her skirts, she kicked off her shoes. Then she stepped to the side of the pool, carefully lowered herself onto the damp tile, and dipped her stocking-covered feet into the water. It felt amazing, better than a warm bath, and she swished her toes back and forth, feeling the tension in the water give as she moved.

He didn't notice her until he completed his lap. Instead of continuing, he swam down and came up directly in front of her. Water cascaded off the planes of his handsome face, his hair slicked back, the wet strands darker than the usual sand color. Air sawed in and out of his lungs, while droplets rolled down his brawny shoulders and along his bare chest, the sight so arousing it should've been outlawed by Mr. Comstock for indecency.

His blue eyes were almost shocking in their intensity as they stared at her, as if he couldn't believe she was real. "Hello."

"Hello," she echoed, not sure what else to say. There was no good reason for her to be here. The two of them weren't friends and she wasn't going to kick him out.

The water was shallow enough for him to stand, though the water line almost reached his collarbones. She wished the pool weren't this full, so she could see the duke in his bathing costume. Gander at the angles and lines of him encased in the tight wet cloth.

I am going to hell.

It was wrong to ogle the man, but he was so ogle-able. Not to mention he had looked—and felt—his fill while she had been naked in the ocean. Turnabout was fair play in her book.

Do you need a rough encounter in the dark to make you feel alive?

How did this man, one who barely knew her, understand her better than nearly everyone else?

"Did you have a nice evening?" he asked as if he couldn't think of anything else to say. Like only years of good manners had forced him to inquire at all.

"Do you honestly want to hear about it?"

His mouth hitched. "No."

There was the real man under the breeding, the one she liked best. "Good. What should we discuss instead?"

"Must we talk? We seem to get into trouble that way."

"I don't need to talk. Are you finished swimming?"

"I could be, if you are in a hurry to get rid of me."

"No hurry," she rushed to say. "I was enjoying watching you."

"Were you?" Water slid down his temples and

along his cheekbones, and he raised an arm to sweep a hand over his wet head. She got a good look at his armpit and biceps muscle, and the delicious sight sent heat rolling along her spine and through her breasts. She hadn't been able to forget the glorious moment when he'd pinned her against the wall, what it had felt like to be at his mercy.

It turned out the duke was rough and demanding in private, which was so different from his public persona. Though she wondered if he was like that with every woman . . . or just her. She quite liked the idea of making him shed his aristocratic breeding, of driving him wild with lust.

He drifted to the side and leaned his arms on the tile, his elbow almost touching her thigh. "And what did you think while you were watching me?"

Was he fishing for compliments? "I think you are an adequate swimmer," she lied.

His brows flew up. "Adequate? I must see about improving my technique, then."

"Why? It's not as if you wish to impress me."

"You think I don't wish to impress you?" He said it as if the idea were preposterous. "Half of New York would dance a naked jig in Central Park if you but crooked your finger."

She shook her head. Poor misguided fool. Still, his compliment earned him the truth. "You are impressive, duke. Surely, you know that."

"My title doesn't impress you."

"No, but your muscles do."

"Are you so shallow, then?"

"Incredibly."

"And here I thought you hated me."

"Never fear, I still do."

That got a small smile out of him. "I don't believe so, not anymore."

"No, not anymore," she admitted, mostly just to see what would happen. Would this change anything between them?

His body grew still. The water rippled around them, intimate and gentle, like the softest touch on bare skin. "I apologize for the other night," he said. "With the waiter."

"Thank you, though it was for the best. I didn't truly want him." *I wanted someone else.*

The moment stretched as his sharp gaze searched her face. "I have a problem."

"Oh? I hear mercury treatments help."

A chuckle fell from his lips then he sobered. "No, the problem is you, Eleanor."

The quiet way he said her name, with reverence and affection, curled her toes. "Because I won't leave you alone?"

"Because I do not *want* you to leave me alone. I am tied up in knots thinking about you. You're invading my dreams, as well. I haven't the faintest idea what to do about it."

Put the poor man out of his misery and sleep with him already.

Aunt Riona's advice had weighed heavily on Nellie's mind for three days. In some ways it felt like this moment was inevitable, that she and Lockwood had been going round and round each other for months just to end up here.

Slowly, she reached out and brushed a droplet from his forehead, his skin warm under her fingertips. The confession was barely above a whisper. "I feel the same and also haven't a clue what to do about it."

"Thank Christ," he swore. "I would hate to suffer alone."

Her fingertips skated along his jaw, now covered with evening whiskers. Her heart skipped a beat at the rough scratch on her skin. What would those whiskers feel like in other places? She heaved a long breath as her fingers continued to wander. "My aunt thinks I should sleep with you. Put us both out of our misery."

"Is that what you think we should do?"

"I haven't decided. It may appear differently, but I don't invite every man I fancy into my bed. You have to earn it."

Oh, it was clear he liked those words. The lines of his face grew taut, his eyes flashing in challenge. He moved closer, angling his body to cage her within his arms, one hand braced on either side of her hips. "I am quite diligent when I set my mind to a task," he murmured. "Some might even say obsessed."

That sounded like a threat, but the very best kind. "What did you have in mind?"

The answer came quickly, as if he'd had it ready all along. "Let me kiss you again."

HE COULDN'T STOP talking, couldn't keep from revealing too much to this woman. She made it easy, so comfortable to confess. If Lockwood wasn't careful, he'd end up spilling all his secrets.

Still, he elaborated, needing her to understand.

"I cannot stop wondering if our kiss in the ocean was as good as I remember."

"You called it trivial."

Of course she recalled that. "I lied—but if we are digging up the past, you said you loathed me. Called me a monster, if I am not mistaken."

"In fairness, you were being rather awful at the time."

"I was anxiously trying to manage a failing engagement," he said. "That buys one allowances, does it not?"

"Not with me."

"You encouraged them all—Harrison, Kit, Preston—merely to thwart me."

"I never encouraged Preston. I tried to keep Katie away from him, in fact."

"You did?" He couldn't help but smile, imagining Nellie going up against the formidable Clarke. It was a wonder the city survived. "I see you were unsuccessful."

She sniffed and looked away. "Well, my friends are capable of making their own mistakes, apparently."

"And you? Do you make mistakes?"

"Many. I once kissed a stranger in the ocean while naked. I'd say that was a mistake."

"Liar. You enjoyed it. And I would wager that kiss was far better than we remember."

"Is this where you tell me we must do it again to make sure?"

As if he'd stoop to such flimsy excuses. No, he didn't need trickery with this woman. He sensed she liked the plain, unvarnished truth.

He dropped his voice. "No. I merely wish to hear you make those little noises against my mouth again."

Her gaze flicked to his mouth, as if imagining what he tasted like, and his skin buzzed with a craving he barely understood, something deeper than lust or longing. It was the need to possess this woman.

She reached out to touch his wet hair, smoothing it. "Will you hold back with me, pretending to be someone you're not, or will you be real? As you were the other night."

"I cannot be anything but myself when I am with you, it seems. Much to my dismay."

She hummed as if his answer pleased her. "I have no interest in the other persona, the one who squires debutantes about and smiles when he doesn't mean it." Her touch moved lower, her fingers boldly tracing the edges of his lips, and he held perfectly still, content to be on the receiving end of her adoration, if only for a short while. She said quietly, "I want the man I see here, the one without artifice."

"Why?" The entire world wanted a duke, even a poor one, if only to rub elbows with the power and prestige that came with his title.

"Because you're much more fascinating than he is."

Nonsense. He was boring, drowning in debt and about to marry a tepid stranger he never planned on loving just to acquire her dowry. Moreover, his defective heart meant he must sire children with a wife as soon as possible, before he died at an earlier age than most, hopefully leaving his family well provided for.

That wasn't fascinating.

It was downright grim.

Desperate to touch her in return, he stroked her thigh, over her dress, uncaring about his damp hands. "You are the most compelling woman I've ever encountered. You are like a shooting star across a dark sky—brilliant and beautiful and mysterious."

"What you mean is something that doesn't belong, something that sticks out from all else around it until it burns out."

Was that how she saw herself? Lockwood couldn't stand to hear it. In fact, he wouldn't hear it. "Do not dare twist my words to make yourself anything less than remarkable, Nellie Young."

"Stern and handsome. Good Lord, Lockwood. You are hard to resist." She dragged her fingers over his head, using her nails to scrape his scalp, and he shivered. *Christ*, yes.

He was already aching and hard, even in the water. This woman had that effect on him, no matter their location. He leaned in to drag his nose across her cheek, inhaling her sweet, flowery scent. Gardenias? "There's no need for you to resist. I've already made it quite clear that I am dying to kiss you."

Her lips parted, so he cupped the back of her head and held her where he wanted. His breath came quicker as this *obsession* for her clawed inside him. It hardly mattered that they didn't much like each other outside of a physical attraction, or that sleeping with her was a terrible idea. He needed it, the temptation too great and his curiosity overwhelming any sense of reason.

He was starved for her.

"So kiss me already," she ordered, and the words washed over him, her command urging him forward.

No doubt she expected him to hurry, to mash his mouth to hers and take, take, take, like the other men she'd been with. That wouldn't do, not now.

Lockwood wanted slow and soft, to let it build. To take his time and explore her, to bring her higher than anyone had ever dared. He needed to map and memorize her, to lay a claim on her mouth so that no other person could ever possibly match it. He wanted to bloody *own* her.

His lips met hers in the softest brush, a mere whisper. He heard her intake of breath, the surprise at his approach, and anticipation crackled between them, an electric spark waiting for a closed circuit. Heat twisted and swirled inside him, a banked need that felt like dark vines in his belly, tightening and pulling, and he teased her again with featherlight kisses.

Her fingers slid along his neck as her arms wound around his shoulders, moving closer. He sealed their mouths together, deepening the kiss, and she met him eagerly, an equal give and take that had his body aching for more. There had been women before her, but he couldn't remember a single one. They were nameless, faceless encounters in this one moment that felt impossibly real, more real than anything he'd ever experienced.

Christ, what was happening to him?

She opened her mouth and he seized the advantage, pressing forward, half-afraid she would take this opportunity away. His tongue met hers and they flicked and swirled, his hands clutching her tighter, stronger, worried she might disappear at any moment.

But she wasn't pulling away. She was kissing him back and melting into his arms as if she belonged there, and desperation edged into the corners of his mind. He wished they were on a bed, where he could lift her skirts and lower his bathing costume . . .

He shoved those impractical urges aside and focused on right now. It was quiet except for their breathing and the lapping of the water against the sides, and she was so soft against him, softer than he ever would've imagined. He wanted to stand here for hours, merely stand and kiss her, explore these perfect lips and warm, slick tongue until the world burned down around them. Drown himself in her and never resurface.

"Damn it," she said, breaking free. "Why must you be such a good kisser?"

"Would you rather I was terrible at it?"

"It would make this so much easier if you were."

He knew precisely what she meant.

They should resist one another, but the knowledge of what they could have dug like a splinter under his skin. It would be explosive between them, probably better than anything either of them could imagine.

What would it mean when the night was over, however? He would have to live with the loss, the ache of marrying another while always missing this. Missing *her*. That was hardly fair to anyone involved.

He couldn't do it.

A meaningless dalliance was one thing, but this had the potential to wreck him. His responsibilities were too great, his life not his own. The time had come for good sense to prevail, even if it pained him.

Easing back, he loosened his grip. "I should return to my swim."

Her lashes fluttered, eyelids lowering to shield her thoughts. Her mouth was swollen and rosy from his kisses, strands of red hair falling around her beautiful face. The wild beat of her pulse at the base of her throat tempted him toward recklessness, so he stared at the water and let her go.

"Do you mind if I stay and watch for a bit?" she asked as he swam to the end of the pool.

"Of course not."

The water felt cool on his overheated skin as he dove back in, rolling his shoulders and kicking his feet, and he punished himself by moving faster than before. Each stroke felt like a penance for wanting a life that was not his, wanting a woman he could never have. And as he pushed himself harder, he knew he had to keep going. He had to exhaust himself until he could think straight once more.

When he finally stopped and looked up, she was gone.

Chapter Nine

❧

From her spot in the corner of the kitchen, Nellie drank a second glass of wine and marveled at the controlled chaos around her. Alice handled it all brilliantly, like a general on a battlefield directing her troops. Alice operated the supper club with her husband, Kit Ward, an enterprise that was always crowded, no matter the night. Alice's food was the most likely reason. Nellie loved everything her friend cooked.

The bustling activity also served another purpose: distracting Nellie from her encounter with Lockwood three nights ago.

Good Lord, that kiss . . .

Why must this particular man kiss like that? A duke, who'd been given every privilege, every advantage, should not have the ability to turn a woman inside out with just his mouth. Nellie had kissed her share of men and none had left her so *shaken*. Decimated and destroyed. The instant she reached her bedroom she'd lifted her skirts and shoved her hand between her legs, the climax so satisfying and necessary.

She wanted him.

If he hadn't pulled away, what would have happened? The question sent goose bumps across her skin, though hard to say whether they were a result of fear or excitement.

"You're awfully quiet tonight."

Nellie looked up from staring at her wine to find Kit standing beside her, his shoulder propped against the wall. "What are you doing in here?" Alice didn't like when her husband loitered in the kitchen. She said he distracted her.

"I was passing on a message to my wife, if you must know." He cocked his head and studied her. "What's got you so down, Young?"

How could she explain it? And even if she could, she wouldn't tell him. "You wouldn't understand."

"Oh, I see. Female troubles."

"It isn't female troubles." Why was that the first thing every man assumed? "I'm . . . I don't know." She rolled her shoulders, her dress suddenly too tight. "Figuring things out, I suppose."

"What things?"

A woman marched up to them and put her hands on her hips. It was Alice, and she looked very unhappy. "You two are making it difficult to focus. I would prefer if you went elsewhere to chat."

Kit kissed her cheek. "Sorry, my love." Then he took Nellie's elbow and helped her off the stool. Nellie tried to resist for a brief second, but Kit was stronger and more determined. "Come along. I have some of that poitín in my office."

They left the kitchen and went through the inner corridors toward the back of the building. "Shouldn't you be out on the floor, overseeing the evening service?"

"That is what my staff is for. I do it because I like it, not because I must." He threw open the office door. "Let's have a proper Irish toast and talk about whatever is bothering you."

"Where on earth did you get poitín?"

"Preston got his hands on some."

It must have come from her relatives in Hell's Kitchen. She would need to ask Finn about this. "If you're thinking to get me drunk so I'll spill all my secrets, I should warn you it won't work. Better men than you have tried and failed."

"You don't need to tell me anything. To be honest, I just wanted to escape back here for a little while and wait on Alice."

Nellie dropped onto the sofa and smoothed her skirts. "Well, that's a relief. No offense, but I'm not certain you could understand, anyway."

"Because I'm a dolt?"

The words were spoken sharply and she knew she'd hit a nerve. "I don't think you're a dolt. I think you're charming and clever, a man who has all the choices and advantages in the world at his fingertips."

He handed her a shot glass full of clear liquid. "You couldn't be more wrong about that."

"Indeed?" Her voice held a good amount of skepticism.

"Indeed. My father was a confidence man who stole all my mother's money then ran off and started another family out west."

Nellie's mouth dropped open. "What? How have I never heard this before?"

"I have no idea." He lifted his shot glass. "Sláinte."

"Sláinte agatsa," she said and threw back the poitín. It burned like hell going down, stealing her breath in a trail of fire to her stomach.

The room was quiet for several minutes as they both struggled. Finally, Kit wheezed, "Jesus, that never gets easier."

Finn could drink poitín like water, but Nellie didn't bother mentioning it. Warmth seeped through her entire body, her head turning light as the liquor mixed with her two glasses of wine. She slumped on the couch and briefly closed her eyes. Maybe this was the answer—getting blinding drunk tonight and forgetting about handsome dukes and reputations and friends who no longer needed her.

"Anyway," he said, leaning back in his chair. "It's why I started this supper club. Because I needed to prove to myself that I was more than what everyone saw."

"A booze-chugging swell who has trouble keeping his pants buttoned?"

"Exactly. Though please do tell Alice to put that on my gravestone."

"Well, I suppose I'm in the same quandary. I don't want to get married and all my friends are married. Soon there will be babies and I'll be invited as a guest . . . until I'm not."

"If you're worried Alice will drop you, that's balderdash. She thinks you hang the moon."

Nellie's lips curled, pleased at this but not

overly reassured. "The two of you will start a family and become your own little island. How long before you or Preston or Harrison tell your wives I'm a bad influence? A wild, unmarried spinster who bucks tradition at every turn?"

He walked over and refilled her glass. "If you think any of us are able to tell our wives what to do, then you don't know your friends very well."

"But you could keep Alice from seeing me."

His brow quirked as he poured himself another drink. "Not if I wished to retain my testicles, which I'm actually quite fond of. Besides, I like you."

Nellie chewed on the inside of her cheek. Kit seemed certain, which took that particular worry off her plate. So why did she still feel this nagging darkness? This uncertainty and unhappiness?

"This isn't what is bothering you, though."

Her head snapped up at his words. "How would you know?"

"Because we're alike, you and I." He held up the glass. "Are you ready? Or do you need your smelling salts?"

"Please. You'll pass out long before I do."

He smirked and downed his drink, slamming the glass onto the desk. She did the same and was pleased when his eyes watered and hers didn't.

"See?" she said when she caught her breath.

"Fair enough." He wiped the corners of his eyes with his sleeve. "So let's get back to what's bothering you. I think you need a purpose. You need to feel like you matter."

The edges of the room softened and her muscles went lax. Hmm. It might be the spirits, but what Kit said actually made sense. "Why are you so certain?"

"It's why I did all this." He gestured to indicate the supper club. "To prove I could. To build something that lasts, to have something that's mine."

Her friends were all passionate about something. In addition to Alice's having the supper club, Maddie had tennis and Katie her art museum. "But there isn't anything I'm passionate about," she told him.

"I find that very hard to believe." He held up the bottle. "Another?"

"I probably shouldn't."

"Me neither. I still have to tally the evening receipts." He dragged a hand down his face. "And that's a struggle when I'm sober."

She snickered. "Which means we definitely should."

"Oh, definitely."

The third shot of poitín went down much easier and she settled into the warmth of the couch. Kit lit a cigar and leaned back in his office chair. Nellie licked her lips, her mouth oddly dry as she said, "I am thinking of engaging in an affair with the Duke of Lockwood."

Kit made a choking sound. "What? No. *Him?*" He straightened and shook his head, as if trying to clear it. "What is it about him that attracts every woman in Manhattan? Is it his title? Because I have to tell you, he is a first-rate asshole."

"Oh, I know that. Perhaps better than anyone. And believe me, I wish he wasn't a duke."

"I can't wrap my head around this. You want to become a *duchess*? Have you lost your mind?"

"Me, a duchess?" She gave a dry laugh. "Absolutely not. But there is something about him . . . And the way he kisses is unlike anything I've ever—"

"You *kissed* him?"

"Stop acting like a prude. You kissed plenty of women before Alice."

"It's not the kissing part, it's the Lockwood part. He certainly gets around."

"What does that mean?"

"It means he's here tonight in the dining room. With the Twombly girl and her parents."

Nellie blinked away her surprise. Lockwood was fond of Alice, so it wasn't all that shocking to learn that he frequented the supper club. Though it appeared tonight he'd escorted another one of his potential duchesses. Now in her second season, Helen Twombly was known for playing the piano and her affinity for cats. She would bore Lockwood to death.

Was he pouring on the ducal charm and making her smile? Or was he miserable?

Nellie had to find out.

She pushed off the couch, steadied herself, then went to the door. Kit stood, as well. "Wait, where are you going?"

"To spy on them, of course."

"Wait, wait, wait." Kit reached the door at the same time. "You can't do that."

"Why not?"

"Because you can't spy on my patrons. What sort of owner would I be if I allowed such a thing?"

"I'm not going to draw attention to myself. No one will ever know."

"All right, but only if you promise to stay hidden."

She put her hand over her heart. "I do solemnly swear."

Dinner service was underway, so loud voices and the scrape of silver on china carried throughout the building. Nellie edged to the corner, still keeping to the shadows, and searched for a tall man with sand-colored hair and obnoxiously wide shoulders.

She found his profile, and her stomach swirled and dipped. The reaction embarrassed her, so she told herself it was the poitín. Anything else was unacceptable.

He wasn't smiling. His attention was on his plate, and Miss Twombly appeared nervous, casting unsure glances his way and biting her lip. The elder Twomblys sat rigidly in their chairs, as if uncomfortable, and Nellie had to assume the chaperones were less than thrilled with the dinner location. After all, a supper club, even one run by a member of High Society, was still scandalous. What had Lockwood been thinking?

This outing was a disaster. Miss Twombly needed an opportunity to shine, otherwise Lockwood would never seriously consider her as a potential wife. And the sooner he married, the sooner he'd leave New York, Nellie's swimming pool and Nellie's mind.

Her gaze drifted to the stage, where a piano rested, awaiting the evening's entertainment.

Looking over her shoulder, she found Kit standing there, observing the room proudly. "Would you mind fetching Miss Twombly for me?"

THE EVENING WAS a disaster.

The supper club had been a terrible idea on Lockwood's part, even if Alice was a talented chef. The Twomblys were clearly horrified by the raucous atmosphere, and Miss Twombly was caught between wanting to please her parents while remaining a viable candidate for a duchess. Lockwood almost pitied her.

In truth, he didn't much care who he married these days. Each of the three heiresses on his list were indistinguishable, too alike to be memorable. None of them inspired interest or passion in him.

Perhaps a red-haired siren had ruined him for all other women.

Every night he returned to the Young swimming pool, but Nellie remained absent. His laps were completed alone, the specter of her chasing him through the water, while his mind wondered where she was and what she was doing. Even what she was wearing. The thoughts had nearly driven him mad, yet he kept coming, hoping to see her.

He was a bloody fool.

I want the man I see here, the one without artifice.

She didn't understand. His life was all artifice, pretending to be something he wasn't—a healthy and happy duke without a care in the world. Only she had seen him stripped bare and vulnerable, and she hadn't even learned the worst of it.

Yet he couldn't stop *wanting* and *craving*, even though it did him no good. None whatsoever.

"Excuse me."

Lockwood turned and found Kit Ward hovering beside their table. His jaw clenched, an automatic reaction he couldn't prevent. Why Alice had chosen this scapegrace was a mystery for the ages. "Yes, Ward?"

"Our chef—my wife—has requested to meet Miss Twombly. Would you mind?"

Miss Twombly's gaze darted between Ward, the kitchen door and her parents. "Me?"

"Yes." Grinning affably, Ward held up his hands as if to say, *I don't understand either, but she's my wife and must be indulged in all things.* "It will only take a moment."

"May I?" the young girl asked her parents.

"I suppose it would be all right, if she's not in the way," Mrs. Twombly said.

"No, she won't be in the way." Ward walked over to the girl's chair and held out his hand. "Miss?"

Lockwood started to stand. "Perhaps I should escort her." After all, the last time he'd sent his companion into a kitchen with Ward all hell had broken loose.

"Not necessary, Your Grace," Ward said smoothly. "We have it well in hand. Enjoy your ox tail."

Ward led Miss Twombly away from the table and through the kitchen door. The whole business struck Lockwood as odd. Why would Alice, who took dinner service more seriously than church, invite a stranger in there to distract her?

She wouldn't even let her husband linger in the kitchen during the hustle and bustle.

Lockwood couldn't very well follow without being rude to the Twomblys, however. He'd check on Miss Twombly if she hadn't returned in a few moments.

"Does Your Grace reside in the country or in London most of the year?" Mrs. Twombly asked.

"In the country, mostly," Lockwood answered. "Yorkshire. Have you been?"

"Oh, I'm afraid I haven't. We've never been anywhere but London. It's frightfully dirty there. I cannot say I'm surprised to hear you prefer the country."

Cleanliness had nothing to do with it. He could breathe in the big manor house, away from prying eyes and wagging tongues. The lake allowed him exercise, and he could better manage the repairs and the land while on-site. If he needed a night out or had an important meeting, London was close.

His grandfather had once owned six estates, and Lockwood's father had lost all but two: Bridgewater Towers in Yorkshire and the house in Mayfair. Right now both were in peril if Lockwood didn't receive an influx of cash. Bloody embarrassing, but he'd inherited the debt, which had only compounded despite his investments and improvements. In this world money begat money, and the same worked with debt. The pile fed off itself, multiplying, until it became unmanageable.

Suddenly, two waiters emerged on the small dais that served as the stage. They went to the piano and maneuvered it sideways, so the audience would have the profile of whoever was to play. The diners quieted, a shifting of silk and wool as everyone adjusted their position to better see the show.

When the waiters departed, Ward was there, welcoming the guests. Lockwood hated to admit it, but the man was charming, perfectly suited to put people at ease.

Wait, if Ward was here, where was Miss Twombly?

"We have something exciting for you this evening. Our short performance from *The Tempest* will be pushed slightly to allow us to present another great talent. I hope you'll indulge me in welcoming two young ladies who are performing together tonight for the first time. I know it will be an event on everyone's lips tomorrow."

Ward began clapping, enticing the crowd to do the same, as he moved to the side of the stage. Two women appeared and Lockwood's heart stuttered. What in the blasted hell . . . ?

Miss Twombly and Nellie Young came out together, the former looking so nervous that it was a wonder she could put one foot in front of the other. Nellie, conversely, walked with all the confidence of a stage actress, head high and shoulders back, soaking in the attention of every person in the room.

Christ, she was magnificent.

Blood rushed south to pool in his groin, sparks igniting in his veins. He clenched his hand on his thigh, fighting the searing desire for her and losing. The things he wanted to do to her luscious body . . . and the things he wanted her to do to him in exchange. *Fuck.* They were lewd and indecent, these things he imagined, far too depraved for a duke.

But perhaps just depraved enough for a rebellious American princess.

"What is she doing?" Mrs. Twombly hissed to her husband. "Go and get her, Mr. Twombly."

"It's too late," her husband said under his breath. "Causing a scene will only make it worse."

Mrs. Twombly huffed and leaned toward Lockwood. "Your Grace, please excuse her. I have no idea what's come over my daughter."

Lockwood had some idea of what had happened. Nellie had happened.

He gave the older woman a small smile, never taking his eyes off Nellie. "Nonsense. I'm looking forward to seeing what the ladies have planned."

Miss Twombly settled at the piano downstage, while Nellie remained more toward the back. Tall and proud, Nellie nodded once at the other girl, who began to play the ivory keys, sending tinkling notes into the quiet room. When Nellie opened her mouth and began to sing, Lockwood almost fell off his chair. Her voice was strong and brilliant, the sweetest sound he'd ever heard. *My God, she can sing.*

The song was "The Simple Ostrich" from *The Merry Monarch*, a popular Broadway show, and Miss Twombly played it perfectly. But it was Nellie who commanded the attention, captivating the room with her sparkling green eyes and full lips forming those gorgeous sounds.

They moved on to another song, then another,

the selections chosen to feature the piano, with complicated solos and rousing melodies. Miss Twombly was accomplished and had no problem keeping up, while Nellie remained in the back, as if content to let the other girl upstage her.

Except it failed.

Nellie's voice was too good, her pitch and tone precisely what each song required, and Lockwood couldn't stop staring at her. More specifically, he couldn't stop staring at her mouth.

He wanted to kiss her. Badly.

More like he wanted to ravish her, to maul her. *Destroy* her. He was boiling over with the need for her, his skin unable to contain these feelings, the desire too great. And he was tired of fighting it.

The battle had been lost.

He willingly surrendered to whatever was happening between them, consequences be damned. *Soon*, he promised himself. *Very soon.*

When they finished he was the first to stand, applauding loudly. It took a few seconds, but the rest of the crowd soon followed, coming onto their feet and clapping enthusiastically. Nellie walked forward, clasped Miss Twombly's hand, and the two ladies bowed. Then Nellie stepped back and clapped for Miss Twombly, who grinned and dipped into an elegant curtsy, her cheeks flushed.

It became clear. Nellie had done this for Miss Twombly. But why? Were the two even acquainted?

The ladies left the stage and Ward announced that dinner would continue, with the second performance occurring during dessert. Meanwhile, the Twomblys were whispering amongst themselves, unhappiness etched in their expressions. He sought to ease the situation before they took it out on their daughter. "She was magnificent. Don't you agree?"

Mrs. Twombly's mouth curled like she'd sucked on a lemon, while Mr. Twombly cringed. "We apologize, Your Grace," he said. "This was entirely unbecoming of a young lady. We have raised her to play the classics, not these . . . sideshow tunes."

Because of his title, people often expected a snob. Lockwood was not, nor did he like those who turned their noses up at simple or popular things. Everyone had varied tastes—including him—which was how it should be. "I say one must play to the audience, and this crowd certainly appreciated the selections. I don't think the heavy classical pieces would have received such a rousing reaction."

The answer didn't appease the older couple, as they exchanged a glance then looked away. Inwardly, Lockwood sighed.

Miss Twombly began threading her way through the dining tables, accepting congratulations as she went, and he could see the pride brimming in her expression. Nellie had caused that, but to what end? Would he ever understand that woman?

As Miss Twombly approached, she seemed to sense her parents' disapproval, and she hesitated. So Lockwood rose, went to her and escorted her the rest of the way. "Marvelous performance, Miss Twombly. You are exceedingly talented."

"Thank you, Your Grace."

Her parents were not as enthusiastic. In fact, they claimed Mrs. Twombly had a terrible headache and the evening must be cut short. Lockwood couldn't argue, but he did reassure Miss Twombly again that he had enjoyed her performance. Soon the three Twomblys disappeared, leaving Lockwood alone.

Instead of finishing his dinner, he went in search of the one person who could provide him with answers.

Chapter Ten

❦

$\mathcal{H}$eart sinking, Nellie watched as the Twomblys escorted their daughter from the dining room. Damn.

At least Lockwood had looked pleased with the young woman, which was all that mattered. Nellie hadn't dared to meet his gaze during the performance, too terrified of what she might see there, but it appeared to have worked. As Miss Twombly returned to the dining room, he stood and smiled, escorted her to their table as if she were precious.

So . . . good. That was done.

Nellie could rest easy knowing she'd helped him to see the other girl's strengths, to appreciate what a competent duchess Miss Twombly would make.

Perfect. Excellent. *Job well-done, Nellie.*

Why did she feel so awful, then?

She retreated into the shadows and started for Kit's office. Alice would be finished in about an hour, so Nellie would wait for her friend there. Lockwood would invariably leave, as well, now that his dinner companions had departed. Perhaps he'd come to the swimming pool after. Better she stayed here, away from temptation.

As she turned the corner, a figure stepped forward, startling her.

Lockwood.

She sucked in a breath and dropped back a step. How had he arrived so quickly? "My God, Lockwood. You scared me."

The dark expression he wore made her shiver. It was intense, a look similar to the one he wore when he pinned her to the wall at the art show. He began advancing on her, the soles of his leather shoes thumping on the worn wooden floor. Unwittingly, she retreated, her heart kicking hard, her lungs suddenly unable to pull in air. This was not fear, however. Definitely not fear.

What was he doing? Would he pin her to the wall again?

Excitement leapt in her chest and she bit her lip as he crowded her into the plaster. "Are you upset with me?"

"No," he said, his brow lifting in that arrogant way of his. "Quite the opposite."

Oh.

A fluttering began in her belly, and her breasts swelled behind her corset. He caged her in, placing both hands on the wall by her head to surrounded her, his handsome face all she could see. Thank the saints the plaster was there to hold her up.

"Here is what will happen now," he said near her ear, his voice soft but threaded with steel. "You will leave and find a hansom. Then you will meet me at my hotel—room 122. When you arrive, I shall remove all the clothing from your gorgeous body and run my tongue over every bit of your bare skin. Following that, I'll remove my clothing and fuck you. I promise to take care with you, Eleanor, and I swear it will be the best goddamn time of your life."

She couldn't speak. She couldn't *breathe*.

Never had she expected such a straightforward approach, not from a duke. She certainly hadn't expected him to use the word *fuck*. Why did she find that so arousing? The word flipped a switch inside her, releasing a flood of want and need until she couldn't hold it back any longer.

She longed to hear him say that word again, slower this time. While he performed the act.

Licking her lips to moisten them, she said, "All right."

His mouth curved in the most sinfully delicious way, as if he'd just received a decadent prize. "Then I shall expect you at the hotel shortly."

"All right," she repeated, incapable of more intelligent speech, apparently.

Without another word, he pushed off from the wall and walked away, his shoulders an unholy masterpiece in his evening coat. She couldn't wait to dig her nails into those slabs of muscle again, feel his strength beneath her fingertips. Swallowing, she straightened and went to gather her things.

Alice was too busy overseeing dessert to pay her much attention, so Nellie waved and promised to visit again soon. Then she went out the kitchen door, into the alley and toward the street.

The night was frigid, her breath gusting in front of her face in cold bursts as she climbed into a cab.

Was this truly happening?

Yes, it appeared it was.

She waited for the hesitation, but it never came. They wanted each other and there was no reason to deny it. Still, she wasn't certain how far she was willing to go. It would be best to keep the encounter light and easy, as impersonal as she could manage. Taking a man inside her body was intimate, a matter of trust and not something she rushed into with a near stranger. Feelings could develop if one wasn't careful.

No chance of that here—she didn't even *like* Lockwood—yet somehow, she wanted him. She wanted to know what a night with him would be like. Based on all she'd experienced thus far, she had a feeling their recklessness would be rewarded.

The hotel was busy with guests returning from their evening out, so no one noticed as she slipped through the lobby and hurried toward the first-floor rooms. Her skin hummed with anticipation as she knocked softly on the door to his room.

The latch turned and he was there, standing in the doorway, tall and handsome, his evening jacket already off. When he stepped aside, she came in and placed her handbag on the table. Without saying a word, he helped her remove her heavy overcoat and hung it on a stand by the door as she removed her gloves.

Then he took her hand and led her through the sitting room and directly into the bedroom. It was large and impersonal as far as decor went, but she took in the little touches of him everywhere, like the book on his nightstand. A half-empty glass of water. Reading glasses. His hairbrush.

Releasing her, he sat on the bed and regarded her. "You may say no, of course."

"I'm aware—and I still might."

"Then I'll see what I can do to convince you. Come here, Eleanor."

She crossed to the bed where he snatched her wrist and pulled her down on top of him. Now flat on his back, he stared up at her with a crystal-blue gaze full of heat and reverence, longing and fascination. His fingertips brushed errant strands of hair behind her ear, his touch lingering on her skin and making her shiver. "I've imagined you here in my bed countless times."

The flattering words caused a fresh wave of desire to snake through her belly and pulse between her legs. "And what did you imagine?"

His hand swept along her spine to settle behind her neck. It was a possessive hold, like he worried she might try to get away from him. "All manner of depravity, most not fit for a lady's ears."

Before she could ask for more, he leaned up and sealed their lips together, while his fingers angled her head to keep her in place. With no preamble, his tongue licked inside her mouth, gliding across hers in a perfect rhythm. The kiss was not the sweet, almost tentative exploration of the other night. No, this was demanding and rough, desperate, like he wasn't holding back from her, and it was perfect. Exactly what she needed.

She sank into him, boneless, melting into the hard angles and taut ridges of his big body as the kiss wore on. The room narrowed to just the two of them and she let him lead as the need spiraled, tightened inside her. Wetness gathered between her legs, and the idea of resisting him seemed distant, too far to even grasp at this point. What would one time possibly hurt? She would satisfy her curiosity and then move on.

He broke off to slide his mouth along her jaw, her neck. She panted, dizzy from the pulsing of her sex, and each place he licked and kissed grew hot, like he was spreading fire all over her skin. A pleading sound she'd never made before fell from her lips, one that would have been embarrassing in any other circumstance.

"I want you naked. I want to take care of you," he said. "May I?"

"God, please. Yes."

They worked together to get the layers of clothing off. Lockwood was no ladies' maid, but he was competent, and they had her down to her drawers and stockings in no time. She reached for the ribbons on her drawers, but he nudged her hands out of the way. "Stop. Allow me."

She relented and relaxed on the bed, while Lockwood loomed over her. He dragged a fingertip over her bare breast, eyes flaring when her nipple puckered at his touch. "You are so bloody gorgeous."

Her fingers swept over his jaw. "You are quite gorgeous yourself, duke."

"Don't call me that," he said, bending to nibble on her throat. "Not here, not now."

"What should I call you, then? Lockwood?"

"It's what almost everyone calls me."

The flat of his tongue dragged over her collarbone and she shivered. "What about the rest? What do they call you?"

"The boys at school called me Stoker."

Some prep school nonsense, no doubt. "That's absurd. What else? Your given name?"

"Andrew, but no one—"

"Andrew," she tried out slowly, examining the feel of it on her tongue. "I like it. It makes you less English."

"Darling, I could never be less English." He moved lower to kiss her chest, then lower even still. "I'm a duke, which is practically the definition of English."

"Don't remind me—I'm trying to forget at the moment."

The tip of his tongue flicked her nipple. "Keep your eyes open, Eleanor. Don't close them. Watch who is pleasuring you out of your fucking mind."

Her toes curled at his crude word, so very unducal and so very appealing. He glanced at her, ensuring she was obeying, as he drew her nipple into his lush mouth. Her breath caught at the tight heat, the pressure, and his cheeks hollowed as he sucked. His lids fell, his long lashes fanning across his skin, and he used his teeth and lips until she squirmed. By the time he moved to the other breast, she was panting, grasping at him, nearly ready to jump out of her skin. No one had taken such care with her before, making her feel worshipped and adored like this. It was heady, and incredibly arousing.

Finally, he released her and began moving in the direction she craved. He kissed and licked her ribs, her stomach, then pushed her drawers down her legs until the silk joined the rest of her clothing on the floor.

He swirled his tongue over her left hipbone. "Would you like my mouth here?" Then he shifted to the right side. "Or perhaps here?"

"Best to cut the difference," she said, barely able to force the words past her scratchy throat.

He chuckled. "Put your hand on my head, then, and place my tongue where you want it."

"Is it because you cannot say the word?" she taunted, sliding her fingers through his soft hair.

"What, *pussy*? *Quim*? *Cunt*? Think I'm too high-brow for those words?"

At his filthy talk, Nellie's eyes practically rolled back in her head, her clitoris throbbing in time with the frantic beat of her heart. Of course he noticed, his mouth curling into a grin. "You like when I use crude words, don't you? Why?"

"Because they are unexpected. *You* are unexpected."

And she quite liked unexpected. Unfortunately.

"Indeed, then. Let's see if I'm able to keep surprising you. Open your legs as wide as you can, Eleanor."

HE COULD SMELL her arousal.

This glorious creature wanted him, *desired* him, and Lockwood felt like the luckiest man in the entire world.

"Has a man licked you before?" He kissed her inner thigh. "Your cunt, I mean."

Her pupils were wide and black with need, strands of red hair hanging loose all around her face like bright slashes of color against his boring bedclothes. She was bloody beautiful. "Yes," she breathed in answer to his question.

Good. He wouldn't need to explain it, then. It had been more than a year since he'd buried his face between a woman's legs, and he was dying to taste her. "Hands, Eleanor. I want to feel your fingers and fingernails as I make you come."

With no hesitation whatsoever, she grasped his head and pushed him down, forcing him exactly to the place where he wished to linger for days. The musky taste of her exploded on his tongue, slick and delicious, better than any dessert or treat he'd ever sampled, and his eyes nearly crossed. "Fuck," he breathed out slowly, knowing she would like hearing the word. "You are absolutely perfect, my darling. Wet and soft and perfect."

He resumed his task, exploring every bit of her with his tongue. He sucked and licked, used his teeth on her folds and his lips on her clitoris. His cock was stiff and aching, but he liked denying himself while seeing to her first. Even if she didn't want more than this, he would be quite satisfied servicing her.

Varying his speed and suction, he quickly learned what she liked. When he pushed a finger inside her channel, her fingernails dug into his scalp, so he added another finger and kept painting his tongue over her swollen nub. Soon she was rocking her hips and holding him tighter, the sting from her nails like hot fire down his back. He could feel her everywhere, his senses overwhelmed with her in the very best way, and it had him nearly humping the mattress.

"Yes, like that," she whispered. "It's so good. Oh, God."

He kept going, not letting up, and her arousal coated his fingers, dripped onto the bedclothes, as he pumped inside her. The sounds coming from her mouth grew louder and her thighs trembled. Finally, her back bowed, her muscles clenching all around him, while her body went perfectly still as if she wasn't even breathing . . . And then she began pulsing and twitching, her cries echoing in the room. Her walls sucked on his fingers greedily, as if trying to bring them inside her body, and he never wanted this to end. He wanted to stay right here, feasting on her, driving her wild, until morning.

When she grew sensitive, he reluctantly pulled off, still giving her soft kisses along her folds as he withdrew his fingers. He swirled his tongue at her entrance, catching more of her wetness, lapping at the swollen tissue.

"Andrew," she said, tugging on him. "Come here."

"Not yet," he mumbled into her flesh, leaving loud, obscene open-mouthed kisses on the most intimate part of her.

"Lockwood." She sounded annoyed. "Please."

The begging did it. Reluctantly, he rose up and dropped beside her on the bed. The clothes he wore itched his sensitive skin, every part of him hot and aching. Still, he didn't undress. He dragged a palm through the red curls on her mound and up her stomach, between her breasts. Her skin was pale cream, unblemished and smooth. "You are without question the most beautiful woman I've ever seen."

She swallowed, the delicate muscles of her throat working. "For a not-nice man, you are being very nice to me."

"Do you hate it?"

"I haven't decided. It's confusing."

"I can be mean and rough, if you prefer."

He did not miss the tremble that went through her at his words. God's teeth, they were so well suited, it was almost scary. *This woman will be the death of me.*

"I've never tried it that way," she said, pulling on his necktie to loosen it. "Every man I've been with has been careful and kind."

"Boring."

"I didn't say that."

"There was no need to. I know you." His necktie now gone, he popped his collar and tossed it to the floor. "You said it yourself—you like the unexpected."

She pushed him onto his back and rose up onto her knees. "So do you. It's why you found me in the ocean. Why you've been chasing me all over New York."

"*I* have been chasing *you*?"

"I don't chase after men. They're too easy to come by in this city." Her fingers went to the fastenings on his trousers. No way she could miss the erection tenting the cloth. "Men chase after me, and I decide whether I'll let them catch me or not."

"So have I? Caught you, then?"

She pulled apart the placket and then unbuttoned his braces on each side. "I'm still making up my mind."

"The earth-shattering climax I gave you didn't sway you at all?"

"It definitely helped swing the odds in your favor."

He rolled one of her taut nipples between his thumb and forefinger, pinching hard. Gasping, she froze, and her eyelids fluttered shut. Yes, she liked that. Just like in the ocean when he bit her lip. He pitched his voice low. "How about that? Does that increase the odds in my favor? Because I should very much like to fuck you right now."

"Jesus, Lockwood." She swayed toward him, her hand resting on his stomach as if to keep herself from falling over.

"We do not lie to one another, Nellie. If I'm to be honest with you, the man without artifice, then I expect the same in return."

"Fine, I'll be honest. I very much want to sleep with you, but I'm worried about what happens after."

"We get dressed and I see you home."

"You know that's not what I mean." She pushed his trousers off his hips, and he lifted to help her. He'd removed his shoes earlier, so he worked the wool down his legs and let it fall to the ground. She was already working on unbuttoning his shirt when she said, "This can only be a onetime thing. I cannot have an affair with you."

"Why not?"

This was taking too bloody long and her touch

was driving him absolutely mad. Standing, he began removing his clothing quickly, not caring if he lost a button or two along the way. She watched intently, still on her knees, her hooded gaze tracking his movements. He liked the way she bit her lip when he was naked from the waist up, her stare lingering on his shoulders, and he slowed a bit as he removed the rest.

When he was completely bare, he stood at the side of the bed and let her look. She took her time, surveying him from head to toe, paying extra attention to his jutting cock. "Sakes alive, you are a beautiful man."

He couldn't help but stroke himself, his whole body on fire. Once would never be enough with her. "I want an affair. For as long as I'm in New York."

"No," she said instantly. "Now, bring that beast here and let me taste you."

His knees shook. He wanted that so badly. "An affair, Eleanor. Tell me I can have you as often as I want for the next few months."

"I'm not some poor actress or chorus girl who needs your gifts and attention, Lockwood." She slipped her hand between her legs and boldly began fondling herself. "I won't be at your disposal."

He watched her delicate fingers strum over her clitoris, enjoying the way her chest rose and fell as she pleasured herself. Bloody hell, that was the most arousing thing he'd ever seen. He stroked himself faster, squeezing harder and twisting his grip over the sensitive head, his breath sawing out of his lungs. The urge to thrust, to take, welled inside him. "Goddamn it," he gritted out from behind a clenched jaw.

"I've never climaxed twice in one night," she said, watching his fist work his erection. "Perhaps this might be the first."

Lust careened through his veins and he caved. Whatever she wanted in this moment, he would grant it if it meant he could have her.

There was a shield in the nightstand, so he located the tin and placed it within reach. Then he crawled onto the bed and covered her, their mouths meeting in a frenzy of lips and teeth, and she smoothed her hands over his shoulders and back. Down to his backside. Around to his front.

When she gripped his cock, he jerked, his body so desperate for her that he wondered whether he would last. Already his balls were tight and heavy, the tip of his shaft leaking, and he needed to make this perfect. Removing her hand, he took both her wrists and pinned them above her head. "I will spend if you keep doing that."

She writhed and panted underneath him, her eyes wild. "Now, Lockwood. Get the shield. I need you now."

In a flash he grabbed the tin, removed the shield and rolled the thick rubber over his erection. She kept her hands above her head, waiting so sweetly for him, and he loved seeing her on his bed. His fiery angel. "Spread your legs," he demanded.

When she obeyed, he settled between her thighs and lined himself up at her entrance. Instead of shoving hard, as his body craved, he stretched out on top of her and, without thinking, held her wrists to the mattress. Then he slowly sank inside, watching her face the entire time. "That's it," he murmured as her tight heat engulfed his shaft. "*Christ*, that feels good."

"Damn, but you are immense." Throwing her head back, she arched her neck. "I'll likely feel you for days."

"Mmm. Quite like the idea of that." He ran his lips over the velvety skin of her throat. Taking her earlobe in his mouth, he bit down lightly on the supple flesh.

"Harder," she said, echoing his words from their ocean encounter back to him, and his cock throbbed in sheer delight.

Did she mean it?

He had to try, had to find out, so he sank his teeth into her skin. Jolting, she gave the sweetest gasp as her walls spasmed around his shaft, allowing him to slide deeper.

Ah, God. *Yes.* There was something about a rough exchange of physical passion in bed that turned him hard as stone. A mix of sensation and desperation that obliterated everything else inside his mind. No heart problems, no debt, no responsibilities. It calmed him much better than swimming, in fact. Unfortunately, he hadn't found many partners with whom to experiment. His last mistress had enjoyed it, but that had been quite some time ago.

Hopeful, he squeezed Nellie's wrists, holding her beneath him, while he examined her reaction. She moaned and rocked her hips, trying to bring him all the way inside her. When their hips met and he was fully seated, she squirmed underneath him. Even though he was sweating with the need to come, he kept still, not releasing her. "Is this all right?"

"So very all right. Move, Andrew."

He put his body to use, then, driving his hips, dragging his cock in and out of her slick flesh to pleasure them both. The sounds in the room were loud and raw—the slap of their hips, their pants and grunts. The bed frame rocked into the wall with a rhythmic thumping. Sparks sizzled along the backs of his thighs, the orgasm building, so he released one of her hands. "Use your fingers. Come while I'm inside you."

She didn't hesitate. Her hand went between them and he could feel her circle her clitoris with every thrust. He rose up on his knees to watch where they were joined, holding her thighs as wide as they would go while his shaft speared into her channel, her slickness glistening on the rubber. Her fingers moved faster over the swollen bud atop her sex, so he slid his hands to her breasts and squeezed hard, bringing blood to her other pleasure areas. The nipples swelled, turning a duller red, and he pinched them as a reward.

Instantly, she seized, her limbs going taut, as a long groan fell from her lips. "Oh, God, yes," she cried as her inner muscles clenched in sweet pulses. He rode her through it, loving every twitch and sigh she gave, trying to stave off his own orgasm.

When she calmed, he put his hands on either side of her head and began riding her, his hips churning and muscles straining, the climax nearly there. It felt so fucking good, better than ever before, and he watched the red fingerprints he'd left on her breasts as he kept thrusting inside her.

"Goddamn it," he whispered, the crest nearly there.

Her hands moved to his chest and before he could prepare for it, she dug her nails into the skin, marking him with little half-moons. The pain punched through his veins and raced to his cock. "Jesus, fuck!" he shouted. It was like she'd flipped a switch inside him, and the climax surged up from his toes and along his shaft. Jets of spend filled the rubber as he trembled, groaning his pleasure to the ceiling as it went on and on.

Finally, the dizziness ebbed and he came back to earth. Slumping, he tried to catch his breath. With clarity came shame as he took in her disheveled state. "I beg your pardon," he panted, tilting his chin toward her breasts. "I believe you'll bruise."

Instead of looking horrified, the edges of her mouth curled. "You're bleeding."

"Am I?" He glanced down and saw that her fingernails had pierced his skin ever so slightly. Christ, he liked that. "You don't mind this?"

Her brows pinched as she stretched her arms, like a cat waking up from a nap. "Did you miss the part when I climaxed? Twice?"

"Eleanor," he said sternly. "This is serious."

"Andrew," she said in the same tone. "If I had an issue with it, I would tell you. I think—"

She bit off what she'd been about to say,

pressing her lips together, but he couldn't let it go. Not about this.

"You think, what?" he asked. "Full truth, remember?"

"I think it might have been the best encounter of my life."

And he fell in love with her right there.

Chapter Eleven

❧

This duke had hidden depths.

Dark hidden depths that were both surprising and naughty. Nellie wasn't repulsed by them, either. Quite the opposite. She found him fascinating.

How was a man raised to be a peer of the realm, the picture of propriety, so rough and forceful in bed? The way he'd held her down . . . She shivered just recalling it. And when she had clawed his chest like a cat, he climaxed straightaway.

She watched as he returned from the washroom, where he'd gone to deal with the shield. The combination of his face and body were something otherworldly and almost unfair. He was built like a sculpture in a museum. A bronze statue. The proud bearing of his ancestors was stamped on his aristocratic features, and the graceful way he moved—with a natural confidence and elegance—spoke of a man who was utterly certain of himself.

It was both admirable and annoying.

Now at the side of the bed, he held out a hand. "Come with me."

"Where are we going?"

"To the bathing chamber. I've started a bath for us."

Biting her lip, she considered it. She liked the idea of him tending to her, this powerful man caring for her after nearly destroying her.

Indeed, she pitied his virgin bride on their wedding night. Poor girl would likely never recover, frightened of her husband's genitals for the rest of her life.

Nellie, on the other hand, felt . . . good. Better than good, actually. Relaxed and refreshed, like she had a lot of energy but could sleep for a hundred years. She wanted to cuddle up next to him and find out all of his secrets.

Dangerous, that.

She couldn't like him. They could be friendly, but not friends. Lovers, but not partners. There could be no feelings between them, no future. No marriage and ducal heirs. He needed someone pure and without a stain on her reputation. Nellie's reputation was so stained it was nearly opaque.

And she needed . . . Well, she wasn't certain what she needed. But it definitely wasn't the title of duchess and a new life in England.

She came up on her elbows. "I'm fine, Lockwood."

He shook his head, color dotting his cheeks. "I was rough with you."

Yes, and praise the saints for that.

"I liked it." She sat up and tried to scoot away from him. "I already told you."

He clutched her ankle and tugged her toward

the end of the mattress as if she weighed nothing. "Do not try to escape, woman. I'm taking you to soak in my tub."

She pictured them, lounging in the tub together, relaxing and laughing. Like a couple.

Friendly, not friends.

Pulling free, she said, "I should go. There's a hot bath waiting for me at home."

"No," he said sharply, uttered like a man who always got his way. "You will stay here so that I may reassure myself you are unharmed."

A delicious tingle went through her at his stern tone, the same one he'd used a moment ago in bed. Lord, she wished she didn't like that so much.

She considered staying. Would it be so terrible? Perhaps after a soak, there could be more games together. Provided she'd recovered, of course. God, she was so weak when it came to this man.

"Fine," she said, "but only if you agree this is just tonight."

"I'll do no such thing. As we've seen, we're compatible. We both enjoyed it. There's no reason to deny ourselves whilst I'm here."

Except that I might develop feelings for you.

He didn't want her. That much was obvious. From the beginning, Lockwood made it clear Nellie wasn't duchess material, that she was unsuitable in every way to be his bride. And until recently, he hadn't been able to tolerate her presence. Which meant only Nellie was in danger of getting hurt.

There had been casual affairs before. Many, in fact. But there hadn't been this absurd pull, an undeniable connection between her and these other men, not like the one she shared with Lockwood. It was dangerous, and must be guarded against at all costs.

When she didn't move, he heaved an aggrieved sigh and tugged her to her feet. "We'll discuss this later. Right now I want to get you into the warm water. Please."

Perhaps it was the *please*, but she didn't argue as he led her to the washroom, nor did she fight when he turned off the taps. And she let him take her hand to assist her into the porcelain claw-foot tub. It was like her independence had taken flight during those two fantastic orgasms.

I'll fight him later.

The hot water wrapped around her sore body as she sank deeper in the tub, her muscles singing in pure happiness. And when he slipped in behind her, his sturdy chest pressed to her back, she thought she'd died and gone to heaven.

His legs surrounded her, his arms resting loosely on the sides of the tub, and neither of them spoke as the water lapped over their naked bodies. Soon her toes began caressing his ankle, while his fingers made patterns on her bare arm. It was intimate, but she purposely kept her thoughts and feelings shoved inside a box, locked away for the moment. For the first time in a long while, she floated on a cloud of nothingness, empty and worry free.

"I had no idea you could sing," he finally said.

"I took voice lessons for years."

"You have a beautiful voice."

She fought a smile at the compliment. "Thank you."

"Why did you do it? Tonight, with Miss Twombly, I mean. Are the two of you even acquainted?"

"Every girl deserves a chance to shine. She looked miserable and you looked bored, so I took matters into my own hands."

"You did it to . . . help her look more appealing to me?"

When he put it that way it sounded ridiculous. "Maybe I did it for her. To give her some self-confidence. Not everything is about you, Lockwood."

He hummed, a deep rumble in his chest that reverberated in her body. "You did a good deed, though I'm not certain her parents appreciated it."

"Will you marry her, then?" She held her breath while awaiting his answer.

"Do you think I should?"

"It hardly matters what I think. It's what you think that counts."

"I think I'd prefer not to discuss my potential brides while I am in a tub, naked, with you."

"Why not? It is the reason you're here, after all. Your Grace."

He slid a palm up her arm and captured a strand of her hair that was hanging loose, then wrapped it around his finger. "Did you have any offers in your first season? I bet you had scads."

Four years ago, yet it felt like eons. "Not a single one, actually. I was too busy causing trouble, determined to make certain no one wanted me." Blast, had she truly just admitted that? She'd never trusted that bit of information to another soul.

"Why?" He didn't sound surprised.

"Because I hated the idea of it, that I was on display for a group of men who would decide whether I was worthy or not. That every year they offer up women like a cheese tray, and these nincompoops are allowed to select a piece to nibble on for the rest of their lives. It's debasing and wrong."

"But the young women hold all the power. A gentleman's suit may be refused. Engagements are broken. You make it sound as if the women are cattle, but the system is designed to favor them."

"You're biased. Perhaps because of your unique experience, you cannot see the process for what it is. Women are bartered and traded—and they willingly do it because society has taught them they must marry and reproduce, otherwise they are lesser creatures."

"What about the men who must marry and reproduce?"

"Again, unique to you."

"Not so. Many American men have legacies to pass on to sons."

"Or daughters."

"Or daughters," he allowed. "Though not in my case."

"What happens if you don't have a son?"

He dragged the end of her wet hair over her collarbone. "Then my third cousin's line inherits the title."

"That doesn't sound horrible."

"He prefers to be called Tooter."

She couldn't help but laugh. "And that is worse than Stoker?"

Strong fingers dug into her ribs, tickling her, and she squeaked in delight, twisting to evade him. His lips met the shell of her ear. "Bite your tongue. It is a hundred times worse."

As she squirmed, his hand brushed over her breast and they both froze. Desire slid through her like warm honey. Lockwood must have experienced the same because his cock began thickening behind her.

"What is it about you and the water?" he murmured, his fingers dancing over her skin, caressing and teasing. "I cannot seem to resist you whenever the two are combined."

She arched into his touch, her nipple pebbling in a shameless attempt to get his attention. "It's something about your bare skin and slippery muscles," she confessed. He rewarded her by taking the nub between his fingers and rolling it.

"No one else gives a damn about my muscles other than you."

"Only because they haven't seen them up close—though they do try. I've watched the women tracking you as you move through a room."

"Spying on me, Eleanor?"

"Do not be your usual insufferable self. You know you attract attention. I bet you have widows and bored wives throwing themselves at you every night."

"I cannot recall. I'm too busy chasing after you, remember?" He pinched her nipple, hard, which caused her to tense.

When the pain ebbed, her muscles loosened, limbs going slack, and her pussy contracted. "My God, why does that feel so good?"

"I haven't the faintest idea, but I'm glad you enjoy it."

There was a note there, a hint of something in his voice. "Have you found many partners who do?"

"A few over the years, yes."

"But you like it, too."

He tensed slightly, but she couldn't tell what he was feeling. "Yes, I do."

"Are you ashamed of it?"

"It's not very becoming of a duke."

"Neither is swimming half-naked in the middle of the night."

"I suppose, but—"

When he didn't finish, she angled to see his face. "What?"

"The reason why I like it is the shameful part—not the pain itself. I don't care what anyone prefers in bed."

"And? What is the reason?"

He cupped water and dribbled it on her breasts, seeming entranced by the way the water slipped down her skin. She didn't speak, waiting for him to gather his thoughts and confide in her. They weren't close, not really, and generally didn't like one another outside of their physical attraction, but she hoped he would trust her.

"I have a heart condition," he said. "It's weak and doesn't beat properly, which is why I exercise regularly."

It wasn't at all what she'd expected him to say. "Were you born with this condition?"

"No, I had an illness as a child. A fever that damaged my heart."

He seemed so strong, so impervious. It was incomprehensible that he was nothing less than perfect.

Dark hidden depths . . .

"And the pain?"

"Makes me feel, I don't know, *alive* somehow. A reminder that I'm still here."

She understood precisely what he meant. "But this heart condition is controlled through exercise." Which explained why he swam so often and so furiously.

"Yes, but I won't have a normal life expectancy. There will come a time when my heart will give out, no matter what I do."

"Have you sought a second opinion? Because there must be new treatments, like with the electric shock—"

He gave a dry laugh that held no amusement. "Darling, I've had fourth, fifth and sixth opinions."

"But not here in America. Our modern doctors are superior to your antiquated quacks over there."

"I believe the renowned physicians at the London Hospital would disagree with such an assessment."

"Will you go, please?" She turned to face him, moving to straddle his hips with her knees as her hands settled on his shoulders. Water sloshed over the side of the tub and onto the floor, but she hardly noticed. His acceptance of his fate bothered her, which was odd considering they weren't friends. "Will you see the best doctors here?"

"It's a waste of time," he said quietly, spanning her waist with his big hands. "And I've had years to come to terms with it."

"You are awfully blithe about dying."

"We all die, Eleanor. My only goal is to leave my children with financial security before I go."

That explained his rush to marry and need for an heir. She stared at his chest, watching for signs that his heart was beating normally.

"Stop." He put a finger under her chin and tilted her face up to his. "Don't treat me any differently or look at me strangely. I can't take it, not from you."

"Does anyone else know?"

"Other than the doctors and my mother, no."

Her chest expanded with a strange emotion, one she didn't have time to examine at the moment. She shoved it aside and pressed a soft kiss to his mouth. When they broke apart, she whispered, "Thank you for telling me."

"No artifice, remember?"

She dragged her nose along his cheek, hiding her smile. It wouldn't do to let him know how much she actually liked him. "So do you prefer spankings and whippings, that sort of thing?"

"Not really. I find it's generally too . . . passive for me. I need it more equal, if that makes sense. I want to be rough with you, but I also want you to be rough with me." When she didn't react, he said, "I cannot believe you are not shocked."

"I'm not a virgin, Lockwood, and I enjoyed what we did earlier."

He traced the marks he'd left on her breasts with his fingers. "You are so beautiful."

Before she could respond, he hitched her higher and took a nipple in his mouth, and the tight suction caused an echoing pulse between her legs. She held on to his head, clasping him to her, and her hips rocked over his shaft. They both groaned.

"Do you have another shield?"

His bright gaze flicked to hers. "Yes."

"Shall we go put it to good use, then?"

AFTER LOWERING HIMSELF into a chair, Lockwood removed his bowler and placed it on the long wooden table. Every seven days he came to this office for a prolonged, but necessary, humiliation as they reviewed the state of the ducal accounts. Digsby was handling the duke's affairs here in New York, and remained in close contact with the bankers in London, as well. There hadn't been good news in a very long time.

"Well, Digsby," Lockwood said. "How do the ducal accounts look this week?" Digsby grimaced and Lockwood's stomach clenched. He tried for a joke. "That good, is it?"

Digsby held up his hands. "I apologize, Your Grace. The totals from last year have arrived and, well, I wish I had better news."

"The fault lies not with you," Lockwood said, bracing himself. "This mess came along far before either you or me."

It was Lockwood's responsibility to fix it, however.

He gestured to the papers spread out on the

table. "Please, present me with the worst of it, will you?"

The accountant outlined what he'd learned, that a fire had damaged much of the stables at Bridgewater Towers. In addition, the tax bill for the previous year had been calculated, an exorbitant sum the estate could never afford to cover without an enormous influx of cash. Lastly, profits on the farms were down almost twenty-five percent over the previous year, the biggest decline since the seventies.

Jesus. Just when Lockwood thought the news couldn't get worse.

He rubbed his eyes. "Might I trouble you for a Scotch? Or a whiskey? Whatever you have on hand. Turpentine, arsenic. Anything at all. It hardly matters."

Digsby did not crack a smile at Lockwood's attempt at gallows humor. "Certainly, Your Grace." He rose and went through the door and out into the corridor.

Numb, Lockwood stared at the wall, the weight of the debt like a stack of bricks on his shoulders. How long before the government seized the estate? Or before his mother was forced from their London residence? When would the creditors begin legal proceedings?

He couldn't avoid his problems forever. He needed to marry as quickly as possible.

Uneasiness settled in his spine. Since leaving the supper club, he hadn't considered his mounting debts or crumbling roofs. Nellie had consumed his thoughts. He even went as far as to contemplate wooing a fiery redheaded vixen instead.

That was madness, clearly. Nellie had disparaged marriage from the moment they'd met in the ocean.

I'd like to retain my name, my worldly possessions and my control over my body.

Would she honestly change her mind for him?

Of course not. She hadn't even agreed to more than one night together. So it would remain an affair. And he wouldn't be satisfied until he'd had her every way he could imagine, in every position his depraved mind could dream up. Somehow, he'd convince her to give him as much time as required to sate themselves, while he courted his future duchess here.

Digsby returned with a tumbler of amber liquid in his hand, thank Christ. Lockwood immediately took the drink and tossed the contents back. Fire trailed down his throat and continued to his stomach. He handed the empty glass to the accountant. "Thank you for that. Ask them how much time I have," he instructed. "A conservative estimate, please."

"Yes, Your Grace. I shall contact them directly."

"Good. Thank you, Digsby. I can be reached at the hotel, as usual."

"About that, Your Grace." Digsby's neck turned a dull red. "I've had a telephone call from the manager."

When the man didn't continue, Lockwood braced himself for more bad news. "And?"

Digsby cleared his throat, beads of sweat appearing on his forehead. "Yes, well. While they do appreciate Your Grace's residence with them . . ."

"They need me to pay a portion of my bill?"

Digsby sagged in relief. "Indeed. Not all of it, of course, but a small amount."

"How small?" He clenched his hands into fists, then shoved them into his coat pockets. There was no use getting angry. The hotel had been gracious thus far regarding payment, so Lockwood wasn't annoyed at them. Rather, he was embarrassed—and furious with his father, who could've done much to prevent this current mess.

Not only had the former duke spent like a Bourbon king before the Revolution, he'd ignored the farmers asking for new machinery and tenants leaving for higher-paying wages in the cities. Everything had been left to rot and ruin. Lockwood had been cleaning up the estate since assuming the title.

And he was fucking tired.

"One hundred dollars should suffice, Your Grace."

Ouch. Lockwood smothered a wince. That was quite a lot of money, considering three dollars would buy him a nice dinner at Sherry's. Still, he'd manage to come up with it. There were silver cufflinks he could sell. It wouldn't cover the full amount, but it would be a start. Or, perhaps his mother could sell a few of the family paintings. She wouldn't like it, preferring to let Lockwood's impending marriage solve any and all financial woes, but desperate times and all.

To be fair to his mother, he should have married by now. If the wedding to Maddie had proceeded as planned, he wouldn't be in this spot.

He gave Digsby a nod. "I'll see they receive it, then."

"Thank you, Your Grace."

Eager to leave, Lockwood strode to the door. As wonderful as last night had been, he needed to think rationally. He couldn't allow the best sexual encounter of his life to sway him into a rash decision, like skipping the Stevens ball tonight. Lockwood had actually considered not attending. With his head full of Nellie, the idea of entertaining vanilla crème sounded as appealing as hearing yet another doctor's opinion about his heart.

But he must go tonight. Today proved that he mustn't wait forever to marry. Though Nellie was tempting, there were practicalities to consider, the many people who depended on him. He could not shirk his duties and responsibilities.

Though he could pursue Nellie while also pursuing the young women on his list. It was the smart thing to do, and Nellie would certainly understand if he escorted debutantes around town while they were sleeping together.

So why was there now an ache between his shoulder blades, as if he were being stabbed with an ice pick?

Because he'd found the perfect woman and he didn't wish to settle for anyone less.

Indeed, it wasn't his choice, though. Which summed up nearly everything in his life at the moment.

Chapter Twelve

꧁⁓꧂

In the conservatory Nellie winced as she rose off her knees. She was sore everywhere, mostly between her legs, but it was the best kind of sore. Lockwood had certainly left his mark on her body last night, both inside and out.

She didn't mind one bit.

Their second time had been gentler than the first. He'd taken her sweetly, slowly, with less desperation but no less passion. After, he put her in a hansom and she came home, exhausted.

He'd surprised her. Not something she could say often happened with other people. Usually, she was the unexpected one, the person who didn't fit the mold into which society tried to place her. The duke was fascinating . . . and she wasn't certain one night would satisfy her curiosity regarding him.

He'd already requested to see her again. She hadn't yet decided. It would be a mistake to grow attached, especially when he had to marry another and return to England.

Tell me I can have you as often as I want for the next few months.

If only it were that simple.

"Nellie!"

A voice broke through the stillness of the plants and trees. Was that Katie? "Back here," Nellie called. "On the right side."

Two pairs of footsteps approached. Had Katie brought someone with her? Nellie put down her gardening tools and went toward the center of the large room. Katie and another woman were coming toward her, and her friend's face broke into a smile. "There you are! I swear, sometimes I feel as though I could get lost in here and they'd need to send a search party in after me."

"Dramatic today, aren't we?" Nellie kissed her friend's cheek before addressing the stranger. "Hello. I'm Nellie."

"A pleasure to meet you, Miss Young." She inclined her head.

"Nellie, this is Mrs. Kimball. She works in the kitchen at the Meliora Club."

"Ah. How do you do? Shall we all sit?"

They followed her to a small table and chairs by the pond. Lemonade awaited, so Nellie poured them glasses while making polite talk. When they were settled, Katie got to the point. "Nels, Mrs. Kimball has a delicate problem to discuss with you."

Mrs. Kimball cleared her throat. "Last month at the club there was a speaker, the one about . . ." She lowered her voice. "Free love."

"Indeed, yes." Nellie nodded. "That was Susannah Mitchell." A friend of Nellie's, Mrs.

Mitchell advocated that women should have as much control over their lives as men do, especially when it came to reproduction and contraception. A dangerous subject, thanks to Anthony Comstock and his absurd obscenity laws, which made it illegal to distribute, discuss or advertise any method of birth control. Therefore, the Meliora Club publicized the event ambiguously, saying issues such as "female complaints" and "changes of life" would be discussed.

"Some of the girls in the kitchens—the married ones, of course—they were very interested in what Mrs. Mitchell had to say. About the items one can use to prevent consequences."

"Of course," Nellie said, even though they all knew some unmarried ladies were interested in these things, too. Present company included.

"Well, they've asked me to find out where Mrs. Mitchell would recommend procuring some of these items."

Sponges, syringes and shields, then. In years past these things could have been shipped by doctors through the mail, but that was no longer the case, lest doctors risk arrest.

"I haven't the faintest idea of where to go," Katie explained to Nellie. "But I suspected you might."

More than suspected, considering Nellie had helped Katie buy a womb veil to use with Preston not too long ago.

Nellie didn't hesitate in answering. "I'm happy to help."

"It wouldn't be too risky?" Mrs. Kimball frowned. "I'd hate for you to find yourself in trouble with the authorities."

Katie snorted as she reached to pour more lemonade. "It certainly wouldn't be the first time."

Nellie ignored her friend. "No, not too much trouble. I know quite a bit about these things, and I like helping women take charge of their lives."

Mrs. Kimball relaxed. "Oh, thank goodness. You see, one girl just came back from her second baby and she—"

"Mrs. Kimball, please." Nellie reached over and grabbed the other woman's hand. "I don't need reasons why. The only reason is that it's a woman's choice when and with whom."

"Of course, of course." She laughed nervously. "You sound just like Mrs. Mitchell."

Yes, Nellie and Susannah agreed on much when it came to women's rights. It was why Nellie had asked the woman to come speak in the first place. "Shall I stop by and ask the ladies what they need?"

That caused Mrs. Kimball to jolt in her seat, as if startled. "Oh! Here." She reached into her small handbag and took out a piece of paper. "They've each told me what they wish to purchase. I can provide you with funds up front or upon delivery, whichever is best for you."

Nellie took the list, smiling to herself. She quite liked the idea of thwarting recreational semen from taking purchase in wombs all across Manhattan. With every woman empowered, it was one step closer to full equality.

She quickly read the items. It was as she suspected: womb veils, sponges and shields. These could all be readily purchased from the midwife

Nellie knew downtown. "I can have these to you tomorrow."

"Tomorrow!" Mrs. Kimball leaned back in her chair. "Goodness, you're a miracle worker."

"See?" Katie said. "I told you Miss Young would know what to do. Thank you, Nellie."

"You're welcome. I'll buy everything today and come to the club tomorrow morning. Perhaps then I can explain to each woman how these items are to be used. They only work if applied correctly."

"That would be very helpful," Mrs. Kimball said. "The ladies would all appreciate it, I'm certain."

"It's my pleasure—which hopefully leads to their pleasure."

Katie choked on a mouthful of lemonade, her skin turning red. "Nellie! I cannot believe you just said that."

"I apologize, but are we pretending none of it feels good?"

Mrs. Kimball blushed. "I've had five children. Told my husband we'd stop after two, but I couldn't help myself."

"I'm unmarried," Katie said. "So I wouldn't know what you mean."

Nellie didn't contradict her friend. Everyone had their own secrets, after all. "It certainly gives you something to look forward to on your wedding night, then. Provided everything is in good working order with Mr. Clarke, of course."

"There is nothing wrong with Mr. Clarke," Katie snapped. "You must get over your dislike of my fiancé."

You needn't play mama bear any longer.

Katie's words from the art show returned to lodge under Nellie's ribs. Her friend had made her choice and Nellie must support her. Through thick and thin, terrible husbands or not. "I beg your pardon," she said. "I'm certain he's a nice man under all that . . . height."

Katie rolled her eyes heavenward, then turned to Mrs. Kimball. "Would you mind if I stayed to chat with Miss Young privately? We have some club business to discuss."

Club business? So that's what Katie was calling gossip these days?

Mrs. Kimball rose off the bench. "Of course not. I can see myself out."

"Nonsense." Nellie walked to one of the many bellpulls she'd had installed in here. The staff was used to finding her amongst the plants. "Someone will see you safely to the door."

After a footman arrived and led Mrs. Kimball away, Nellie returned to her seat. "Club business?"

"A flimsy excuse, I realize, but I wanted to check on you. How are you?"

"Fine. Why?"

"Because you left the art show abruptly and didn't come by afterward. Alice said you snuck out of the supper club in a hurry, as well. Is there anything I should know?"

Nellie didn't bother keeping it a secret. Not from one of her few close friends. "Lockwood is the reason I disappeared."

Katie's mouth parted before she recovered, but her gaze remained confused. "The duke, you mean."

"Yes."

"I don't understand. Are you saying you and he . . . ?"

"Yes, I am. Twice."

Katie's brows climbed toward the ceiling. "Twice! My goodness. How have I missed this?"

"It just happened. But . . ." Nellie took a deep breath and let it out slowly. Was she really going to confess the entire history? She decided to keep it brief. "We have been circling one another for some time. It almost feels inevitable."

"You're going to become a duchess?" Katie's voice rose in tone, as if this was an absurd notion.

"Good God, no. Lockwood's made it clear I don't fit his qualifications for a bride."

"What does that mean?" Katie actually looked offended. "You are perfectly qualified to be a duchess. Has he actually told you that you are—"

"Stop." She reached to clasp Katie's forearm affectionately. "I appreciate what you are trying to do, but we both know I'm not the type of respectable innocent he must marry. Not even close. Furthermore, the idea of relinquishing my freedom and moving to England gives me hives."

"So this is an affair? Nothing more?"

"It only happened last night. I haven't decided if we'll repeat it."

"I wondered why you look so refreshed and happy today."

"I definitely feel relaxed," she said with a small laugh. Swallowing, she looked down to avoid Katie's eye. "I think I could really like him, Katie, and that terrifies me. I cannot let a duke break my heart. I have a reputation as a reckless hoyden to maintain."

Katie didn't share her amusement. "Or you could both fall in love."

"Oh, for the love of Pete." Nellie pinched the bridge of her nose. "You are not listening to me."

"I am listening, but you need to open yourself up to the possibility. You've kept your heart guarded for a long time, and I understand why. Losing your mother—"

"Don't." Nellie could not handle that conversation. Not at the moment. "Please."

Katie held up her palms. "You've loved and lost. You don't want to experience it again. I understand. Truthfully, I do." Katie had lost her mother, too. "But there is joy awaiting you out there, Nels. You just have to be brave enough to let it in."

Bravery had nothing to do with it. And she wasn't stupid enough to let Lockwood into her heart. She stood, more than ready to put an end to this conversation. "I should get back to the plants. Do you know the way out, or shall I ring for a footman?"

"Fine, I'll go," Katie said. "But this conversation is far from over."

STANDING AGAINST THE wall of a drawing room he'd never see again, Lockwood tried to hide his annoyance. What was he doing? Why was he amongst these boring people instead of tracking Nellie down and dragging her off to his hotel room?

All he wanted at the moment was to kiss and

fuck her until they both passed out. Instead, he was circulating amongst New York's crème de la crème and trying to pretend as if he wished to be here.

"Surprised to see you standing alone instead of mingling with the ladies, Stoker," said a voice at his elbow.

Lockwood didn't look over at Potter Pierce. "Evening, Potsie. I trust you've been well?"

"Yes, I've been enjoying the city. They're much more uninhibited, these American girls, wouldn't you say? Though I do miss the food back home. They drown everything in sauces here. Have you noticed?"

No, Lockwood hadn't noticed.

"How goes your search for a bride?" the other man asked. "Any closer?"

"A bit," Lockwood hedged, not wanting to give anything away lest it get repeated. "You?"

"Five or six I've got my eye on. Wouldn't do to settle on the first one, you know." He snickered. "Though you're aware of that, I suppose."

Outwardly, Lockwood maintained a polite expression, but his hands curled into fists. What would happen if he punched Potter in the middle of this ball? He wouldn't, of course, but that didn't stop him from imagining the immense satisfaction he'd derive from doing so.

Does no one else see you for the monster you truly are?

No one except Nellie, apparently. She'd seen through his polish and charm right from the start, perhaps because he'd let his guard down around her. With everyone else, he always had to maintain appearances. But not her. She possessed the uncanny ability to get under his skin, to poke and prod until he lost all civility. With her, he'd been real and rough, and she hadn't seemed to mind in the least.

I think it might have been the best encounter of my life.

"Lockwood." Potter nudged his arm.

"I beg your pardon. You were saying?"

"I was telling you of this house I've found in the Tenderloin district filled with the most gorgeous women. I'll be going later. You should join me."

Lockwood could think of a thousand ways he'd rather spend his time. "No, thank you."

"Are you certain? Because these American whores are unlike anything we have in England, my friend. Uninhibited and accommodating. The most outlandish request is treated just as if one's asking for tea."

Lockwood was no prude—he'd enjoyed his fair share of women over the years—but he didn't care for Potter's tone or words. He stared out at the dancers, wondering how quickly he could extricate himself from this conversation. "Tempting, but I'll pass."

"Ah, I see." Potsie leaned in. "Got yourself a bit o' fluff already. Smart of you. I like to keep it varied myself. Keeps me from getting bored."

Jesus. Lockwood pushed off from the wall. "I should start circulating. Have a pleasant—"

Cornelius Young suddenly appeared in front of Lockwood and struck out his hand. "Your Grace!"

"Mr. Young." Smiling, Lockwood shook Nellie's father's hand. "A pleasure to see you once more."

"You, as well. I wanted to check—"

"Hello." Potsie edged his way into the conversation, forming an unwelcome triangle with the other two men. He studied Mr. Young like a science experiment. "Have we met?"

Neck growing hot, Lockwood gestured to Potsie. "Mr. Young, this is his lordship, the Earl of Harkness."

"Young man," Mr. Young greeted with a nod, not bothering with the honorific, and Lockwood's opinion of Nellie's father rocketed skyward.

Potsie's face slackened in disbelief. "Cornelius Young? Of the railroads? I am quite pleased to finally meet you, sir."

Nellie's father frowned, not looking pleased in the least. "Oh?"

"Yes, indeed," Potsie continued. "Been thinking about investing in railroads myself. I wonder if you might give me a few—"

Mr. Young didn't even let Potsie finish before he returned his attention to Lockwood. "I wanted to check in with you regarding the swimming pool, see how it's going. Everything all right?"

Lockwood nodded. "It's exceptional. Really, I cannot begin to thank you enough."

"Good, good. If the water's not the right temperature or there's too much dirt, you tell Eleanor and she'll see that it's taken care of."

Was Mr. Young aware that his daughter had been coming down to watch Lockwood swim? "I will, sir. Though I doubt it'll be necessary. Your staff does an excellent job maintaining the pool."

"I am pleased someone is finally using it again. Eleanor hasn't been in since her mother died."

That was surprising. Lockwood could still picture Nellie in the waves at Newport, splashing and rolling, her naked skin glistening in the moonlight. She'd seemed to love the water.

So why never use the swimming pool in her own home?

"Oh?" he asked.

"Indeed. My wife loved to swim. A regular fish in the water."

"You must miss her," he murmured.

Mr. Young's mouth twisted into something wistful, his eyes going unfocused as if he was remembering. "I do. Choose wisely when you marry, Your Grace. Find a woman who makes the sun rise and set with her smile. Life's too short to spend it with anyone else."

Nellie's face sprang unbidden to Lockwood's mind, her fiery red hair spread out on his bed as she looked up at him last night. His chest squeezed like he was trapped under water. He knew precisely what Mr. Young meant, because something about Nellie's smile made Lockwood feel invincible. All-powerful, with no heart condition or mountains of debt.

"Precisely what I've been telling him!" Potsie lied. "Just because a man has to build up the family coffers doesn't mean he can't also choose the perfect woman."

No one paid the earl any attention. Instead, Young shook Lockwood's hand again and bid him a good night. He didn't bother addressing Potsie before disappearing into the crowd.

Lockwood rubbed his jaw and considered the exchange. Had Young suspected an attraction between Lockwood and Nellie? No, impossible. She'd visited the swimming pool only once when Lockwood was there, and last night happened suddenly. No one spotted them at the hotel when he put her in a hansom in the wee hours this morning.

"Say, Mr. Cornelius Young." Potsie's voice was full of speculation. "I would love to pick his brain a time or two. Then maybe I could save the estate without marrying. Too bad about his daughter."

That got Lockwood's attention. "What on earth does that mean?"

"Oh, you haven't heard?" Potsie leaned in, like he was sharing a great secret. "Reputation's in complete tatters. They say she's loose, with affairs up and down the island. There are even rumors she's had a child or two." Potsie waggled his brows, as if this statement required additional drama.

The bloody fucking nerve. Lockwood's body clenched, expanded, his muscles seemingly doubling in size as his indignation and loathing mounted. He advanced on Potsie, and whatever the other man saw in the duke's face had him backing up. Potsie held up his hands. "Say, Lockwood. What's this—"

Lockwood reached out and dug his fingers in Potsie's collar, taking care to press his knuckles into the other man's windpipe. "Listen, Potter. If I hear you spread one falsehood or repeat one tale about that woman, I will throw you under the nearest streetcar. Are we clear?"

"I won't, I promise! I had no idea you even

knew her." Potsie choked and tried to dislodge Lockwood's hand, but Lockwood was stronger.

"I don't," Lockwood lied. "But she doesn't deserve to be disparaged in such a crude manner."

With a final shove, he released the earl and turned on his heel. That was enough socializing for one night. He had the sudden desire to go swim instead.

Chapter Thirteen

❧

She couldn't stay away from the swimming pool that night.

Earlier, Nellie traveled downtown to see the midwife, then returned to spend the evening alone. Her father had a social engagement with Mrs. Paulson, so Nellie ate in her room and then tried to read. Except reading was boring, unless it was one of those racy novels with plenty of kissing. Unfortunately, she'd loaned those books to Maddie ages ago. It was past time for Nellie to get them back. Maddie certainly didn't need those books anymore, not with a husband and lawn tennis career to keep her occupied.

No, Nellie was the only one adrift. The others seemed to have their lives all sorted.

Must be hard to watch everyone find love but you.

Rosemary Whitney, that evil witch.

Nellie tried to push the words away, to lock that particular trunk back up tight, but it was too late. The black thoughts had escaped, a heaviness that compounded to press on her chest and make it difficult to breathe. She wanted company—and a sandy-haired, broad-shouldered duke sounded perfect.

She found him, but he wasn't in the water. He was reclining in a chair next to the swimming pool, arms folded behind his head, staring up at the ceiling. He was still in his black evening suit, which meant he'd been at a party, wooing his heiresses. She tried not to think about that. For now, he was here. With her.

"Hello, Eleanor. I was wondering when you'd arrive."

God, the sound of his deep accented voice plucked across her nerves, making her entire body vibrate with longing. Her heart was already racing and she'd just arrived. Clasping her hands at the small of her back, she drew closer. "Hello, Andrew. Why aren't you swimming?"

"I've been waiting for you." He sat up and toed off his dress shoes. Then he slipped out of his evening jacket.

Distracted by his disrobing, she finally caught on. "Waiting for me? Why?"

"Because you're going to swim with me."

She instantly took a step back, her blood turning to ice. "No, thank you. I'd much rather watch you."

His bow tie now off, he removed his cuff links as he came toward her. "You will swim with me."

The absolute arrogance. Anger was the easiest emotion to express, so she snapped, "No, I won't. You cannot order me about merely because you gave me a few orgasms, Lockwood. You're good, but you're not *that* good."

Instead of looking offended, he smiled. What on earth? Now she was really confused.

This was too much. All she'd needed was to blissfully watch his strong arms cut through the water and maybe kiss him for a bit when he finished. Why did he have to ruin everything? Well, she wasn't going to stick around to find out.

Just as she whirled for the exit, he clasped her arm. "Wait, darling. I know this has to do with your mother—"

She stiffened and tried to pull away. "Let me go, you pompous prig."

His palm cradled her cheek and he moved in, closer, until his forehead met her temple. The heat from his body wrapped around her, his warm breath gusting on her cheek, and it felt like a cocoon for the two of them where no one else existed. In here she could almost believe he cared about her.

"I've seen you swim. I know you love the water. And I also know you haven't been in the pool since your mother died. Come swimming with me, Eleanor. Just me and you, surrounded by the stars. I want to hold you in my arms and lick the water from your bare skin. Please."

"We don't need to swim for that. I can lay on the bed and dump a glass of water on myself."

His lips were soft as they pressed to her forehead, the bridge of her nose. He kept going, kissing her cheek and then down to her jaw. It was like he was mapping her, memorizing her skin. When he finally reached her mouth, she was panting slightly, eager to kiss him again.

She angled her head to join their lips together,

but he evaded her and started the entire process on the other side of her face. Up her jaw he went, the softest of kisses along her cheek. She was clinging to him by the time he returned to her forehead, her knees trembling. Never had she expected this much . . . tenderness.

Especially when this was temporary.

"Please, for me," he said quietly. "I'll take very good care of you, I swear it."

She softened, melting into him like hot wax. Why couldn't she ever resist this man? It was like he knew precisely what to say to bend her to his will. She wasn't certain she liked it.

Though she didn't hate it, either.

"Why does it matter to you?" she whispered.

"Everything about you matters to me. And I think it will make you happy to be in the water."

It would also make her sad, and the weight on her chest was heavy enough at the moment. Why must he add to it? She tried to put it into words. "We did this together when I was a girl. She said everyone should know how to swim, especially an Irish lass."

"Why?"

"Because we're too stubborn to drown."

He chuckled. "See? She would want you to enjoy the pool."

"I'll most likely cry."

His thumbs swiped over her cheeks, his bright blue gaze burning with an intensity that scared her. "Then I'll hold you even tighter."

Jaysus, this man.

She swallowed the lump in her throat. "And if I change my mind and want to get out?"

"I'm not going to force you to stay in, but I hope you'll trust me. Perhaps you just need someone to lean on once in a while."

The backs of her eyelids burned, the idea of leaning on him so appealing she could almost taste it. But he wasn't here forever, only long enough to find a bride. Then he'd return to England and his ducal matters and heirs, and Nellie would be forgotten, the American woman he'd once slept with.

He's going to break my heart.

She licked her lips. "You really must stop being so nice to me."

"I hate to disappoint you, but I quite like it. Much better than being at odds with you." He kissed her nose. "Come. I'll be as mean as you like when you get into the pool with me."

She nodded and the two of them began to undress, separately, while their eyes tracked the other's progress. When he was down to his undergarment—which hugged him in all the very best places—he paused. "Should I leave it on?"

"No one will come in, if you're worried about preserving your ducal modesty."

"I didn't wish to assume . . ."

"Don't dare tell me you've suddenly found your nobility when it comes to me, because I won't believe it."

The edge of his mouth hitched arrogantly and he stripped out of the undergarment, leaving him gloriously bare, the perfect male specimen. Before she could ogle him too long, he dove into the swimming pool and disappeared beneath the water.

She finished more slowly, taking her time with her clothing. Yes, procrastinating, but who could blame her? The specter of her mother loomed large in here, and the memories were bittersweet.

A splash of water hit her chemise-clad back. Spinning, she gaped at Lockwood, who was treading water and wearing an innocent expression that didn't fool her in the least. "Did you just *splash* me?"

"I haven't any idea what you mean. Just finish up and get in already."

To torture him, she removed her drawers and stockings, then lifted her chemise over her head. This left her naked and completely exposed. Lockwood's gaze darkened as he swam closer to the side of the pool. "Fucking hell, you are a vision. How can I possibly swim when all the blood's gone to my cock?"

Dirty, filthy man. She adored this side of him.

She peered down as if trying to see his erection for herself, but he sank lower into the water. "You shall have to get in if you want to see it, darling."

"Tease. I'm too sore, anyway."

He winced. "I was afraid of that. No matter. The warm water will make your quim feel better. Get in already."

"Your tongue would also make it feel better."

"True, but my tongue is here with me in the pool. If you want it, you have to get in, Eleanor."

NEVER TAKING HIS eyes from her, Lockwood followed Nellie around to the shallower end of the swimming pool. The water came up to his waist, so he knelt to hide his erection. The comment about all of his blood rushing to his groin the instant she removed her clothing hadn't been in jest.

She was bloody gorgeous. Porcelain skin, full breasts with rose-tipped nipples. Long legs and round hips, with vibrant red hair that streaked like fire. She'd been crafted by demons to make men weak . . . and Lockwood was incapable of resisting her.

Sitting at the edge, she dipped her toes into the water. Her bottom lip disappeared between her teeth, and he could see the way her shoulders hunched, as if drawing in on herself. He wouldn't allow her to feel small. Not this strong and powerful woman who could rule the world if she so chose. "Keep going," he encouraged. "Come out here with me."

"Give me a moment," she snapped. "What's your rush?"

He lifted his legs and let his body float on top of the water. His hard cock lay on his belly, the cool air like a caress over the warm skin. Though he wasn't looking at her, he could feel her eyes dragging over the thick column of flesh between his legs. "No rush. I've got all night."

He heard her blow out a breath and mutter something. His heart leapt into his throat, but he didn't move. She needed to do this herself, not be dragged into the pool kicking and screaming. That wouldn't be fair. Then water splashed. He shot up and braced his feet on the floor of the pool. She did it. She was in the water, albeit standing near the edge, her body trembling.

He was at her side in an instant.

"I'm here. I have you." He wrapped his arms around her, then repeated, "I have you."

She pressed her nose to the hollow at the base of his throat and exhaled. "It's silly. She's been gone a long time."

"It's not silly. There's no expiration on grief."

"I miss her."

"I know, darling." He stroked her back and kissed the top of her head. "Tell me about her."

At first, she was quiet and he worried that he'd pushed too hard. "She was beautiful, with a huge personality. She owned any room she occupied and made everything prettier. Brighter. My father worshipped her. My Aunt Riona reminds me of her quite a bit."

"This is your mother's sister?"

"Yes. I have a lot of Irish relatives. They're over in Hell's Kitchen."

"Do you see them often?"

"I try to go over once a month."

He tried to picture her surrounded by red-headed Irish relatives. If they were anything like her, it was undoubtedly entertaining. "Perhaps I could meet them one day."

She made a sound in her throat. "You would hate them."

"Why? I'm not a snob. I don't care how people live."

"It's not that. They're . . ." She leaned back to see his face. "They run the Saints."

Lockwood's mouth fell open. Even he had heard of the Saints. "You're related to an Irish street gang?"

"Indeed, I am. Proudly, too."

A chuckle escaped his throat as he pulled her closer. "Christ, I should've known. Trouble runs in your blood, woman."

"You're not horrified?"

She seemed genuinely surprised, so he cupped her cheek and smiled softly at her. "Nothing about you could ever horrify me. I find you endlessly fascinating and appealing in every way. Haven't you realized as much by now?"

"Well, I believe the appealing part," she said as her hips nudged his erection.

"Ignore it."

"I'm not certain I can when it's displacing most of the water in the pool."

He let out a bark of embarrassed laughter. "Bloody hell, Nellie."

She slid her arms around his neck and came up on her toes, their mouths hovering close. The soft mounds of her breasts rested on his chest, slippery skin everywhere his hands touched. "I like when you call me Eleanor," she whispered.

"I'm glad. Now, kiss me, Eleanor."

Her lips, wet and soft, ghosted over his, plucking gently, and he let her lead. She deepened the kiss, angling her head to seal their mouths together, and the knot between his shoulder blades eased, as if this was what he'd been waiting for all night. Right here, this woman, back in his arms, kissing him. He would never tire of it.

Slowly, he drifted them into deeper water. He could still reach the bottom but she couldn't, so her legs wrapped around his hips as they continued kissing. The warm water blanketed them on all sides, enveloping them, a world where no one else existed. There was only her mouth, her luscious body and her bold spirit, which drew him like a moth to a flame every single time.

He was in love with this woman.

He knew it as surely as he knew his own name. What he felt was beyond lust or obsession. She'd carved a place for herself in his heart and head, and he couldn't begin to extract her. Didn't even want to try. She was fucking perfect, the match he needed to bring light and joy to his ordered world.

Somehow, he sensed she wasn't ready to hear it.

He would tell her soon, though. He wanted to win her over first.

"Are you ready for my tongue?" he panted against her mouth, his hand sliding to cup her breast. He pinched her nipple and was rewarded when her back arched, her pussy dragging over his belly.

"I'm still sore." She gasped as he rolled her other nipple between his fingers.

"I promise to keep to the outside." He sank his teeth into the top of her breast and bit down gently until she moaned. "I won't put my fingers inside your pussy."

"Oh, God." She writhed in his arms, her nails digging into his scalp exactly as he liked. "Yes, please. I need you."

He swam them to the side and sat her on the edge. Leaning back on her hands, she widened her thighs in welcome, unabashedly eager, and he didn't waste any time before lowering his face to her quim. The folds were slick and swollen, and he gave her deep, open-mouthed kisses, tasting her arousal, before licking her clitoris. Christ, she was delicious, a treat he could devour every single day, morning and night.

It didn't take long before her thighs clamped around his ears, nearly cutting off his air. He didn't mind in the least. They'd find him dead with his mouth attached to her cunt, covered in her juices, and his cock stiff as a pike. No more preferable way to go, as far as he was concerned.

Satisfaction filled him as she trembled and shouted, and he rode her through the climax until she twitched. Easing off, he kissed her thigh. "Absolute perfection."

"Yes, I agree." She was still out of breath when she slid into the water again. "Your turn, you talented man."

He shook his head, though his bollocks were screaming for him to take up her offer. "That's unnecessary. It'll eventually deflate." As soon as he was alone and could frig himself.

Her fingers disappeared beneath the surface of the water and wrapped around his shaft. His eyes fluttered closed, the streak of pleasure so strong it weakened his knees.

"I want to suck on you. It's a glorious challenge and I'm not one to back down from a challenge." She twisted her hand around his crown. "Do you want it?"

He might beg if she rescinded the offer. "God, yes."

"Then up you go."

Pressing up on his arms, he heaved himself onto the side of the pool, taking care not to crush his bollocks in the process. He expected her to hurry, to lunge at him as he'd lunged at her, but she surprised him. Instead of coming closer, she swam away and dove beneath the water. Suddenly, she surfaced and flipped her hair, much as she'd done that night in the ocean, and water cascaded down her face and over her round tits. He fisted his cock, stroking, as he watched her run her hands through her wet hair. The irregular pounding of his heart echoed in his ears, and he grew light-headed from all the craving coursing through his veins.

Then she moved her hands lower, over her shoulders to her breasts, which she cupped in her palms. Eyes closed, she massaged and squeezed them, then pinched the tips. "Fuck," he whispered, his hand picking up speed. "Eleanor. Come here. *Now*."

"Yes, Your Grace?" She drifted closer but continued to mold her breasts. "How may I serve you?"

His cock jumped and he groaned. "I need you. Please."

Laughing lightly, she dove beneath the water again and reappeared between his legs, her skin glistening with water droplets. She trailed her wet fingers over his knees and thighs, green eyes twinkling. "I like when you need me."

"Then you should be very pleased, because it's nearly every minute of the day. Put my cock in your mouth." He angled the crown toward her. "Suck hard."

Instead, because she was the most contrary woman he'd ever met, she went slowly, gently, licking him from root to tip. She bathed his shaft with her tongue, then did the same with his bollocks, tormenting him, and his eyes nearly rolled back in his head. He moaned, the sound bouncing off the tile walls. "Darling, I'm begging you."

Taking the base in her hand, she held his gaze then opened her mouth over the head. Wet heat enveloped him and he had to clench his jaw to keep from coming right then. Fuck, she was so beautiful. Her lips swallowed his length, and he felt a surge of lust and protectiveness the likes of which he'd never experienced before. He wanted to hold her and fuck her and bite her, then listen to every thought in that gorgeous head. "That's it. God, you are perfect. Take more, as much as you can."

When he reached the back of her throat, she paused then carefully pulled up, swiping her tongue over the crown. "How was that?" she whispered, paying extra attention to the sensitive underside.

His skin prickled, the pressure in his groin building. "More. Hurry."

She gave a husky laugh. "I quite like you desperate."

"Goddamn it. Finish me, Eleanor."

She must've taken pity on him. She began moving fast, bobbing up and down, her cheeks hollowing with her efforts, and he gasped and hissed, unable to keep quiet as sparks raced down his legs. Then she took his hands and placed them atop her head.

Oh, hell.

Though his fingers tightened in her hair, he had to be sure. "Are you certain?"

She nodded, then paused. Waited with him in her mouth.

Don't hurt her. Not too rough.

Then she fondled his bollocks—and all his gentlemanly instincts deserted him. He was no longer a well-bred duke, her a gentle lady. They were partners in this madness and though he might regret it later, he would take her mouth rudely, if she would allow it. "Stop me if it's too much," he said.

He began guiding her, setting the pace, and she widened her jaw to fit more of him in, then moved her tongue in the most arousing manner. The result left him awash in sensation, wave after wave of pleasure rushing through him, and his fingers tightened in her hair. Her saliva coated his cock, the slick skin disappearing between her lips as he moved her faster. She offered no resistance, just gave herself over to him, and he couldn't last. It was too bloody perfect.

His muscles coiled with the inevitable orgasm, so he forced his hands off her head. "I'm coming," he gasped, assuming she'd pull away.

Instead, she moaned and the vibration cascaded all the way down his shaft. Then she dug her nails into his thighs, sending pain up his legs.

His climax exploded.

His limbs jerked as he released in her mouth, and it went on and on, the high unlike anything he'd experienced before. It was as if she'd unlocked something inside him, as if she'd discovered the secret to unraveling his mind and his body, and he gave her everything he had in exchange.

When it finally ebbed, he wanted to fall at her feet, worship her like a deity. If he wasn't careful, he'd promise her everything in his power to keep her by his side. He had to press his lips together to keep from spouting nonsense—or worse, make a declaration neither one of them was ready for.

Chapter Fourteen

❧

$\mathcal{H}$e insisted on cuddling afterward.

Nellie tried to escape upstairs, but Lockwood refused to allow it. He wrapped them in towels and carried her to a chaise by the water. Then he reclined with her, his strong arms holding her close. She buried her face in his throat, not wanting to admit how nice it felt to lie here with him.

She couldn't become accustomed to this.

Girls like her did not end up with dukes.

Besides, she had her father here. Her friends and her plants. She had roots in New York—literally and figuratively. There was no place else for her.

The lapping of water in the pool was the only sound other than their breathing. Lockwood's hand caressed her spine, and she wondered what he was thinking about. His potential brides?

"Where were you tonight?" she asked, returning to the topic of his purpose for being in her city.

"At the Stevens ball."

Ah. Another social event to which she hadn't

been invited. How surprising. She toyed with the coarse hair sprinkled across his broad chest. "And which of your heiresses were in attendance?"

"I don't care to discuss this with you."

"Why not?"

His voice sharpened slightly. "Because I find it distasteful."

That was odd. "I'm not sure why. You're here to marry an heiress. It's no secret, Andrew."

He shifted to stare down at her, his face so close she could see each long eyelash. "Because I'm with the most beautiful woman I've ever seen, one who just gave me the best orgasm of my life, and I'd rather not discuss other women at the moment."

Oh. That was a fairly decent answer.

Her toes curled into the soft cotton surrounding her. *Do not fall in love with him. He will only break your heart.*

She angled to kiss him and his lips met hers, brushing and skimming, while their noses scraped. The kiss was light and slow, with no purpose other than to maintain a connection between them. There was none of the desperation from moments ago, yet it was memorable all the same. Heart swelling in her chest, she was certain down to her soul that she could kiss him for days and never tire of it.

She was in trouble. The urge to run bubbled up once more, but she beat it back. She was not a coward. Usually.

"You never got in your swim," she murmured against his mouth a little bit later.

"I did raise my heart rate, though." He bit her bottom lip gently. "Rather, you raised my heart rate."

"Did you like it?"

"Like it? I came faster than a teenaged lad, darling. It was almost embarrassing."

She'd gone on instinct, shifting his hands to her head and allowing him to control her. "I'm glad. I suspected you might enjoy it."

He hitched her closer and she could feel the growing hardness against her belly. "I loved it," he said. "We're going to do that again. Often."

There went the flutters in her chest again. She tried to keep her voice dry and uninterested. "Oh, we are, are we?"

"Yes, we are," he said arrogantly. "That, and quite a lot of other things. I plan to have you in every way I can imagine."

A smile threatened, so she buried her face in his shoulder. "You're supposed to be focused on a bride, Lockwood."

"I am. You needn't worry."

Bully for his efficiency, then. She wouldn't think about that. What mattered was right here, right now. "I haven't agreed to an affair."

"Yes, you have. The moment you entered the room tonight, then again when you swam with me."

"Your arrogance is appalling."

"Hmm." His hand disappeared into the cotton cloths and she felt him probe between her legs.

"What are you doing?" she asked, even as she parted her thighs to give him room.

"Seeing if my arrogance is well-founded." His

finger found her entrance and played in the slickness gathered there. "Oh, yes. Very well-founded, indeed. You're wet for me, Eleanor."

She licked her lips. "That's merely water from the pool," she lied.

He chuckled darkly, like the devil on holiday. "Let's taste it and find out, shall we?" His hand emerged from the towel, then he brought the finger to his lips and sucked on it. His eyelids fluttered shut. "Christ, I like that. And it's definitely not pool water."

"Fine, I'm aroused. Blame your shoulders and your very large—"

He kissed her again, cutting off more falsehoods. Yes, she liked those specific things, but it was more than that. It was everything about this man, like his sense of nobility and the way he cursed with her. His bad heart. How he made her feel. She poured what she could never tell him into her kiss, twining her tongue with his and clutching him close.

She wished it could go on forever.

By the time he pulled back, she was panting, rocking her hips against his erection, desperate for friction. "I should go," he whispered.

Go? She held on to him even tighter. "Don't you dare. Come upstairs with me. I have shields up there."

He shook his head and pushed up on his arms. "You're sore."

"I don't care. It'll be worth it."

"I care," he snapped, brows knitting as he disentangled their legs to sit up. "And there's no rush. I'll see you tomorrow."

She clasped the towel around her nakedness. "What's tomorrow?"

"I'm taking you to dinner."

The words fell into her stomach like a lead ball. "Dinner? Have you lost your mind?"

Naked, he stood and went to the chair that held his clothing. She tried not to let her eyes drift over his bare back and ass. This was no time to let his body distract her from the conversation.

"Yes, dinner, Eleanor. It's a thing people do when they'd like to spend time together."

"I know, but why do you wish to do it with *me*?"

"Because I like you. I want to sit across from you and enjoy a meal together."

"Then I'll have someone bring us some sandwiches and we can do so right now."

"In public," he amended as he pulled on his undergarment.

This was madness. He couldn't mean it. An association with her would ruin his social standing. The family of any potential bride would frown upon it, and the town would start gossiping about him. The scandal would make his broken engagement last summer seem like a trifle.

She sat up and wrapped the towel around her body. "Lockwood, think about what you are suggesting. Your chances at forming a decent match with the right young woman would be dashed."

"Perhaps I don't care."

"Well, you should. I don't mind having a quiet affair. You needn't court me. I'm perfectly fine doing this," she said, sweeping her hand out toward the pool.

He busied himself with pulling on his clothing. "It's too soon and you're not ready. I can wait."

The man was speaking in riddles. "You'll wait until Armageddon before I meet you at Sherry's for dinner."

"I suppose we shall see, won't we?"

His stubbornness was both annoying and flattering. Her scandalous reputation didn't bother her—she'd cultivated it with reckless behavior, after all—but she was aware of the effect it could have on others. She tried to mitigate the damage whenever possible, which meant she had to do the right thing for Lockwood's sake. He would never find a proper bride if he was squiring Nellie about town.

She didn't wish to argue with him, not at the moment. Tonight had been too perfect to ruin, and she was enjoying watching as he put back on his evening suit. "I didn't realize dukes knew how to dress themselves," she murmured as he fastened his trousers.

"It's not so difficult, and I can't tote my valet around every time I wish to go swimming."

Fascinating. Lockwood was so much more than he appeared on the surface. She suddenly wanted to know everything about this man. "Do you have a mistress back in England?" The question surprised even her. No idea why it was the first thing she'd asked, but she couldn't take the words back now.

"No," he said and dragged on his vest. "Personal luxuries such as that were beyond my reach. I gave the last one a necklace and my fond wishes more than a year ago."

Nellie tried to imagine Lockwood entertaining an actress or an opera singer, but couldn't picture it. "Who was she? Anyone I'd know?"

"The wife of a high-level cabinet official."

He dropped the news casually, as if this wasn't shocking. "She was married."

"Yes. I found it neater that way."

"Neater, how? When her husband arrived with a pistol?"

He tied his bow tie expertly, clearly not needing a mirror. "Her husband was aware of the arrangement. They weren't in love. It suited all three of us."

Nellie's jaw fell open. "I do not understand you British at all."

That earned her a deep chuckle. "I suppose that's fair, because we hardly understand you Americans, either."

He slipped on his evening jacket, perfectly put back together. No one would know, other than his wet hair, that the two of them had been naked in the pool moments ago. She liked sharing this secret with him. There was no need for dinners or carriage rides or dances. This was enough right here.

"Come here and kiss me goodbye, Eleanor."

The demand slid under her skin, and goose bumps quickly followed on the surface. How could she possibly refuse? Towel secure around her body, she stood and walked over to him as if mesmerized. His intense gaze tracked her every movement, locked on her like no one else existed in the entire world. Like he couldn't wait to lunge at her, push her down onto the ground and thrust inside her. She shivered. God, she wanted that, as well.

She slid her hands up his chest and onto his shoulders as she rose up on her toes. "Goodbye, Lockwood." Moving closer, she pressed her body flush with his and kissed him. He took over, his tongue finding hers, and the kiss quickly turned hungry, their teeth clashing in desperation. His palms cradled her jaw, making her feel treasured even as he destroyed her with his mouth.

When he finally pulled back, she was boneless, clinging to him as if he were a rope. "Jaysus, Mary and Joseph," she panted. "Was that necessary?"

"Very." He pressed his lips to her forehead. "Don't worry, darling. I'll fuck you tomorrow night. You'll come more than once, I swear."

She swayed toward him, more than ready for him to make good on that promise. "Where?"

"Meet me at my hotel. Eight o'clock."

"Haven't you a social engagement?"

"Nothing I cannot break for you." He gave her a swift kiss on the mouth, then turned and headed for the outside door. "Eight o'clock. Do not keep me waiting."

NELLIE DROPPED HER large carpetbag onto the wooden workbench. "Good morning, ladies!"

A circle of eager faces surrounded her in the Meliora Club kitchen. Most were women Nellie didn't know, but there were a few familiar faces, such as Mrs. Kimball and Katherine, who was standing in the back and attempting to look virginal.

"Good morning, Miss Young," Mrs. Kimball said, coming forward. "Thank you for helping us."

"I'm quite happy to do it. I have everything with me, so is there an office we may use for private discussions?"

"Of course. Would you like to speak with the group first, or handle these one by one?"

The women in the kitchen were of varying ages and backgrounds, yet they all stared at her eagerly. Knowing how little education women received when it came to their own bodies and sexual matters, she decided to give a group talk first. "There is some general knowledge I should like to impart first, if you don't mind. Then we may each meet separately and I'll answer questions."

This was followed by lots of nods, so she began. "First of all, engaging in sexual activities is normal. It's what our bodies are designed to do for reproduction, in fact, which is why it feels good. But we don't always want to reproduce, so therein lies the dilemma. Men don't have this problem, obviously, so we as women must do what we can to educate and protect ourselves."

She patted the carpetbag in front of her. "I have the requested items in here that will offer each of you protection from conception. However, they only work if applied correctly. I'll show you how to use them privately. For whatever reason, if these tools fail you, I will leave a pack or two of Mrs. Pinkham's tablets with Mrs. Kimball. I think that's it. Please, ask questions. I'll keep them in confidence. I'm here to help you."

"Thank you, Miss Young." Mrs. Kimball gestured to the rear of the kitchen. "Chef said we could use his office. Follow me."

Once Nellie was settled in the small room, Mrs. Kimball brought the first woman in. She looked young, probably seventeen or eighteen. "This is Mrs. Ingram," Mrs. Kimball said. "She's one of our kitchen maids."

"Hello, Mrs. Ingram. Won't you have a seat?" Nellie gestured to the chair.

The young woman sat, looking nervous but resolved. When the door closed, she said, "Thank you for doing this, miss. I've been married for four years and already have three children. I don't know what I'll do if I get pregnant again. We can't afford the ones we have."

Nellie reached over and squeezed her hand. "I understand. Which item did you request?"

"The sponge."

Nellie reached in and found the wrapped package with the sponge inside, as well as a tube. "Here is your sponge and the antiseptic." Then she took out a sample. "I want to show you how this works."

"Before you do that," Mrs. Ingram said. "I have to ask. Will my husband know I have it in? He won't like that I'm trying to, you know, prevent his seed from taking purchase."

Nellie smothered the curse that rose up in her throat. Oh, how she'd love a few minutes alone with Mr. Ingram. Instead, she smiled reassuringly at the other woman. "He won't know. You may insert this an hour or so before intimacies, then remove shortly after. Everything is marked

as 'feminine hygiene' so I don't think he'll become suspicious if he stumbles across them in
your personal items."

Mrs. Ingram appeared relieved and Nellie
showed her how to apply the antiseptic and insert the sponge. When they finished, Mrs. Ingram
said, "I would like to ask an indelicate question,
if it's not too embarrassing for you."

Embarrassing for Nellie? Please. As if there
was such a thing. "Ask away."

"I was wondering, if these items go into my . . ."

"Vagina," Nellie supplied.

"Yes, there. Then how do I prevent a baby when
he deposits in other places?"

Nellie tried not to react. Lord have mercy, the
lack of education in this country for women was
enraging. "The only way you can conceive is
when your husband's spend is deposited in your
womb, where your ovum are. If we prevent the
spend from reaching the womb and fertilizing
an egg, we prevent a baby."

Mrs. Ingram's eyebrows flew up, her cheeks
turning bright red. "But I thought . . ."

"No. If he spends in your mouth or your rear,
you won't conceive."

"Sakes alive, I had no idea."

"You're not alone." Nellie patted the other
woman's arm. "Which is why I like helping other
women. The more we know, the less power men
have over us."

After thanking Nellie profusely, Mrs. Ingram
left. The rest of the women came in one by one,
and Nellie gave tutorials and answered questions. Mrs. Kimball brought in some tea at one

point because Nellie's throat grew dry. Still, the entire morning was fulfilling in ways Nellie couldn't begin to explain. She collected the money for the items, which she'd take to the midwife tomorrow, and some of the women asked for more items based on Nellie's recommendations.

When she finished, Nellie came out into the kitchen to find Mrs. Kimball and Katherine waiting. "I cannot thank you enough," Mrs. Kimball said. "These young women aren't able to ask their family doctors and they can't risk ordering things through the mail any longer, either. It's getting harder and harder to take matters into our own hands."

"Which is a dashed shame," Katherine put in. "So, yes. Thank you, Nellie."

Nellie put her nearly empty carpetbag on the workbench again. "It was my pleasure. I hadn't imagined I would enjoy it this much, but it was wonderful."

"I'm happy to hear it," Mrs. Kimball said. "Because we might ask you back. Once these girls start talking to their friends and neighbors, you might have a whole new group to educate."

"I would love that." Nellie put her teacup in the sink. "I'll return anytime."

"You should become a midwife," Katherine suggested.

A grimace twisted Nellie's lips. "Heavens, no. I don't like blood and I like my sleep, thank you very much. Also, not that fond of babies."

"Right," Katherine said with a chuckle. "How could I have forgotten?"

"Well, we should let the girls get to work," Mrs. Kimball said. "We've got a busy day ahead of us."

"Of course!" Katherine grabbed Nellie's carpetbag. "We'll get out of your way. Take care, Mrs. Kimball."

"A good day to you both," the older woman said. "And thank you again, Miss Young."

"You're welcome."

Nellie followed Katherine into the drawing room, where they collapsed onto the sofa. "There's an event here tonight?" Nellie asked.

"Yes. Are you coming?" Katherine put the carpetbag at Nellie's feet.

"No, I have plans."

When Nellie didn't elaborate, Katherine leaned in and peered into Nellie's eyes as if trying to discover a secret. "Are these plans with a man? A duke, perhaps?"

Nellie sighed and smoothed her skirts. "Yes, if you must know."

"Will you be using any of the tricks from your carpetbag, then?"

Leaning her head back, Nellie laughed. "I have my own tricks at home."

"So this is a regular thing, then. You're officially having an affair."

"Will you lower your voice, please. I'm not shy, but there's no reason for the entire world to know."

A noise escaped Katherine's mouth. "Forgive me, because you normally brag about these things to anyone who'll listen. Is this modesty or embarrassment?"

"He's here to find a wife, Katie. I have to keep this quiet, else he'll be ruined along with me."

"You can't be serious. You're worried about Lockwood's reputation?"

Nellie huffed in irritation. "I fail to see how this surprises you. I am capable of discretion every now and again."

"Oh, my God."

Katherine's tone had Nellie sitting up straight. "What? What is it?"

"Oh, my God," Katherine repeated. Excitement lit her expression like a child who'd been given a new toy. "You're in love with him."

Nellie didn't say anything. How could she, when she suspected it was the truth? "It doesn't matter. I'm a temporary diversion for him until he returns to England with his new duchess."

"Have you asked him how he feels?"

"Between orgasms? No, Katie, we haven't had time to delve into our feelings yet."

"You are being very prickly about this—which means you're avoiding the conversation."

The back of Nellie's neck burned in irritation. "I don't need to hear his plans to marry a virginal bride and return to England. I already know all of that."

"Plans change. Look at Preston and his company. How he wanted to build the world's tallest building. He put all of that aside for me."

"Katie, I say this with all of the love and respect in the world, but Lockwood is not Preston, and I am not you. The circumstances are totally different."

"Because he's a duke?"

"That's one reason, certainly. Lockwood's choices are not his own. I've come to terms with it, so please don't try to matchmake. This does not have a happily ever after."

"Nonsense." Katie's lips pressed together as she studied Nellie. "You're afraid to fight for him, afraid to take a risk on a man. Too afraid of leaving New York. The house, your father, the judgmental biddies you can ignore—everything here is comfortable for you. But if you go to England, it's all unknown, an uphill climb. You're afraid of the change."

The words were too much. While there might've been an element of truth to them, Nellie didn't want to hear of her failures. Her cowardice. Her heart was too raw and too vulnerable for that. Nellie needed her friend's unconditional support, not a lecture on her deepest, darkest fears.

The backs of her eyes began burning, a familiar misery settling in her throat, and Nellie knew she needed to leave unless she wanted to break down in tears right there in the Meliora Club. Grabbing her carpetbag, she pushed to her feet. "I have to get home. I'll catch up with you later."

"Nellie, wait," Katherine said, but Nellie was already halfway to the door. "Come on, let's talk."

"I can't right now," Nellie lied, her chest tight with suppressed emotion. "Have a good day, Katie."

Nellie escaped out the front door and darted into a hansom. She had the driver take the long way home, going through the park, just in case Katie tried to follow. She didn't want to be around people right now, not even her closest friend.

Chapter Fifteen

❦

She was early.

Strange, as Nellie was never early, but she found herself knocking on Lockwood's door at a quarter to eight.

He answered, perfectly put together even in his shirtsleeves, vest and trousers. Her belly warmed and softened, the sight of him cutting through her like a hot knife to cold butter. She could almost sigh, he was that handsome.

Without saying a word, he extended a hand and tugged her inside, then closed the door behind her. He crowded her into the wood, trapping her, and took her mouth in a very thorough kiss. He surrounded her, his big body casting off heat that sank into her bones, and she wanted to lean into that strength, crawl inside it until all her problems and insecurities disappeared.

His tongue swept inside her mouth to caress hers, his hand grabbing her hip to keep her where he liked. She wrapped her arms around his neck, perfectly happy to let him lead tonight. All day she'd been thinking of this moment right here, the one when they first saw each other and their hunger and need consumed them. She felt drunk on him, dizzy and weightless, their breath mingling in the quiet space as they panted and gasped.

Finally, he pulled back, though he remained close. His big chest heaved with the force of his breaths. "I've been dying to do that for hours," he said, and Nellie's toes curled in her shoes.

"I've been looking forward to it, as well." Then she realized he was dressed in evening clothes. "Are you going out?"

"*We* are going out. I told you."

Oh, he couldn't be serious. "Nonsense. We are doing no such thing." She slid her hand to his crotch and found a delicious present waiting. God, he was so big and so hard. It made her mouth water. "Get naked and let me suck on you again."

He swallowed audibly but stepped back. "Not yet. I told you I'm taking you out. You are not some dirty little secret I am hiding. You are not a mistress."

Where was this coming from? "No, but I'm your lover, Andrew. Nothing more. You're not courting me. There is no need for dinner and the theater."

"I'm not demanding a night at the Metropolitan Opera House. However, I do wish to spend time with you—outside of a bed."

"And we have. The pool last night, remember?"

He didn't appear amused. "I want to know you better. I want to see inside your life, hear your thoughts."

"Why?"

He exhaled and shook his head a little, as if exasperated. "You are a bloody frustrating woman. Why is this so difficult?"

Because it didn't make any sense. He wanted to see inside her life? Hear her thoughts? To what end? There was no need to forge stronger ties between them. She already had feelings for the man. It was irresponsible to allow them to deepen.

He's going to break my heart.

"You are the one who is frustrating," she said. "Perhaps I should remove all my clothing and you'll change your mind."

His bright blue gaze glittered in challenge. It was the same look he'd worn on the croquet court in Newport and again when he found her with the waiter at the art show. "I am walking out that door in one minute. You may either come with me or stay here by yourself until I return."

The tips of her ears burned. "I don't care for ultimatums, duke."

"A bloody shame, that. And don't think I'm bluffing, either, Eleanor."

No, she didn't think he was bluffing. But perhaps she could change his mind. She grabbed the hem of her skirts and began lifting them, revealing her shins. Then her knees. His eyes tracked her progress, but he didn't move. When she reached her thighs, he turned away and found his evening jacket, slipped it on over his shoulders.

Then he started for the door, his focus on her face. "Time's up. What will it be?"

Defeated, she let her skirts fall to her feet. "I hate you."

"No, you don't," he said with all the arrogance of a handsome man. "Far from it. Now, where shall we go?"

Was she really doing this? She narrowed her eyes on him. "This was your idea. Why do I need to decide?"

"Because I want to choose something that appeals to you, instead of making you miserable. Otherwise, I am quite happy to have dinner in the dining room downstairs."

Nellie's skin crawled at the idea. All those judgmental stares? Everyone whispering about her, wondering why Lockwood would bother, speculating about an affair. News of his unfortunate choice in dinner companions would be all over Fifth Avenue tomorrow. He'd never find a suitable duchess then.

So where could they go that would satisfy him without also ruining him?

The answer popped into her mind and she had to fight to keep from bursting into laughter. Oh, it would serve him right. To be fair, it was everything he'd asked for, a peek inside her life. He would regret forcing her hand.

Yes, she was going to enjoy this.

Straightening, she opened the door. "I've just the place in mind."

"That's the spirit. Where?"

She went out into the corridor and waited for him. "It's a surprise."

Lockwood closed the door and locked it, pocketing the key to his room. "It has to be a public place."

"It is." She patted his chest. "I'll meet you in a

hansom out front. That way no one will see us wandering the hotel together."

His brow furrowed, but he didn't argue. Likely, he thought he was protecting her reputation. Little did he know that she was actually protecting *his* reputation.

She took the stairs instead of the elevator, arriving on the ground floor quickly, where she had the doorman hail a hansom. This allowed her to give the driver their direction before Lockwood arrived. He'd never agree, so better to surprise him. It would be too late by the time he figured it out.

He came out the front doors looking like Apollo, beautiful and strong, drawing attention from everyone around him. Arrogance and entitlement dripped off his frame, so much that she doubted he was even aware of it. He was the complete opposite of what she should have found attractive in a man . . . and yet she couldn't resist him. She was weak around him, a piece of clay with no spine or critical reasoning of any kind. Her plants possessed more intelligence in his presence than she did.

The doorman directed him to where she waited and Lockwood soon climbed aboard. He left no space between them, every bit of his body snug to hers. Her skin buzzed where they touched, an electric charge hovering just above the surface. As the carriage wheels began to move he settled deeper into the seat. "Well, where are we going?"

"You'll have to wait and see."

"Hmm." He watched through the window as they turned west. "Am I going to regret this?"

"Most likely, yes." She rolled her lips between her teeth to keep from smiling. "And you have no one to blame but yourself."

"Are you dragging me to a bordello? Or a gaming hell?"

"No. Gambling is a silly way to lose money, and I don't fancy watching you with another woman."

His head swiveled toward her and his voice pitched low. "Would you be jealous, darling?"

She wasn't about to answer that question, not even to herself. When she remained quiet, he chuckled. "I see."

Ignoring him, she kept her attention on the streets. Let him think whatever he wished. He would not be amused in a few minutes when they arrived at their destination.

"I've not traveled to this part of the city before," he noted as they crossed Seventh Avenue.

"I'm not surprised. Not many debutantes or heiresses running around in these parts."

"Except for you, apparently."

When they headed north, the number of tenements increased, from one on each block, to three or four. The buildings were packed tight, with men out loitering on the stoops. The saloons grew rowdier, the streets dirtier. There was a lawlessness, a stubborn rebelliousness on this side of town that existed nowhere else.

She loved the energy here, the resilience of the immigrants who worked on the docks and in the slaughterhouses. No matter the hardships or the struggles, these residents would never accept defeat. They'd fight to survive until their last breath.

The carriage began to slow at the corner of Eighth Avenue and West Forty-Eighth Street. "Wait," Lockwood murmured. "Are we . . . ?"

"Welcome to Hell's Kitchen," she said proudly, then patted his knee. "Better tighten your suspenders, Your Grace. You're in for a wild night."

LOCKWOOD SHOULD HAVE known. Nothing was ever simple or easy with this woman.

Which explained why he liked her so damn much.

He smothered a grin as he followed her into the King's Saloon. The minx clearly hoped to shock and horrify him, as indicated by her smirk, but she should know him better by now. He wasn't a prude or judgmental arse. If she wanted to take him to an Irish saloon full of her relatives, he was game.

A cheer went up when the crowd saw her. "Red!" several young men called, raising their hand in greeting.

Lockwood stepped out from behind her and the pleasantries instantly died. The place turned deathly silent, the piano halting mid-F sharp. Chairs scraped as men came to their feet, every eye narrowed on him. He leaned down and put his lips near Nellie's ear. "Something tells me they don't care for Englishmen here."

The tallest man in the room started toward them, his expression so menacing that Beelzebub himself would quake in his boots. He carried an air of importance. Was this the Saints' notorious leader, Finn O'Callaghan?

Without taking his gaze off Lockwood, the

man said quietly, "Caethrair, it looks as if you've brought a feckin' gombeen in here tonight."

Nellie placed herself directly between Lockwood and the other man. "Back off, Finn. He's harmless and he's with me."

Ah, so it was O'Callaghan. The gang leader was known for his ruthlessness and height, both of which he used to terrorize the city's West Side. And he was Nellie's cousin, apparently.

O'Callaghan sneered. "He's English. They're as thick as a pile of shite but only half as useful."

Though his heart thumped erratically in his chest, Lockwood didn't say a word, nor did he look away. He wouldn't cower or retreat. Years had passed since his last fistfight, but he remembered how it was done. If O'Callaghan wanted to have a go at him, Lockwood was more than happy to oblige.

"Oh, boy-os," O'Callaghan called out darkly. "This one's asking for trouble. You ready to taste the leather of my boot, English?"

"Go right ahead, Irish," Lockwood said smoothly. "I dare you to try it."

"Jaysus," Nellie exclaimed as she pushed on the other man's chest. "Will you two knock it off?"

"What the hell's goin' on out here?" a feminine voice boomed.

A redheaded woman emerged from the back, and Lockwood sucked in a small breath. It was like looking at an older version of Nellie. The woman came toward them, a frown on her beautiful face. "Finn O'Callaghan, what are you doin' to Nellie's beau?"

O'Callaghan's lips curled into a sneer as his

eyes raked over Lockwood. "Beau?" Then he looked at Nellie. "Tell me you aren't tupping this one, Red."

"It's none of your business." Nellie stepped around O'Callaghan and embraced the older woman. "Hello, Aunt Ri."

"Hello, love. Now, introduce me proper before Finn loses his shite."

Nellie brought the other woman over. "This is His Grace, the Duke of Lockwood. Lockwood, may I present my aunt, Riona O'Callaghan."

"A bloody duke!" Finn snarled. "Have you lost your feckin' mind?"

"Quiet," Riona snapped at the gang leader, and O'Callaghan pressed his lips together. She studied Lockwood's face. "Your Grace, we're honored. Welcome to the King's Saloon."

"Please, call me Lockwood." He took her hand and kissed it. "And the honor is all mine, madam."

She blinked a few times, seemingly at a loss for words, and then turned to Nellie. "Oh, love. You *are* in serious trouble."

Had Nellie discussed him with her aunt?

"Stop," Nellie said. "All of you need to behave yourselves. He's a friend."

O'Callaghan spun and marched back to his table. The men all sat slowly, the threat apparently over, and Lockwood's shoulders relaxed a tiny fraction.

"Come on." Nellie took his arm and began dragging him to the bar. "Let's get a drink."

"Let me finish up some work and then I'll join you," Riona said.

"I'd like that," Nellie told her. "We'll save you some whiskey."

"That was your mother's favorite, too." Riona kissed Nellie's head. "Sometimes you're so much like her that I could cry with it."

Nellie bit her lip, eyes sparkling, and it was clear the comparison meant something special to her. "Thanks, Aunt Ri."

Then the other woman was gone, leaving Nellie and Lockwood at the bar. The other patrons drifted away after casting Lockwood suspicious glances, and the two of them were soon alone. He leaned against the wood. "I'm making friends fast, wouldn't you say?"

"My aunt likes you. That's all that matters." She lifted her hand in the direction of the bartender. "Peg, two whiskeys, please."

The woman named Peg took out two glasses and reached for a bottle behind the bar.

"The real stuff," Nellie amended. "Not the watered-down bottle."

The bartender sighed, her brow furrowed in apparent unhappiness. "Even for him?"

"Yes, even for him."

Lockwood chuckled. "Good thing I didn't come in alone."

"You'd be bleeding on the floor already, if you had," Nellie said.

"I can tell you spend a lot of time here. They love you."

"I come over once a month or so. It's nice to be around family."

He nudged her boot with his foot. "You spoke to your aunt about me."

"Only for advice on how to avoid you."

She was lying, but he let it go. For all her adventurous and bold personality, Nellie was a private person, her true thoughts and feelings locked up tight. It would take time and patience for someone to truly get inside her heart and mind.

Lockwood was up to the challenge.

Peg slammed two full glasses in front of them. "Here you go."

Lockwood reached into his pocket and took out several coins. Peg waved him off. "Your money's no good here, amadán."

"Keep a tab for us, Peg," Nellie said. "I'll settle up at the end of the night."

"Very good, Red. Let me know when you're ready for another."

Nellie lifted her glass toward him in a toast. "May the winds of fortune sail you. May you sail a gentle sea. May it always be the other fellow who says, 'This drink's on me.'"

He chuckled. "Sláinte."

She looked at him through her lashes, her full lips curving and begging for a kiss. "Sláinte agatsa."

They both downed the glass in one swallow. Smooth fire slid all the way down to his stomach, a glorious burn. He licked his lips. "I like that."

"The bottle, Peg!" Nellie called over her shoulder.

"Oh, you're in trouble, amadán," Peg said as she put the bottle down. Lockwood ignored the barkeep, staring down at Nellie instead.

"What does that word mean, amadán?"

"You don't want to know," she murmured. "Finish your drink."

"Should I be worried? Are you going to get me drunk and take advantage of me later?"

A flash of heat flared in her moss-green eyes. "Only if you're very good tonight."

He moved closer, almost touching her but not quite. "Then I shall be so very good, Eleanor."

He heard her swift intake of breath. She edged in, her breasts brushing his arm, and it was his turn to suck in air. She drawled seductively, "Even though I prefer you mean and rough?"

His cock twitched in his trousers, blood pulsing through his veins like a drumbeat. Forcing himself to ease back, he said, "Something tells me your cousin won't like it if I sport a cockstand right here."

The edges of her mouth curled and she looked mighty pleased with herself. "So I shouldn't tell you that I'm no longer sore?"

"Oh, Christ," he muttered, dropping his head into his hands. This was not the time to tell him such information. He tried to think of all manner of non-arousing things, just to keep from getting hard.

"Drink up," Nellie said, nudging a full glass toward him. "The whiskey will take your mind off it."

"Doubtful, not with you standing next to me, looking good enough to eat." He lifted his glass in a toast. "May we never go to hell, but always be on our way."

She laughed, a genuine delightful sound that

wound through him and settled into the pit of his chest. "Lockwood, you may just fit in here yet."

He wanted to kiss her then, right here in the midst of her relatives, even if it earned him a fat lip and a knife to the ribs. Leaning closer, he focused on her mouth, a familiar ache gnawing at his insides.

"What are you doing?" she whispered, her slight frame going perfectly still.

"Think your relatives would cut off my bollocks if I kissed you right now?"

"You can't kiss me here. Have you lost your mind?"

Before he could make a decision one way or another, Riona was back, shouting, "Peg, hand me a glass. Looks like I need to play chaperone."

Nellie rolled her eyes toward the ceiling. "I've never needed a chaperone, Aunt Ri."

"I'm not chaperoning you. I'm chaperoning *him*." She hooked a thumb in Lockwood's direction. "If your man doesn't mind his manners in here, he might not make it out alive."

"He's not my—"

"Thank you, Riona," Lockwood said, interrupting Nellie's ridiculous denial. "I often lose my head around your niece."

"I can tell. Let me give you a word of advice, duke. Flanagan women don't like to be pushed or backed into a corner. The best way to love us is to give us a little bit of lead, understand?"

"You make me sound like a donkey," Nellie grumbled.

"Stubborn as a mule," Riona said with a nod.

"And don't you dare deny it, missy. I've known you since the day you was born."

"You don't need to give him advice." Nellie reached for the bottle and filled all three glasses on the bar. He could hear the Irish lilt in her voice now that they'd been here several minutes, and it only made him want to kiss her more.

"And why not?" Riona asked, accepting the full glass from Nellie. "The English are about as romantic as a clod of dirt. The man needs all the help he can get."

"We're merely friends. This isn't anything serious. Remember? He has to find a suitable heiress and return to England."

"Cold and miserable there," Riona said. "And you're a suitable heiress."

"Hear, hear," Lockwood said and lifted his glass.

Nellie's face paled slightly and she searched his gaze as if looking for hidden meaning there. He didn't bother hiding his intent. She was a suitable heiress, at least in his eyes, and anyone who didn't agree could go to the devil. After a long second, she shook her head. "Now I know you've gone mad."

Riona held up her glass. "Here's to whiskey, scotch and rye—amber, smooth and clear. It's not as sweet as a man's lips, but a damn sight more sincere."

They all drank and set the glasses back on the bar. The burn wasn't quite as fierce this time, like a pleasant wave of heat throughout his entire body. Riona took Nellie's hand but kept her attention on him. "Duke, if you don't mind, I'd like to steal my niece for a bit."

"Of course," he said automatically.

"What for?" Nellie asked. "And I'm not sure I should leave him alone in here."

"Aye, he'll be fine, love. Come along. You can spare your old aunt a few minutes."

Nellie cast a worried look over her shoulder. O'Callaghan and his crew were watching Lockwood carefully, whispering amongst themselves. He knew they were waiting to get him alone—and Riona probably knew it, as well. They would want to see what he was made of, to test his mettle. Well, if they thought he was a soft aristocrat, he would take pleasure in quickly dissuading them of that notion.

"Go," he urged Nellie gently. "I'll be fine. Don't worry about me."

Riona began dragging Nellie away. "See? The man knows what he's about. Let's go back to my office for a moment."

Nellie regarded him carefully, like she was memorizing him before he left for the battlefield. "Finn O'Callaghan," she shouted as she neared the back. "Not a scratch on him, do you hear me?"

Chapter Sixteen

❧

 Jhey're going to kill him," Nellie said as soon as they were alone in Aunt Riona's office. "What are you thinking, leaving him out there by himself?"

Her aunt pointed to the velvet sofa along the wall. "I'm not worried about your duke. I'm worried about you. Sit down."

Nellie dropped onto the sofa, while her aunt went over to the cabinet with the liquor. She returned with two glasses full of amber liquid. "Try this," her aunt said. "It's even better than the stuff Peg serves."

Nellie sipped it and agreed. "Oh, this is good. Where do you get it?"

"A few sailors bring it over from Galway for me. Now, about your duke."

"He's not my duke, and there's no reason to be worried. I'm fine."

"You're in love with him."

"Bollocks." After taking another sip of whiskey, Nellie smoothed the silk pleats in her skirt. "I like him, yes. But I'm not stupid enough to fall in love with him."

"And now you're lying right to my face. Do you think I don't recognize a girl who's head over heels for a fellow?"

"Please, Aunt Ri. You're making this into something it's not."

"I don't want to see you hurt, is all. You've never brought a man over here to meet us. That tells me you're serious."

"No, it's not serious. We're having fun. He needs to marry a debutante with a spotless reputation, a virgin he can take back to England as his duchess."

"A virgin," Riona sneered. "Men and their obsession with purity. As if it's a bloody crime for women to like the same things they do."

Indeed. "Still, his bride must be above reproach."

"You know, when your mother met your father, it about knocked her sideways. 'I'm not fancy enough for him,' she liked to say."

Nellie had heard this many times, how the lovely Irish lass and the railroad magnate fell in love during a chance meeting one rainy night. A barmaid in a saloon, Mama had served Daddy a drink when he came in to get out of the storm. He'd been smitten from the instant they'd met. The tale was one of Nellie's favorites, but it was hardly applicable here. "Please. I'm fancy enough for a duke. I could out-duchess any of those boring sticks who call themselves ladies over there. But I'm too scandalous for him to even consider."

"You've given it some thought."

Nellie squirmed under her aunt's keen regard

that saw too much. "Not seriously. More like I'm reminding myself of all the reasons I can't keep him."

"You could, if you were willing to marry him and move to England."

Nellie took a long swallow of the whiskey to wash the idea from her mind. "Give up my independence? Give up my life here? Why on earth would I do something so foolish? I would hate living over there. It's full of snooty aristocrats."

"Oh, love. There is no limit to the foolish things we do for men." Aunt Riona sighed and settled deeper into the sofa, cradling the near-empty glass of whiskey in her hand. "And weren't you here not long ago cryin' about the snooty girls at your society party? What's the difference if you're here or there? At least there you'll have that big brawny man to keep you warm at night."

Dangerous hope began welling inside Nellie's chest, and she jumped to her feet and began pacing across the worn floorboards. "I can't believe you of all people, someone who refuses to remarry, would push me toward a damn duke."

"Now, wait a minute, missy. I had my Colin, spent thirty-three years with the man and I wouldn't change a day of it. We built a life together, had our children. Took over and expanded the Saints. So I've had my great love. What do I need another for?"

"Well, don't think I've forgotten what you told me during my last visit. You said I was setting myself up for heartbreak if I wanted a future with him."

Aunt Riona waved this away with one hand. "That was before I saw the way he looks at you, like you're the moon and the stars. Like he's about to drag you to an empty closet and screw your brains out. He's either in love with you or well on his way."

I want to know you better. I want to see inside your life, hear your thoughts.

Why had Lockwood said it earlier? Did he have deeper feelings for her? Nellie didn't want to believe it. She couldn't *let* herself believe it, because then their situation would become even more complicated. And she hated complicated.

She finished her drink and set the glass on Aunt Riona's desk. "I'm not in love with him. It's a short affair and I won't get hurt. There. Does that reassure you?"

Her aunt tossed back the rest of her whiskey and got to her feet. She put her glass down then came to stand in front of Nellie, her face as serious as Nellie had ever seen. "Lie to me if you must, but don't lie to yourself. If he makes you happy, then be happy. All of us have such a short time to be alive, so grab all the happiness you can with both hands."

A lump worked its way into Nellie's throat. No doubt her mother would've liked more time—and Lockwood's heart condition meant a shortened lifespan. Another reason he needed to marry and reproduce quickly. Some poor woman would lose him much too soon and be left to grieve all that could've been.

Nellie had experienced that grief once. She didn't intend to go through it again.

Besides, this was too grim a subject for tonight. "I know you mean—"

A rousing shout erupted from out in the bar. Nellie's eyes widened and she grabbed her aunt's arm. "Oh, God. They're killing him. I knew it."

Then she was out the door, Aunt Riona right behind her, as the sound of fists smacking flesh echoed, followed by another cheer. "Shit, shit, shit," Nellie said, breaking into a run until she burst into the bar.

She drew to an abrupt halt.

All the tables and chairs had been moved to the edges of the room to clear space. Two fighters circled each other on the worn floor, their coats off and sleeves rolled up, surrounded by the crowd.

Lockwood and Finn were fighting in the bar.

"Jaysus, Mary and Joseph," she breathed and took a step toward the two idiots.

"Wait a moment," Aunt Riona said, putting an arm around Nellie's shoulder. "Just watch. Let's see if he can hold his own."

"That's absurd. Finn won't fight fair."

"Your duke might not, either."

Was Lockwood . . . smiling? Blood trickled from the side of his mouth, but he didn't look angry. Neither did Finn, come to think of it. What on earth was happening out there?

Their shoes scraped on the floor as they kept moving. Then Finn lunged and attacked with a right hook, but Lockwood blocked it and countered with a punch to Finn's ribs. "Fuck me," Finn wheezed as he dropped a step. "That was a good one, English."

"Plenty more where that came from, Irish," Lockwood called, beckoning Finn closer with his hands.

"Is he cracked?" Nellie whispered to her aunt. "Taunting Finn like that?"

"Let's see how it plays out."

This time it was Lockwood who advanced, faking a left jab before landing a right hook on Finn's chin. The men in the crowd all cheered. Wait, they were cheering for Lockwood? This made no sense.

Finn got in a few punches of his own, and Nellie winced, even though Lockwood barely reacted. They continued, trading jabs back and forth, and she began to relax, impressed with Lockwood's technique. He was a decent fighter. In fact, Finn looked the worse for wear between the two of them.

The men in the bar began trading money, making bets on the fight, but Nellie could hardly look away from Lockwood. Sweat dripped down his face, his thin shirt and silk vest clinging to his torso, and the heft of his shoulders bunched and shifted with his movements.

He was fighting the leader of the Saints . . . and winning.

It was surprising. And very arousing. Lockwood's hidden depths never failed to intrigue her. While she didn't want him hurt, she was quite enjoying the view.

"Jaysus, those shoulders," Aunt Riona murmured. "He didn't get those from lazing about."

"He swims. God, you should see him, Aunt Ri. It's like he's carved from marble."

"And you worried he wouldn't be able to handle Finn. You clearly don't know him as well as you thought."

No, she clearly didn't.

Lockwood punched Finn in the cheek and sent her cousin stumbling back. Instead of pressing, Lockwood held his ground and waited, his chest heaving with the force of his breaths. Finn held up his hands. "That's enough, duke. I think it's been settled."

The crowd broke out in a rousing cheer, then everyone surrounded Lockwood, slapping him on the back. Nellie frowned. "What's been settled?" she asked her aunt.

"Whether your duke deserves you or not. Finn's just given a Saints' blessing."

Nellie's throat closed with a mix of emotions. The whole thing was ridiculous, some bizarre male ritual that was nonsensical, but it was also flattering. Like they were two knights on a jousting field and Lockwood was trying to win her favor.

The wall around her heart cracked open the tiniest bit, her chest swelling with pride and affection. Lord, this man. She'd never felt this way about anyone before. It was both thrilling and terrifying.

"Remember what I said, love." Aunt Riona pressed a kiss to Nellie's head. "Grab that happiness with both hands before it's too late."

"Oh, I intend to grab something with both hands," Nellie said, her gaze never leaving Lockwood's ass.

Her aunt laughed. "I'm serious, love. You let

that one get away and you're a fool—and your mother did not raise a fool."

"Thanks, Aunt Ri."

"Aye, you have it bad." Her aunt released her and nudged her toward the crowd. "Go. Go and get your man."

FINN THRUST OUT his hand as the men slapped Lockwood's back. "I never would've guessed it," Finn said. "Consider me impressed, English."

Lockwood's side ached, and he'd have a swollen lip and black eye tomorrow, but he still smiled and shook Finn's hand. "I can give you some pointers any time you like, Irish."

Finn chuckled. "You've got some stones on you, I'll say that much. Come, let me get you a drink."

They ended up at the bar, where Peg produced a fancy bottle with clear liquid and two small glasses. "I figure it's time to give him some Irish milk," the barkeep said.

"I'd say he's earned it," Finn said as he poured.

"Wait!"

Nellie was pushing her way through the crowd to get to him. The pain in his body instantly disappeared, replaced by tenderness and affection, the need to hold her so strong that he had to grip the edge of the bar to keep from reaching for her.

"Don't drink that," she blurted, gesturing to the clear liquor.

"Why not?" he asked.

She took the glass out of Lockwood's hand. "Because it'll tear a hole in your stomach."

"Stop scaring the man," Finn said. "He can handle it, caethrair."

"Anyone who fights like that can handle a bit of poitín!" someone shouted.

Lockwood quickly plucked the glass from her hand and held it up. "To the queen!"

Groans erupted all around him. "That'll earn you another beating, English!" one of the Saints called.

Finn just shook his head. "Sláinte."

They downed their drinks and Lockwood actually felt his heart stop beating for a few long seconds while fire ignited his insides. *Christ,* that burned. He knew of poitín, so he'd braced himself for the worst. No amount of bracing could've truly prepared him, however. It was like swallowing a lit flame that never extinguished, and instead roared like the fires of hell in one's stomach.

They all watched him closely for a reaction, which he carefully masked. After all, no man on earth had perfected that skill better than he.

Grinning through the excruciating pain, he slammed his empty glass on the bar. "Another!" he cried, and the crowd let out a rousing cheer.

"You can't be serious," Nellie said, peering at his face carefully. "Your eyes aren't even watering. I don't understand it."

"Nothing to understand." Finn refilled the glasses. "Your duke's a real man, is what."

"A real *English*man," Lockwood couldn't help but add, which earned him lots of good-natured ribbing from the Saints.

The next glass of poitín went down easier, as did the third. The edges of the room started to waver at that point, but he didn't let on. Thankfully, Nellie stepped in before a fourth.

"That's enough. I'm taking him home."

"Are you?" He leaned closer to her, not caring that the room tilted slightly. "Taking me to your home, I mean?"

"Damn it, Finn," she snapped at her cousin. "You got him drunk."

"Sorry to ruin your plans," Finn said with a chuckle, which Lockwood didn't understand at all.

"You did it on purpose." Nellie grabbed Lockwood's coat off the bar. "You aren't fooling me, Finn O'Callaghan."

Finn bent to press a kiss to her cheek. "I've got to protect your virtue somehow, caethrair."

She pushed him away playfully. "That ship sailed a long, long time ago."

"Thank fuck," Lockwood murmured.

"Oh, God. That's our cue to leave. See you all soon." Nellie began towing him toward the door, and he let her lead, because of course he did. He'd go anywhere with her.

A hand dropped onto his shoulder, stopping him. Finn was there, his face dangerous and intense, even if a bit blurry. "Hurt her and I'll come looking for you, duke. They'll find little pieces of you sprinkled all over the island like ticker tape. Hear me?"

Lockwood held the other man's gaze, needing him to understand. "I would never hurt her. I think I love her."

A gasp sounded nearby, but his eyes remained

on Finn. Nellie's cousin nodded and stepped back. "I figured, but it still needed to be said. Enjoy your night, Red!"

Nellie led them into the cold night and soon hailed a hack. Lockwood's limbs felt uncoordinated and heavy as he climbed inside the vehicle, and he slumped onto the seat. Were they moving yet? He couldn't tell because everything was spinning.

"Move over, duke," Nellie snapped and shoved at his legs. "Why are you so dashed big?"

The comment caused him to chuckle. "I thought you liked my size. A beast, you called it."

"Unbelievable. I'm not talking about your penis." She sounded annoyed so he tried to shift over to make room for her.

"Why don't you sit on my lap?" he offered. "It would save us both the trouble."

"Because I fear you'll drop me. You're as coordinated as a day-old foal at the moment."

"I apologize. I don't usually drink to access." Why did that word sound funny? "*Excess*," he tried again. "It's not good for my heart."

"What?" Nellie settled next to him and he noticed she was frowning. "What does that mean, not good for your heart?"

He attempted to lift a shoulder. "The doctors say not to overimbibe. That it can throw off my heart rhythm even more. Makes me lightheaded."

"Are you light-headed now?"

"Yes."

"Oh, for Pete's sake. Andrew, I can't believe you!"

"Don't be angry, Eleanor. I had to."

"No, you didn't. You didn't need to impress Finn at the expense of your health."

Was she serious? "Of course I did. I need to impress your family. I want them to like me."

"Why? Who cares whether they like you or not?"

"Because I like you. Therefore, I need the people you care about to like me."

She turned and stared out the window, the gentle column of her throat working as she swallowed. "You stupid man."

"Are you cross with me?"

"Yes." She dabbed at the corners of her eyes with her fingertips. "Very."

"Is that why you are crying?"

"Don't be ridiculous. I never cry."

"Everyone cries, darling."

Instead of answering, she opened the slat and spoke to the driver. When she returned to her seat, he said, "What did you tell him?"

"I'm taking you to my house."

"Why?"

She lifted her chin and kept her gaze on the passing street. "Because someone needs to keep an eye on you."

He struggled to get closer to her, but there wasn't enough space for him to move around. He ended up with his head in her lap. "You like me. Admit it."

"I like sleeping with you—which you aren't even capable of at the moment."

He closed his eyes, but the spinning only increased. He forced himself to look up at her.

"Is that all you like, Eleanor? My cock and my tongue?"

He hoped it wasn't the case. They were weirdly compatible in the bedroom, and Lockwood loved fucking her, but he needed this to be more. He'd decided at some point tonight, right about when she took him to meet her family, that he wanted to *marry* this woman. Have her bear his children. Spend his life, however long it lasted, with her.

"Of course. That's all men are good for."

Disappointment burned in his chest worse than the poitín. Was he wasting his time in trying to win her over? Hell, he'd fought her cousin and nearly drank himself stupid tonight just to impress her. There wasn't a damn thing she could ask that he'd refuse. But he needed this to be two-sided. He couldn't drown alone.

"Then why not drop me at the hotel?" he asked, needing to push, hoping for a crumb.

"Because I don't need the guilt of your death on my soul."

"Really? You don't strike me as a pious woman. Except for when you climax and you call out—"

"Stop," she said, smiling, and threw up her hands. "Fine, I like you."

His lungs inflated with the joy of her admission, and warmth lit him up from the inside out. It was like the clouds had parted on a rainy day to give the first glimpse of sunshine. A grin stretched his mouth and he cuddled closer to her stomach. "Good, because I'm going to win you over, sweetheart."

She brushed his hair off his forehead, not

meeting his eyes. "What am I going to do with you, you poor misguided man?"

"You're going to stay with me."

"You know why that can't happen."

"Balderdash. I know nothing of the sort." His lids were too heavy to keep open. He let them fall and murmured, "I'm keeping you, Eleanor Young."

"Except that I'm not the keeping kind," was the last thing he heard her say before the darkness swamped him.

Chapter Seventeen

❦

She didn't leave his side all night.

Two of the footmen helped Nellie get the nearly asleep duke into the mansion and settled in a guest bedroom. Then she undressed him and put him to bed, after which there was nothing to do but pull up a chair and watch the steady rise and fall of his chest as he slept. It was terrifying, knowing that his heart could stop at any minute.

Why the hell had he drunk so much?

Because I like you. Therefore, I need the people you care about to like me.

No one had ever gone to such lengths to impress her or her family. Yet, Lockwood had—at the expense of his own health, the idiot. Like some weak ninny, she nearly cried in the hansom when he told her, her heart and mind overcome with emotion. Lockwood did that quite a lot to her these days.

I would never hurt her. I think I love her.

He couldn't really mean it. No, he'd said it merely for Finn's benefit, as a way to allay her cousin's fears. Lockwood couldn't *love* her. Yes, she'd let her stupid heart fall for him, but she wasn't about to change her mind about marriage merely because a gorgeous pair of sculpted shoulders swam by. Granted, the shoulders were attached to other impressive assets, as well, but they had no future together. When he was sober, no doubt he'd forget about these declarations. Lockwood was a logical, reasonable person. Full of duty and responsibility, with visions of a scandal-free bride dancing in his head. He didn't truly want *her*.

The hours dragged as she kept watch over him. Every now and again she reached out to touch his forehead or cheek, just to feel his warm skin. She let his breath coat the back of her hand. And yes, she pressed her fingers to the pulse in his neck, reassuring herself that his heart continued to beat. His poor future wife. Whoever she was, she would undoubtedly spend many nights like this, at his bedside, sick with worry.

He should consult with doctors here in America. Perhaps Nellie could make an appointment and force him to go. It was the least she could do, because she'd never be able to tell him how she felt. They wanted very different things out of life, and Lockwood needed to save the ducal estates back home. Keeping this a temporary, casual affair was best for both of them.

In the middle of the night he stumbled to the washroom, and when he returned she forced him to drink a prairie oyster: an egg, pepper sauce and a tiny amount of whiskey. He chased it down with a big glass of water. Then he dropped back down on the bed, mumbling, "Get into bed with me, Eleanor. Now."

Exhausted, she could hardly argue. The clock showed three-thirty, so she figured he was through the worst of it. Just to be safe, she crawled close to him, staying on top of the covers, and put her hand on his chest, right atop his heart. The steady beat lulled her to sleep.

The next thing she knew, warm breath and soft lips were brushing along her throat. Morning whiskers scratched deliciously over her skin, and her mind came fully awake. He was nearly covering her, his bare torso gleaming in the early light. "Hello, beautiful," he whispered between kisses. "What a wonderful way to wake up, hmm?"

She couldn't agree more. "What time is it?"

"Just after six."

Turning her head to give him better access, she moaned when he sank his teeth into her flesh. "How do you feel?"

"My head feels fine. My cock on the other hand . . ." As if he needed to prove it, he shifted his hips and pressed his erection into her thigh. Even through the bedclothes, she could feel him.

"Indeed, that does seem like a sorry state."

"Very sorry," he murmured as he licked behind her ear. "Were I alone, I would already be stroking myself and thinking about you."

Her toes curled at both the image and the compliment, and she slid her hands over his shoulders, skimming his muscles. "Fortunate you're not alone, then."

"Yes. I have the real thing right here with me. No imaginings required. Except . . ." He paused and leaned back. "You're wearing all this blasted clothing."

She started to lift her skirts, but he stayed her hand, rising slightly. "I want to take my time with you, and I want you completely naked." The tender light in his eyes was new, intensely honest, and it scared her down to her very soul.

I'm keeping you, Eleanor Young.

She swallowed past the lump in her throat. This was just an affair. Nothing more.

"We should hurry," she said. "Before someone notices you're here."

"Will anyone walk in here unannounced?"

She couldn't lie. "No."

"Is this room next to your father's?"

"No. We're in the opposite wing."

"Oh, darling." His smile turned positively wicked. "You shouldn't have told me, because now I'm going to make you scream."

Jaysus, this man.

Then Nellie lost the urge to complain because Andrew was removing her clothing, his touch patient and reverent, as if she were important and precious. Like he treasured her. No one had ever treated her so solemnly, with such care. He kissed the skin he uncovered and seemed in no hurry whatsoever to fuck her, even though his cock made its demanding presence known between them.

"I adore your skin," he said, licking the top of her breast when he finally removed her corset and chemise. "I want to kiss it and mark it and come all over it."

Then he took her nipple into his mouth, sucking gently at first, then increasing the pressure until she writhed underneath him. "I love your breasts," he murmured. "Have I told you?"

"No, I don't think so."

"I have been remiss, then. Tell me if this becomes too much." He sank his teeth into the heft of the soft mound, biting down. Hard. Shocks of pain spread throughout her body, centering in her core, where liquid heat began to pool. She panted, the air in the room turning thick in her lungs.

When he let go, he eased up to see the results. "Oh, indeed. I quite like that." His blue gaze was bright with lust and possessive arrogance as he regarded her. Whatever he saw in her expression caused him to grin. "I'm going to cover you in bite marks, darling."

He continued around the same breast, sinking his teeth deep, more animal than man, each jagged arrow of discomfort meant as a claiming. The effort was successful. She felt *his* in a way no one had attempted before, like he wanted the world to know she belonged to him.

And for a weak moment she longed to surrender and give all of herself to this man, to capitulate to his every whim and desire as long as he kept pleasuring her.

"Please, please, please," she begged, restless, and his hand found its way between her legs.

"You're utterly soaked," he whispered, circling her entrance with the tip of his finger. "You like this as much as I do."

"Yes, now put yourself inside me."

"Patience, my greedy Eleanor."

He switched to her other breast and began leaving marks deep in her skin, his fingers teasing her folds but never quite stroking where she needed. It was maddening and thrilling and so very Lockwood. Frustrated, she slid her hand to his crotch and grasped his erection. Instead of stroking him, however, she merely clasped the root, denying him the friction she knew he craved.

"Witch," he murmured against her breast. "Pump your hand." He tried to move his hips and push his cock through her fist, but she didn't allow it.

"Stop tormenting me and I will."

"You like my torment." He pushed inside her entrance, now slick and full of moisture. "See? You're dripping."

She could torment, too. Moving her hand to the top of his sac, she pulled gently away from his body, squeezing. He froze, a strangled gasp escaping his lips. He didn't pull away or tell her to stop, though, so she tightened her fingers, and his back bowed, eyelids slamming shut. "Oh, Christ."

When she eased her grip off his bollocks, he flew into motion. The rest of her clothing disappeared and he quickly mounted her, his erection heavy against her belly. "Shield?" he asked through panted breaths.

"Not here," she said, gripping his hips. "Just don't spend inside me."

"I promise." He lined himself up at her entrance, then pushed in. The crown stretched her, and she felt every thick inch of him as he tunneled into her channel. He was a lot to take, but it was the best kind of pinch.

"You're perfect," he whispered against her

mouth when he was fully seated. "Just bloody perfect."

She wrapped her legs around him, deepening the angle, and they both exhaled. "Make us both come, love," she said, the endearment falling from her mouth so naturally that it should've frightened her. But she was too far gone, too needy and ravenous for him, to keep the word inside.

He began to move then, with hard and measured thrusts that hit exactly the right spot every time. Something was different this time, something she couldn't put her finger on, but he held her close, their noses nearly touching as he continued to work his cock in and out of her body. He surrounded her, inside and out, their shared world all that mattered. Even their breath mingled, mouths hovering barely an inch apart as they huffed and wheezed, both of them straining to help the other finish.

"Please, darling. Hurry," he urged.

"I'm so close." The angle was amazing, but not quite what she needed to climax. "Get on your back."

He climbed off and fell onto the mattress. Rising up, she threw a leg over his hips and straddled him. Heavy-lidded blue eyes watched her as she lowered herself onto his erection. He filled her once again, replacing the yawning loneliness inside her, burrowing his way under her skin.

"Yes, that's it. Use me," he murmured. "Use my body to pleasure yourself. Goddamn, you are fucking gorgeous."

She began rolling her hips, moving faster

and faster as the pleasure built. The friction was exactly what she needed, the view of him stretched out beneath her too good to be true. He reached his arms above his head to brace his hands against the wooden headboard, but his gaze never left her face. It was like he saw into her mind, with every thought and feeling in her head bared for his inspection, so she closed her eyes, lest she reveal too much.

But that meant she could only *feel*, and soon the climax gathered in her toes, at the base of her spine, and then it rushed over her, her body spasming as her walls contracted around his length in sweet pulses. "Oh, God," she shouted to the ceiling, and he thrust up, riding her through it, until she collapsed onto his chest.

In a heartbeat, he flipped them and sat on his haunches between her splayed thighs. His hand flew over his shaft, twisting and pulling, and in seconds, he was shooting on her belly, coating her body in his spend. Muscles taut, he groaned through clenched teeth as the orgasm went on and on. "Fucking hell," he gasped, shivering as the last of his climax dripped onto her skin.

He slumped and braced his hands on her thighs, his chest heaving. "I am utterly wrecked, Eleanor."

A small, happy smile twisted her lips. "Same, Andrew."

After cleaning her up, he dropped to the bed beside her and pulled her close. The winter sun was shining through panes of frosted glass. The household would soon rise. There were a thousand things she should've been worried about right then, but at the moment she couldn't think of a single one.

WHEN SHE FELL back asleep Lockwood rose and dressed. He had things to accomplish today, and he didn't intend to let Nellie interfere.

Besides, she was exhausted. She'd been sitting up with him half the night before he made her lie down. His chest swelled as he looked at her, red hair spread out on the pillow, sweetly curled onto her side. Had anyone ever worried over him like this before? Not enough to keep vigil at his bedside for hours, certainly. His own parents hadn't sat with him during his childhood illnesses, not even the worst one that damaged his heart.

He and Nellie had turned a corner last night and this morning, whether she realized it or not.

"I'm keeping you," he whispered into the quiet room.

Once he was perfectly put together in his evening dress, he left the room, went downstairs and found a footman. "Is Mr. Young up and about yet?"

"No, sir. Is there a message you'd like to pass on?"

"Would you please tell him the Duke of Lockwood is waiting in his study? I'd like a moment of his time."

The young man's eyes widened. "Yes, Your Grace."

"Thank you. Now, can you point me in the direction of the study?"

"Third door down on the right."

With a nod, Lockwood went to the described

door and entered. The room was large and airy, bright, with rows and rows of books stacked on shelves. He couldn't help but examine the titles, curious what sorts of books a railroad baron would stock in his home. It was an impressive collection, with first editions of many rare titles. They weren't alphabetized, which struck him as odd. How did anyone find anything in this system?

"She has it organized by year," a voice behind him said.

Cornelius Young came in and closed the door behind him. Lockwood went over to shake the older man's hand. "Ah, I see," he said. "That makes sense, I suppose. Good morning, sir."

"Morning, Your Grace. I understand you were a guest last evening."

"I was, so my thanks for your hospitality. I had a bit too much to drink last night."

"Eleanor would've worried over you, then. No wonder you ended up here." He gestured to the seats by his massive desk. "Shall we sit?"

Nellie's father was an intimidating man. He owned most of the railroads on the east coast and some out west, as well. His fortune was stuff of legend, with no one quite sure exactly how much wealth he had, but it was more than anyone else in the world, even Carnegie and Vanderbilt.

But it wasn't Young's money that Lockwood found intimidating. No, it was the relationship he shared with his daughter. Nellie was obviously the most important thing in Young's life, and something told Lockwood the man wouldn't tolerate anything but the best for her.

Lockwood was far from the best, but he would somehow prove himself worthy.

When they settled into chairs he came right to the point. "I am in love with your daughter."

Young's brows climbed ever so slightly. "I see. Does she know?"

"Yes, but no doubt she's written it off as drunken ramblings."

"Does she return your feelings?"

Lockwood studied the grooves in the wooden desk in front of him. He wasn't certain how to answer. "I believe so, yes, but she hasn't admitted as much. Yet."

"I like your confidence," the older man said. "You'll need it, if you have any hopes of winning her. She's not one to suffer fools, though, and she'll work hard to drive you away."

It was a spot-on description. "Why do you say so?"

"Because she's just like her mother." Young's expression softened. "Greatest woman who ever lived, my Siobhán, but I had a devil of a time catching her."

Lockwood stroked his unshaven jaw. "I thought you'd try to scare me off."

"Why would I do that?"

"Because I'm a penniless duke who wishes to take your daughter across the ocean to a crumbling estate."

"You won't be penniless if she agrees to marry you. I'll see to that. But I should warn you that the decision is hers. I promised never to force her into a marriage, and I meant it. She'd only fight me, even if it would make her happy."

This Lockwood well knew. Nellie was the most stubborn person he'd ever met, and convincing her to change her opinion on marriage was undoubtedly a Herculean task. But Young hadn't reacted to the penniless part, which was what concerned Lockwood most. "You don't care that your money will go toward an estate drowning in debt? That your daughter marries a pauper?"

"Money is just paper, Your Grace, not happiness. I'd let her marry a dirt farmer if I thought they loved each other."

"Indeed, if I cannot convince her to marry me soon, I may end up a dirt farmer."

Young looked down his nose and leaned in slightly. "No offense, but you might have an easier time winning her over that way. I'm afraid a duke will be a hard sell to Eleanor."

Figured Lockwood would fall in love with the one woman on the planet who didn't care to become a duchess. "Not one for the aristocracy, then?"

"No, or society in general. She's taken some knocks since her debut and that's probably my fault. I let her have too much freedom, too much independence, but she's all I have left of Siobhán and I'll be damned if I'll see my daughter's spirit squashed."

"I think she's perfect, sir," Lockwood said quietly. "I wouldn't change a thing about her."

"Then I wish you luck, son. Because you're going to need it."

"Thank you. Seeing as how she's like her mother, do you have any advice on how best to proceed?"

Young stroked his white beard, his eyes seeing

but not seeing, like he was remembering a fond memory. "All I can say is you have to learn when to push and when to back off. If you push too hard, you'll lose her for good."

Lockwood blew out a long breath and flexed his fingers. *What if I fail?* What if he couldn't convince her in time and he was forced to marry vanilla crème, as she'd once called his other marriage prospects?

No, he couldn't think that way. Not yet. He had to find a way to convince her.

He rose and held out his hand. "Thank you, sir. It is much appreciated."

Nellie's father rose and they shook. "I'll be rooting for you, Your Grace. Incidentally, that is a hell of a black eye."

"Yes, sir, I know. Compliments of Finn O'Callaghan last night."

Young's mouth slackened. "She . . . took you to meet her mother's family?"

"She did," he said, then chuckled. "She took me out of spite. I told her I wanted to escort her somewhere in public. I'd intended dinner at Sherry's, but she surprised me with Hell's Kitchen instead."

The older man pressed his lips together, and for a moment it seemed like he might break down in tears. Eventually, he cleared his throat and said, "Well, I'll be damned. She really does love you back."

"What makes you say so?"

"She'd never take you to the O'Callaghans otherwise, spite or not. It was a test. Considering she brought you to sleep here, I'd say you passed."

Lockwood certainly hoped so. "I didn't wish to leave without thanking you for allowing me to stay, as well as for the use of your pool. You've been very generous, Mr. Young, and I'm grateful."

"You're welcome—and you best start calling me Cornelius, son. I have a feeling I'm going to be seeing a lot more of you."

Chapter Eighteen

❧

"Nellie? Where are you?"

Nellie glanced up from her plants at the sound of Katie's voice. For the first time in her life, she considered not answering her friend, hiding from her problems instead of facing them head-on.

But that wasn't like her at all.

"Near the frog pond," she called, continuing to dig in the dirt. "Two lefts then a right."

She wasn't ready to see Katie—or anyone else—this morning. While she'd been sleeping, Lockwood snuck out and went to speak with her father. Papa wouldn't say what was discussed, only that he liked the duke quite a bit.

Same, Papa. Same.

And therein lay the problem.

Still, Nellie was trying to imagine the conversation between the two men, but she couldn't fathom what had been discussed.

I'm keeping you, Eleanor Young.

Nerves and dread bubbled in her stomach. Had Lockwood declared his intentions to her father? Without speaking to her about it first?

Even if he had, it was pointless because she'd never marry him. How could she leave her father or her mother's plants? Who would care for everything without her here?

"Oh, Nellie." Katie rushed toward Nellie, not stopping.

Nellie put up her hands. "I'm all dirty."

"I don't care," her friend said and threw her arms around Nellie's shoulders. "I need to hug you."

"Whatever for?" Nellie did her best to squeeze her friend in return without using her muddy hands.

Katie stepped back. Were her eyes shiny? "I owe you an apology. I hurt your feelings yesterday, even though I didn't mean to. I am so sorry, Nels."

Nellie pressed her lips together and tried to wave it off. "It's fine. I'm a bit oversensitive these days."

"I had no right to criticize you or point out your personality flaws. I shouldn't have meddled."

"Well, you wouldn't be Katherine Delafield soon-to-be Clarke, if you didn't meddle."

"I'm serious. Please, may we forget I ever said anything about you and Lockwood?" Katie put her hands together as if in prayer. "Pretty please, with penis on top?"

Surprised, Nellie burst out laughing and the trowel fell from her hand. This was why she loved her friends. They were small in number but big in personality.

She retrieved the small trowel and set it down. "I'm not mad at you." Nellie stripped off her gardening gloves, then removed her apron. "Come on, let's sit."

"You needn't lie on my account," Katie said as they walked to the refreshment table. "I saw it on your face yesterday. I've been sick to my stomach ever since."

Nellie dropped onto the iron bench. "Honestly, I wasn't mad. I was feeling vulnerable and you picked at a scab. That's all."

"Honey." Katie sat down and clasped Nellie's hand. "I completely understand and I'm so sorry. It's just . . . I want you to be happy. The rest of us are all settled, or soon to be settled, and I want you to be settled, too."

Nellie's chest suddenly ached like a fifty-pound weight rested there, her throat so tight she couldn't speak. *They don't want to worry about me. They don't want a spinster hanging about.* They preferred for her to join the club, with marriage and babies and a new last name, even though Nellie had resisted it for years.

"I've said something wrong again, haven't I?" Katie was studying Nellie's face. "Oh, heavens. I'm so sorry. Let's just talk about the weather instead!"

The burning in Nellie's lungs compounded and she could feel tears pressing behind her eyes. Shit, shit, shit. She did not want to cry. First with Lockwood last night, now again this morning with Katie. What the hell was wrong with her?

She drew in a few deep breaths and decided she owed it to Katie to tell her the truth. "It's me. I've been feeling this . . . dark cloud inside me for a few months now. It's like I can't shake it, no matter what I do."

Well, that wasn't entirely true. It disappeared when she was with Lockwood.

Setting that aside for the moment, she continued to explain as best she could. "I'm watching everyone around me fall in love, and then you said you didn't need me to play mama bear anymore, and I'm just . . . sad and adrift. Worried. I have no idea what the future holds for me, and yes, maybe you're right. Maybe I'm too scared to find out. Maybe this is comfortable and safe, living here in my father's house surrounded by memories. Maybe I can't bear to lose anyone else."

Eyes huge and round, Katie covered her mouth with her hand. "I didn't mean I don't need you anymore. God, Nellie. Is that what you thought? You're . . ." Tears welled in her friend's eyes again. "You're my rock, my sister by choice. There isn't a day that goes by where I don't think about you or wish to talk to you about something, no matter how small. I don't know what I would do without you."

Nellie couldn't prevent the two tears that slipped down her cheeks. "I feel the same. I do. But Katie, you'll soon have a husband and children. Tell me, how often do you see or speak to Maddie? I hardly hear from her anymore. Alice is busy with Kit and the supper club. You're all going your separate ways and I'm . . . here. And please don't think I begrudge any of you your happiness. God, I don't. I'm thrilled for all of you. But it hurts to be left behind and forgotten."

"You think we've forgotten you? I can't speak for the others, but that will never happen between you and me." Katie grabbed Nellie's arm. "Do you hear me? Never."

"Never is a long time. Women get swallowed up by their husbands, the life they build together. And that's how it should be, I suppose. I think I'm merely feeling sorry for myself."

"Husbands also get swallowed up by their wives—wait, that didn't come out the way I intended. Let me start over." Katie shook her head and wiped her eyes. "It's probably natural for a couple to get caught up in one another while it's still new. But I don't think this cloud of yours has anything to do with Maddie, Alice or me. I think it has to do with you and Lockwood. There, I said it. Don't yell at me."

Nellie started to dismiss it out of hand, but she forced herself to think about this weight she'd been carrying and when it started. It first appeared over the summer, after she returned from Newport. After the run-in with Lockwood at the house party.

Damn.

"You might be right," she said, picking at a loose flake of paint on the bench. "As much as I don't want to admit it."

"Talk to me. I won't make any more assumptions and I won't matchmake. Just please, tell me what's going on in your head."

What could it hurt at this point? She hadn't talked to anyone, other than her aunt, and perhaps her friend could offer some much-needed perspective.

So she told Katie everything, from swimming with Lockwood in the ocean to last night in Hell's Kitchen. She left out the private bits and Lockwood's heart condition for obvious reasons, and ended with how Lockwood met with her father today. "My father won't tell me what they talked about."

"You," Katie said excitedly. "Obviously, they talked about you. My God, Nels! I can't believe you've been sitting on all of this. He's in love with you."

"As if that is a good thing. It's a disaster. I can't marry him."

"Because . . . ?"

"First of all, he hasn't asked. Second, weren't we just discussing being swallowed up by your husband? I wouldn't even have a name. I'd be the Duchess of Lockwood. And move to England? Absolutely not. I love it here." She stood up and began pacing. "But really, all that is inconsequential because he needs a bride with an unblemished reputation. I would be the absolute worst choice in a duchess."

"Not if he loves you. Would you really care whether London society accepts you or not?"

"No, but Lockwood would care."

"Something tells me he might not. Do you know how rare it is to find someone you love? Even more rare is finding someone who loves you back. Your parents had that kind of love, and they came from wildly different stations in life."

"Yes, in America. My father was filthy rich by then and Mama never cared about New York society."

"Well, there are more and more American women over there now, with the British aristocracy in shambles. So I think you'd feel right at home."

Nellie stopped pacing and crossed her arms over her chest. "Why must I bend on this? If we married, Lockwood would get everything he wanted—a rich wife, his title, living in his ducal home. What is he giving up for me?"

Katie's mouth opened, then she closed it. "The unblemished bride part, I suppose."

"Fine. What else?"

"Would you give him heirs?"

Nellie's temples began pounding, so she rubbed them with her fingers. "Damn, I forgot all about those."

"I don't know how, with all the practicing you two have been doing."

"Bite your tongue." Nellie exhaled. "We've been very careful."

"I believe it. Oh, by the way." Katie dug in her handbag. "Here is a list of more contraceptive items to procure. Apparently, some of the girls went home and talked to neighbors."

"No problem. I do love thwarting Mr. Comstock and his ridiculous laws at every turn." She took the list and studied it. This was much longer than the one from yesterday, which only showed how desperate women were to control their own reproduction. "I need to go down to see the midwife today, anyway. Do the women know how to use these properly?"

"I'm not certain. Can I tell them you'll do another one-on-one demonstration session?"

"Would they be willing to come to the club?"

"I don't see why not. I'll ask."

"If there's a better location, have them suggest it."

"I will." Katie closed her handbag. "Are we done discussing the duke?"

"Please, yes. I can't bear to think about it any longer."

"I figured you might say that. But, Nels, you need to decide on an answer because I know Lockwood. If he's decided on you, nothing will stop him from trying to accomplish his goal. He's incredibly stubborn."

"As am I, and I stand to lose in this arrangement."

"Except you gain a husband who loves you. You get joy and happiness every day of your life."

To Nellie's mind, that wasn't enough. No, he needed to marry some other young girl and Nellie would get over him eventually. Then she could resume her wild affairs and raucous parties. There would be new friends who weren't in relationships, women who liked to gamble and drink, as Nellie did. Her life would go back to normal.

"I'm going to leave you to your plants, but think about what I've said." Katie walked over and held on to Nellie's shoulder. "And you are never getting rid of me, Eleanor Lucinda Young. Husbands, babies, different countries, I don't care. You're important to me, mama bear."

Nellie threw her arms around her friend and hugged her tight. "Good, because you're never getting rid of me, either, Katherine Eloise Delafield."

"Even when Lockwood steals you away to England?"

"Stop." Nellie stepped back. "Why did you have to go and ruin a perfect moment?"

Katie just laughed. "Listen, in all seriousness, he's a good man. I like him a lot. But maybe he'd be better off marrying a boring debutante without any ambition or intelligence. If you're not serious about a future with him, then let him go so he's free to make a life with someone else."

Nellie's stomach soured at the very idea of Lockwood with one of his vanilla crèmes. He would be miserable, but why was that her concern?

And why was she still thinking about how much she hated the idea long after Katie left?

STARING IN THE looking glass, Lockwood smoothed his hair and tried not to dread the day ahead. He'd been invited to a tea at Mrs. Richard Leary's, which made sense considering their daughter, Grace, was twenty-two and unmarried. Richard Leary was a wealthy investment banker, and the purpose of the tea could not be more obvious.

A month ago Lockwood would've relished the opportunity to court the Leary girl. Now, however, he longed to send his regrets and find a certain red-haired vixen instead.

You have to learn when to push and when to back off.

Lockwood had taken Cornelius Young's advice to heart, giving Nellie a few days of silence after their night—and morning—together. Even though he was running out of time, he didn't wish to scare her. This needed to be handled gently.

But he had to see her—soon. It was killing him to stay away from her. After his swim tonight he'd find her in that huge house one way or another. Until then, small talk over tea.

His collar was suddenly too tight. "Wilkins," he called to his valet, who was in the outer room. "I want to switch out this blasted collar. Can you find—"

A knock sounded on the hotel door. Lockwood went to select another collar as Wilkins dealt with the guest. "May I help you, miss?" he heard his valet say.

Lockwood paused while opening the wardrobe. Miss?

"Miss Young to see His Grace, please."

He closed his eyes, the sound of her voice washing over him. Bloody hell, he was besotted. Every instinct screamed for him to run out there and take her into his arms. But he was in the midst of a strategic campaign, one he intended to win, and he could not scare her away.

So he forced himself to stand perfectly still as Wilkins instructed her to wait. Then his valet entered the bedchamber. "Your Grace, a lady by the name—"

"I'll see her. That will be all, Wilkins."

"But your collar," Wilkins protested.

"Nothing is wrong with my collar. I shall ring for you later, after tea." He strolled into the sitting room, where he found Nellie standing by the door, looking fresh-faced and gorgeous. His lungs compressed as his heart kicked, like it was restarting, having been frozen in her absence.

He couldn't wait to touch her. Closing the distance quickly, he lifted her gloved hand and brought it to his lips. "Eleanor. What a pleasant surprise."

Color stained her cheeks and she cleared her throat. Flustered? He could only hope. "Hello, Lockwood. I'm relieved to find you in. We have an errand this afternoon."

He frowned, running his calendar appointments through his head. "We do?"

"Yes. I apologize for not giving you much notice, but I've just been told he has an opening."

"He, who? And an opening for what?"

"Dr. Janeway, and an appointment."

The nape of his neck pulled tight and he cursed his stupid collar again. "Who is Dr. Janeway and why do we need an appointment?"

"He's the friend of a friend of my father, and the premier physician in New York regarding cardiac conditions. I was able to secure you an appointment—"

"No."

The word came out more harshly than Lockwood intended, but he couldn't restrain himself. His muscles were now clenched, his entire body locked in protest. He'd been down this road before and the experience was humiliating. Not to mention soul crushing and distressing. There was no need to ever endure it again.

Her gaze narrowed as she studied him. "Lockwood, I realize this is a surprise, but I can't see what it would hurt."

His pride, for one. His good mood. Any sense of control over his own life.

"No," he repeated.

She folded her arms. "Why?"

"Because I said so. Now, I must leave shortly for tea, but I have a few minutes to spare. How quickly are you able to remove your clothing?"

"I'm not sleeping with you and you are not going to a blasted tea. Sit down and let's discuss this."

He walked over to the looking glass where he smoothed his hair again. "There is nothing to discuss."

"Stop preening and get over here, you daft man."

Annoyance prickled over his skin like ants. "If you think to sweet talk me into attending, you'll find yourself disappointed, darling."

"What if I offered you something in exchange?"

He slid her a glance. "Oh? And what would you be willing to offer?"

"I'll swim with you again."

"Not even close to a fair trade. Give the doctor my regrets, will you?"

"God," she exclaimed to the ceiling. "You are impossible. Fine, I'll sleep with you now."

She started to stand, but he held up a hand. "There will be no trading of sexual favors for doctor's appointments. Try again."

"Are you certain? Because I promise to do all the things you like."

As good as that sounded, and as much as he craved having her again, he would not bend on this issue. The bad news he received today from the doctor would haunt him for weeks, perhaps months, and he needed to focus on winning the woman in front of him, not falling into a pit of despair. "You'll do all of those things anyway, because you like them, too."

"True." She bit her lip. "Then, what can I do to convince you to come with me? There has to be something."

Marry me.

It was on the tip of his tongue, but he knew she'd run screaming from the room if he said it. Confirming his heart condition wasn't that important to her.

Then it came to him. It was the perfect answer, something he desperately wanted, but also something she'd never grant.

Staring her down, he said, "I'll go—if you agree to supper. At Sherry's. With me. Tonight."

Nellie's lips parted as she sucked in a breath. "That's . . . absurd."

"Is it? I suppose, then, you'll need to cable Janeway and tell him we will not be coming."

She didn't flinch or look away, their gazes locked in a silent battle of wills. He could see her thinking, turning it over in her mind, but he didn't waver. If she agreed to dine with him in public, then he would endure the humiliation of a doctor's examination.

The clock ticked on the mantel, and noises from the lift in the corridor could be heard through the walls. Neither of them moved, except to breathe and occasionally blink. He felt a little like Lord Nelson squaring off against Villeneuve.

Finally, she flopped her hands and exhaled.

"Fine. I'll share a damn supper with you at Sherry's tonight."

"In the dining room," he qualified.

"You're going to regret it," she said, flicking a piece of lint off her skirts. "But all right. Why not?"

He wouldn't regret it. He wanted every person in New York to know he was going to marry this woman, whether they approved of it or not.

"Wilkins!" he bellowed, suspecting his valet wouldn't be far.

"Yes, Your Grace?" The valet appeared in the adjoining door, confirming Lockwood's theory.

"Send a note to Mrs. Leary with my regrets, will you? And then I'll need a table for two at Sherry's this evening in the main dining room. Let's say eight-thirty."

"Very good, Your Grace. Will there be anything else?"

"No. I'll return shortly to dress for dinner. After that take the evening off. I might be quite late." He turned back to Nellie and gestured to the door. "Shall we, then?"

She rose and went out into the corridor. "Am I allowed to change before this dinner engagement?"

"If you like. I want you to be comfortable, so wear whatever you wish."

"Well, I can't very well show up in a jacket and shirtwaist." She gestured to herself.

He leaned closer as they approached the lift. "I think you look gorgeous."

"Annoying man." She reached to smooth his collar, fussing over him, and he stood still, relishing her attention. He couldn't get enough of her hands on his person, no matter the reason.

She tilted her head toward the end of the hall. "I'll take the stairs and meet you out front."

He grabbed her wrist before she could dart away. "Absolutely not. No one is taking the stairs today."

"Lockwood, that's absurd. Think about what you are doing."

He took her arm and placed it on his. "I know precisely what I am about."

She tried to pull away, but the lift arrived and he quickly hustled her inside. The attendant closed the gate and took them to the ground floor. "You are being exceedingly difficult," she stage-whispered as they entered the lobby. He took her arm again, unwilling to let her put any distance between them. It was the first time they'd left his hotel together, and he didn't care what anyone thought.

After he helped her into a hansom, she asked, "I will regret this, won't I?"

"Most likely, but there's no help for it now."

Chapter Nineteen

※

Nibbling on her lip, Nellie glanced over at a brooding and silent Lockwood. He was in his evening dress, as handsome as ever, his face a blank mask, while they rode in a hansom to Sherry's for supper.

He'd said hardly three words since leaving Dr. Janeway's office this afternoon. Instead, he reported the appointment went "as expected," and promised to collect her at seven-thirty sharp.

Now they were on their way to dinner, and she couldn't stop wondering over the afternoon's appointment. Why wouldn't he share Dr. Janeway's diagnosis? Was it so terrible? Was Janeway's prognosis for him considerably worse than the doctors in England?

Regret squeezed around her chest like a vise. She never should've pushed him to go. What had she been thinking, meddling in his life like this? The hubris of believing she knew better than he—

"Stop," he said quietly, reaching over to take her hand. "Whatever you are thinking, please. Just stop."

"I can't. I am terribly sorry I made you go. I never should have insisted on it."

"It's nothing I haven't heard before. And I chose to go."

"I had no right."

He angled toward her, his thumb stroking her gloved palm. "You have more right than anyone else in my life, Eleanor."

That was a statement best left to deconstruct later. She squeezed his hand. "Did he give you worse news than the other physicians?"

"No." A muscle in his jaw clenched. "Same prognosis. Except he advised that I go to Austria or Germany this summer."

"Why?"

"It's where all the medical innovation, especially in cardiology, is taking place."

"Go, then."

"No. I won't allow them to poke and prod at me," he said, his voice sharp. "They can have my heart once I'm done with it and not a moment before."

The pressure behind her ribs increased, so strong it nearly stole her breath. He talked so cavalierly about his death. "Don't you wish to prolong your life? Think about your children, your wife. All those ducal responsibilities. Are you so eager to kick up your toes and become worm food in the ground?"

"The family has a mausoleum, darling."

"Goddamn it, Andrew." She turned away, torn between the urge to cry and scratch his eyes out.

"Eleanor," he said softly. "Look at me." When she turned, he gave her a tiny smile, the haunted expression from earlier replaced by a tenderness that sank into her bones. "Thank you for caring. I know you meant well and I love that you tried. Let's forget it and move on, shall we? I wouldn't like for this to ruin our evening."

Unable to help herself, she leaned over and pressed her lips to his. They shared a long, deep kiss before she broke off. "Consider it forgotten."

"Good, because we're here."

Seconds later the carriage wheels came to a stop and the duke handed her down to the walk. Lights blazed from inside the popular restaurant and she wished he'd asked for anything else. Lockwood would regret this, far more than his doctor's appointment. This would ruin his social credibility and ensure that the task of finding a wife from a decent family became much more difficult. If not impossible.

Perhaps they would get lucky and tonight's crowd would consist of only actresses and theater types. Her people, those who loved a good party and cared nothing about society. It seemed unlikely, but stranger things had happened.

Then she spotted faces she recognized through the glass—several matrons of High Society. Women who would not appreciate seeing her, a reckless hoyden, with the prize of the social season. She paused on the walk. "Are you certain you wish to do this?"

He rolled his eyes and towed her toward the entrance. "Get inside, Eleanor."

Stop worrying. If he doesn't care, then why should I?

Because she loved him and wanted to see him

happily settled with his proper and virginal vanilla crème. That would never happen after tonight, and he was acting as if it didn't matter.

The maître d'hôtel looked up as they entered. "Your Grace. Miss," he said. "Good evening. We have your table waiting."

"Thank you," Lockwood said graciously. They handed their coats to the attendant and then followed the maître d'hôtel to the dining room.

Nellie could feel eyes on them the instant they stepped inside. Still, she did not cower or blush. She kept her shoulders back and walked proudly through the tables, letting them all stare. She'd worn a daring green Worth evening gown that set off the color of her hair and eyes. At least she would look fabulous while these snobs pilloried her.

Their table was in the center of the dining room—because of course—and Lockwood helped her into a chair, then settled across from her. They took menus and Lockwood ordered champagne to start. Nellie studied the evening's offerings and tried to pretend like Tessie Oelrichs and her younger sister weren't sitting three tables away, with a gentleman Nellie didn't recognize. Mrs. Oelrichs was a gossip and one of Mrs. Astor's devoted followers on the strict rules of society. News of this dinner would be all over Fifth Avenue by breakfast.

Even worse, Rosemary Whitney was dining with her husband and another couple in the back. Nellie peeked at them through her lashes and noticed that Rosemary was already throwing dark glances her way.

Excellent. The evening was off to a fantastic start, then.

The champagne arrived and Nellie lunged for her full glass gratefully. Lockwood, being more civilized, held his up in a toast. "To the most beautiful woman here."

She tried not to react to the compliment. Perhaps if she appeared nonplussed, no one would suspect this was romantic in nature. "Thank you," she told him primly and downed a large mouthful of champagne.

"You are acting strangely." He set his coupe back on the table. "Tell me, is there something wrong?"

She hated that he saw her so clearly. Avoiding his eyes, she stared at the menu. "Nothing is wrong. Shall we order?"

"Are we in a rush?"

"No, of course not. I'm hungry, is all."

He sighed and picked up his menu. "I won't scuttle out of here as if I've done something wrong. I'm quite proud to have you sitting across from me. I had thought you might feel the same."

Oh, hell. Was that what he thought? She put down her menu and gave him her full attention. "I am proud, Lockwood. But you have to realize what this means for you. I'm a walking scandal in this city, and you've just sent your reputation up in flames tonight."

"I don't care to hear it any longer, Eleanor. You're wrong, and even if it were true I hardly care."

Was he being deliberately obtuse? She wanted to argue with him, but she couldn't very well do that here. No matter her reckless tendencies, she was determined to be the perfect, proper dinner companion this evening. The old biddies would find no fault with her behavior tonight. She would not embarrass Lockwood.

She shoved down her objections. "You're right."

One sand-colored eyebrow quirked. "Did you just tell me that I am right?"

"I'm able to admit it every now and again, you know."

"Under duress, perhaps."

She could feel her cheeks begin to heat under his teasing regard. "Stop. Everyone will think you're flirting with me."

"I *am* flirting with you."

That made her blush harder. No doubt her pale skin ensured everyone noticed.

"My God, you're beautiful," Lockwood murmured. "How could you possibly care what any of these people think of you?"

"I don't."

"If that were true, you wouldn't have attempted to hide your face in a menu."

"I was trying to spare *you*, not myself."

"You needn't protect me. I want everyone to see us together."

Had he gone mad?

Thankfully, the waiter returned, preventing the need for a response. After they ordered, he leaned in. "Talk to me. I want to know everything about you."

He already knew far too much. More than anyone else, in fact. She decided to focus on him, instead. "Tell me about London. What is your life like there?"

He shook his head, as if he knew exactly what she was doing, but he answered her. "When there, I stay in Mayfair with my mother. I hate Parliament, so I mostly avoid it and go for only the votes I care about. My time is generally spent in meetings regarding the estate and visiting my clubs."

Everything he described sounded so . . . dull. "And when you're not in London?"

"Then I'm at the estate in Yorkshire, meeting with tenants and overseeing the finances, swimming. In fact, this is the longest I've been away since I was at Eton."

"Were you a troublemaker at school?"

"I was not." The edges of his mouth curled ruefully. "And after I grew ill, they brought me back home and I remained there, educated by tutors. I didn't leave again until Oxford."

"This sounds awfully dreary, Lockwood."

"It's the life I was given." He lifted a shoulder and reached for his champagne. "And it's one of great privilege, even if I am on the precipice of losing it all."

"You won't lose it. Any of these women here tonight would chew off an arm to marry you."

He gave her a tender smile, the kind that caused her stomach to flutter. "But I only want one of these women."

I'm keeping you, Eleanor Young.

She could see the truth in his steady blue gaze and it scared her witless. The man needed to be set straight on the impossibility of their future. Not here, but soon.

Before he did something truly foolish.

Tonight, however, she would enjoy their single dinner out in public. The memory of it would need to sustain her for years to come, during the days when she missed him with a terrible ache.

Their first course arrived, and soon she forgot about the whispers and stares. Lockwood was too charming and the food too delicious. Louis Sherry himself stopped by to speak with the duke, fawning over Lockwood as people were often wont to do with the aristocracy. Nellie didn't mind. She fawned over him, too, but for entirely different reasons.

Lockwood was polite and proper, his table manners impeccable. Seeing as how she'd been kicked out of two different finishing schools, she wasn't as perfect, but he didn't seem to notice.

While they were waiting on dessert, she excused herself to the ladies' retiring room. After she finished, she overheard female voices at the sinks. "Can you believe she is here with him?"

"What is the duke possibly thinking?"

Nellie's stomach sank. Rosemary Whitney. She would recognize that sharp tone anywhere. Which meant Rosemary and her friend were in the retiring room to gossip about Nellie, who was trapped in one of the small toilets.

The first woman continued. "He cannot truly be interested in her, is he?"

"Please," Rosemary said. "No decent man is truly interested in her. She's good for only one thing. Remember when she tried to seduce Charlie Appleton away from poor Mary? He said she was all over him in the gardens, like some Bowery strumpet."

Nellie's hands curled into fists. That wasn't what happened in the gardens *at all*, but women like Rosemary were rarely interested in the truth.

"The duke had best be careful," Rosemary went on. "He'll have a hard time with the Twomblys and the Shermans after tonight. Not many families will overlook an association with her."

It was what Nellie had feared. This right here, that her presence would ruin his standing in New York society.

Why hadn't he listened to her?

"Exactly," the other woman said. "He's been thrown over twice. Not certain how much more scandal his reputation can handle, even if he is a duke."

"Well, I can't wait to tell everyone. I'll tell them how he made cow eyes at her and embarrassed himself, while she giggled and flashed her bosom at him. I think I even saw him touch her leg under the—"

That was it.

Nellie threw open the door with a snap, her ears ringing with the sound of her pounding heart. Both women jolted and glanced over, then shrank as Nellie marched toward them. Rosemary recovered quickly, her mouth curving into a satisfied smile, like she didn't care if Nellie had overheard them.

"Miss Young, how nice to see you," Rosemary purred, while her friend looked on, stupefied.

When Nellie reached the sink, she calmly washed her hands and accepted a towel from a bewildered attendant. "Thank you," she politely told the older woman, then stared directly at Rosemary.

"If I hear you spread one tale about His Grace, true or not, I will tell everyone why your husband spends so much time in Hoboken." Mr. Whitney had another family in New Jersey, complete with three children. Rosemary's mouth fell open, but Nellie didn't stop. "Say whatever you like about me, but do not dare to mention the duke's name, Rosemary. Not even a whisper, not once. Because if you do I will hear about it and I will destroy you."

Turning, she checked her reflection in the mirror, smoothed her hair and walked out of the retiring room.

THE FACE OF Potter Pierce suddenly appeared across from Lockwood. "Evening, Stoker! Fancy seeing you here."

The back of Lockwood's neck tingled, his skin turning hot with annoyance. "Hello, Potter. Have a care. That is my companion's seat."

"Aw, I'll move when she returns." He leaned in as if to share a secret. "A redhead. Nice. Who is she? An actress? A chorus girl." He snapped his fingers. "I bet she's an opera singer."

Lockwood's hand curled around the edge of the table, squeezing. "She is Miss Young, the daughter of Mr. Cornelius Young, and watch your mouth."

Potsie's jaw fell open, his brows climbing up his forehead. "Are you—?" Then he shook his head. "No, I see how it is. She's keeping you company whilst you search for a proper bride."

The description, while initially apt, no longer applied, and Lockwood had the desire to punch Potsie's face. "She is a proper lady and you should cease speaking."

Though Lockwood had already issued a warning regarding Nellie the last time he saw Potter, the earl still appeared confused on the other side of the table. "You can't be serious about her, Stoker. I've heard the stories. London society would sharpen its claws on her. And your mother . . ." He let the words hang, as if they knew exactly what the current Duchess of Lockwood would have to say about this choice.

Except Lockwood wasn't giving his mother an opinion on his bride. It was Lockwood's decision—and he'd decided on Nellie. His mother would need to accept it—and London society could go hang for all he cared.

Leaning in, he growled, "It is none of your concern, Potter. Furthermore, I plan on marrying her, so I'd shut my mouth were I you."

"My God, you've lost your mind." Potsie sat back and stared across the table as if he'd never seen Lockwood before. "I wish you luck, then. Has she any idea what she's in for back home?"

A whisper of uncertainty crawled along Lockwood's spine, but he wouldn't give it a chance to grow roots. He rushed to defend his choice. "She's strong and resilient. Nor does she care about society and gossip, which I would naturally shield her from there."

Potsie shook his head and pushed up out of the chair. "Not sure how that'll be possible. You know how some of those hens are. But I'm sure you'll discuss all this with her. It would be cruel to keep her in the dark."

"Of course," Lockwood said through clenched teeth. He didn't need advice from Potsie, of all people, who was as sharp as a marble and hadn't the first clue about Nellie's fierce bravery. "Now, do run along."

Potsie's mouth flattened. "I'm leaving. I should mention, though, that I'll need to distance myself. Though we're friends, I cannot allow a scandal to color my own matrimonial chances. You understand, I'm sure."

Lockwood said nothing and Potter took the hint. He nodded once and disappeared into the crowd, where he rejoined a table of three other gentlemen.

A flash of red caught Lockwood's eye, and his throat tightened as she crossed the dining room. She was worth a hundred scandals, a thousand lost friendships. Every bit of gossip and innuendo. Nothing mattered except being on the receiving end of her smile every day.

She wasn't smiling now, however. Something was wrong.

Lockwood could see it in her closed expression the instant she reached their table. "What's happened?" he asked as he assisted her into her chair.

"Nothing."

He knew she was lying and he hated it. "Nellie," he started.

"Leave it, duke." She placed her serviette in her lap and arranged her silverware, ignoring his gaze.

The waiter chose that moment to bring their dessert, a glorious charlotte russe. Nellie waved hers away. "I've changed my mind," she told the waiter. "Please, take it back with my apologies."

Frowning, Lockwood drummed his fingers on the table. What had happened in the—

Movement coming from the direction of the retiring room caught his eye. Mrs. Whitney and another woman were walking across the dining room, returning to their table.

It would be wise of you to stay clear of that one. She's nothing but a troublemaker.

Mrs. Whitney's warning from the night of the art show still bothered him. She had no right to interfere in Lockwood's life. He'd neither needed nor asked for her advice.

Had there been some sort of run-in between Nellie and this woman in the retiring room?

"Did she annoy you?" he asked. "Say something about you?"

A dismissive sound escaped Nellie's lips. "I don't care what Rosemary says about me."

"About me, then."

Her mouth flattened and she fixed her stare on the window, looking out to the street. "I said to let it go, Lockwood."

So it had been about him.

Had she been defending him? The idea of it sent a giddy rush along his spine, even if he hated that it had been necessary in the first place. "Thank you," he said simply.

"Someone needed to put her in her place. Shall we go?"

"You want to leave?"

"Yes."

He didn't argue. She'd given him what he asked for. Glancing around, he searched for their waiter. "I'll settle the bill."

"I've taken care of it," she said. "Earlier, when I went to the retiring room."

He hadn't expected that. Heat singed the back of his neck. "Why?"

"Do not get prickly. I have the money, so allow me to treat you."

"The entire point was for me to treat you."

"And I am happier treating you. Stop arguing."

Maddening woman. Everyone in the city knew of his pathetic finances, so he shouldn't care. But he wanted to shower her with gifts and favors, offerings made in tribute to her beauty. Someday, he vowed. Someday, he would drown her in jewels and all the finery she could stand.

After rising from his chair, he helped her out of hers. "Thank you for dinner, darling," he whispered very close to her ear. He was pleased when he saw her shiver slightly.

They left and soon he had her in a hansom. Without thinking, he gave the driver the address for his hotel. When he climbed in, she said, "I'd like to go home, Lockwood."

He studied the unhappy set of her shoulders, the lines bracketing her mouth. Seeing her like this shredded the inside of his chest. He picked up her arm and kissed the bare skin between her glove and her gown. "Don't let her ruin our evening."

"She hasn't. It's been lovely. For the most part."

"Then why not come back with me. Let me

show you how much I've missed you." He nipped her elbow.

"Lockwood," she said, "we should talk."

A weight settled in his stomach at the edge in her tone. She wasn't ending this, was she? Well, he wouldn't allow it. He wasn't done trying to win her. "No."

"You can't order this problem to go away. It doesn't work like that, even for dukes."

"There is no problem."

Instead of answering, she opened the slat and redirected the driver to her address. The carriage instantly swung around and began heading north on Fifth Avenue. When she sat back, he said, "Was that truly necessary?"

"I told you I want to go home. And we shouldn't see each other anymore."

There it was, exactly what he'd been dreading. He pushed aside the panic and tried to keep calm, breathing steadily so his heart didn't race. "I don't agree."

She angled toward him, her brows lowered in challenge. "What do you mean? This is not up for debate."

Stalling, he smoothed his trousers. "You don't get to arbitrarily decide unless there are good reasons. So let me hear your reasons."

"I needn't explain myself to you. We should not continue to see one another. It's harmful to us both. The end."

"Harmful, how?"

"You are perfectly aware, so do not force me to recount it."

"If this is about my reputation again, I will

put you over my knee, lift your skirts and spank you."

She snorted. "I'd like to see you try."

Her reaction didn't fool him. He cupped her jaw, forced her to look at him, then gave her a wicked smile full of promise. "Darling, based on all I've done to you already, I know you would love it. Shall we try?"

"You are not listening to me, you arrogant man." She jerked out of his grasp. "Pull over and let me out."

"I'll do no such thing. If you want to have an argument, then I'll give it to you, you stubborn woman. I don't give a goddamn about my reputation or my marriage prospects or what anyone in this country thinks about me, except for you."

"That right there. That is why this is a bad idea." She pointed at him. "You are losing focus. We are spending too much time together and your priorities are off-kilter."

Balderdash. She was his only priority, but he couldn't very well tell her that. Not yet. Not until she was ready to hear it. "Let me manage my priorities, if you please. I am aware of what needs to be done."

"Are you?" Her nostrils flared, her green eyes like emerald fire in the dim light. "Because I sincerely doubt it. How many heiresses have you wooed in the last week?"

He couldn't lie. "None, though I was on my way to a tea party this afternoon. Does that count?"

"No. You are too busy wasting time with me."

"Not a thing about you could ever be considered a waste. And you needn't worry. I know what I am doing." Indeed, this was all part of his plan.

"This is ridiculous. You're thinking with your cock, not your head."

By no means was this the case. No, he was thinking with his heart. "You must calm down. You have become overexcited by your run-in with Mrs. Whitney—"

"Do *not* say that woman's name to me, and do not tell me to calm down. Absolutely nothing is more offensive than a man telling a woman to calm down!"

This was unraveling fast. He pressed his lips together and swallowed what he'd been about to say. Had he pushed too hard, too soon?

Dr. Janeway's voice rang in his head.

There's no telling how long until your heart gives out, Your Grace. It could be a week or a year. Or ten years.

But not twenty. No one expected him to live that long.

He would back off for the moment, but he couldn't wait forever. The clock was ticking and nothing else would do except for this woman becoming his wife.

"We shall discuss this later," he said.

She threw her hands up and let them fall in her lap. "No, we will discuss it now. I don't wish to continue seeing you. We've had our fun and now we both need to move on."

Move on? The very notion of her sleeping with another man caused homicidal rage to bubble in Lockwood's gut. "Are you so tired of me, then?"

"Yes, exceedingly. You are British, after all, so

it only stands to reason you'd be much too dull
for me."

"Dull? Was that how you'd describe it when I
made you scream yourself hoarse from orgasms?
You didn't sound very bored, Eleanor."

"I had to make them sound believable," she
snapped. "I'm an excellent actress."

He ran his tongue along the backside of his
teeth, shoving down the irritation. She was lying.
He'd felt her body convulse each time.

I will not give up on her.

She could try to push him away for noble
reasons, but it wouldn't work. Only if she truly
didn't care for him, and only then, would he surrender. But he knew she felt something deeper.
While she didn't say it in words, her actions spoke
loudly, from swimming with him and taking
him to Hell's Kitchen, to arranging that doctor's
appointment. Her heart belonged to him.

He was close to getting her to admit it, as well.
Whatever happened tonight had upset her, so he
would give her a tiny bit of space. Then he would
charge ahead, full speed.

The carriage began to slow. He wasn't ready to
let her go tonight, but he needed to retreat. She
was in no mood to tolerate any further emotion
at the moment. But how long was he expected to
wait? Was an hour enough?

"I think I'll come in and swim," he said, glancing through the window at the huge house.
"Would you mind?"

"Of course not," she snapped. "Do as you like."

"A pity I forgot my bathing costume."

She said nothing, merely fidgeted in her lap.

Was she imagining him swimming naked? God, he hoped so. "You are welcome to come and watch, you know."

"I'm tired."

He exhaled in frustration, but remained undeterred. Picking up her hand, he kissed her gloved knuckles tenderly. "Then I'll bid you good night."

Chapter Twenty

❦

She didn't come to watch him swim.

Lockwood dried off and redressed, his mind churning. In the water there had been nothing but time to think about his day, to rehash all that had been said and done. The doctor's visit. Their dinner at Sherry's. Mrs. Whitney. The carriage ride.

Heart racing, he wondered if he'd blundered by walking away tonight. Nellie needed a man to fight for her. To stand up and claim her, uncaring of reputations or gossip. She was an incredible woman—smart, beautiful and fearless—and it was New York's loss that they had turned their backs on her. So instead, he was going to marry her and make her a duchess. Take her to England and worship her every day for the rest of his short life.

Just as soon as he could convince her.

He wiped the sweat off his brow with a handkerchief. Though he was done, leaving didn't feel right. Her family advised giving Nellie space, but hadn't he just given her two days apart? He didn't want to give her any more. He wanted to feel her skin and drink in her sighs, taste her slick pussy and make her come. There was an ache inside him that only she could ease.

Perhaps he could apologize and they could discuss their relationship further. He would convince her to keep sleeping with him, then use his considerable charm to get them both naked and in a bed. Yes, that sounded much better than returning to his hotel and frigging himself.

The house was quiet when he arrived on the ground floor. No servants loitered about, which was for the best, really. He didn't wish to frighten anyone on his way up to her bedchamber. When he passed the large set of windows in the center of the house, lights in the distance caught his eye. The end of the massive home was lit up, a glass room, nearly every pane fogged with condensation. Was that a conservatory? Who would be in there this late?

Instantly, he knew.

She had once talked of her love of plants, how soothing she found it to dig in the dirt and prune leaves. Had she needed soothing this evening?

Thrusting his hands into his coat pockets, he walked through the large home, winding through the corridors, until he found the conservatory. It was immense, with glass surrounding it on all sides. Huge trees and plants formed a neat jungle, complete with rocks and ponds, birds and insects. Had she done this? He began strolling along the path, taking it in, inhaling the sweet scent of flowers and earth.

Remarkable.

Stopping, he listened for sounds to determine her location in the cavernous space. One could easily get lost in here.

"Damn it," he heard about twenty yards to the left.

Smiling, he wandered in that direction. When he found her, she was still in her evening gown, an apron tied around her front, pruning a bush. "Hello," he said gently, not wishing to startle her.

She jerked and looked up, hand pressed to her heart. "Jesus, Lockwood. What are you doing in here?"

"This is where you are," he answered simply as he leaned against a tree trunk. "Couldn't sleep?"

"We discussed this. I told you we were moving on. This is over."

"And I refuse to allow what happened tonight to come between us. Do not throw this away because of that woman."

She put down her shears. "This is not just because of Rosemary. It's more than that, and you know it."

"I know nothing of the sort."

"Stop being obtuse. We're both . . . developing feelings for one another. It's unhealthy."

He well knew this was more than an affair, but it pleased him to hear her admit it. "I disagree. Not about the feelings part—that's definitely true—but rather about it being unhealthy. There's nothing wrong with letting yourself love someone."

She was shaking her head before he even stopped speaking. "There is if he's a duke, he must marry someone respectable and he lives in England."

"Well, this duke may marry whomever he likes."

"Bully for you, then. I wish you luck in finding her."

"I've already found her." He hadn't meant to say it, but she was pushing him, as she always did, and he would not lie. Not about this.

Her skin paled, her eyes filled with panic. "Don't."

He started toward her, needing to touch her, desperate to be connected to her. Thankfully, she didn't move, and he was soon cradling her jaw in his hands. "I've found her, Eleanor, and I won't pretend or lie about it. I lo—"

"Don't say it." She ripped out of his grasp and whirled away. "How many times have I told you this was a terrible idea?"

His skin grew hot. Why was she making this so difficult? Then he saw her wiping the corners of her eyes, and his heart stuttered. He hadn't wanted to make her *cry*.

In an instant he was at her side, pulling her into the cradle of his arms, her back against his chest. He kissed the top of her head. "Eleanor, please. Everything is going to be all right."

She trembled, her breath ragged. After a long moment she seemed to compose herself because she stepped out of his embrace, and he clasped his hands behind his back to keep from reaching for her again. When she met his gaze, he saw the resolution there and his blood turned cold. No, she wouldn't, would she? He knew this meant something to her, that *he* meant something to her. Whatever she was thinking, he would talk her out of it using logic and reason. "Nellie," he started, until she held up a hand.

"I can't do this any longer. Please don't ask me to try."

"I have to. I have to keep asking and asking until you agree, because I love you and I want to marry you." There. He'd finally told her.

"Oh, for Pete's sake," she whispered, screwing her eyelids tight. A single tear escaped from the corner of one eye. "I just told you not to say it."

"I cannot hold it in any longer. I've been thinking about it for a long time, and I know you feel this, as well. I want you by my side, day and night. I want to hold you and kiss you and share a life together—"

"You want, you want, you want. Have you even stopped to ask me what I want? How I feel about all of this? I can think of nothing worse than being a duchess, with its limitations and rules, and moving to a country where I know not a single soul. It's like I would cease to exist."

"That's nonsense," he said automatically, his stomach roiling with panic. "You will be with me, as my wife. Would that be so terrible?"

"But then you'll die. You'll *die*, Andrew, much sooner rather than later. And I'll be left alone." There was genuine fear stamped all over her face, and he realized how afraid she was of losing someone else she cared about.

His damn defective heart. Never had he resented it more than at this moment. "That's true," he said quietly. "I won't try to paint a pretty picture for you. But I would think the time we have left together is more important. It's why we shouldn't waste a single day."

"You are asking me to give up everything to become someone I'm not. To leave my entire life behind for you. Would you do the same in return for me?"

"You know that is impossible. There are hundreds of people counting on me to save the estate. I cannot shirk my responsibilities or the title. It would be the height of selfishness."

She held out her hands as if to say, *Exactly my point*.

His ears began to ring with frustration, his heart struggling to maintain a constant rhythm. He put his hands on his hips. "What is so preferable about New York that you must stay? They treat you abominably here. Other than Katherine and your father I can't imagine what this godforsaken country holds for you."

"Do you think it would be any better in England? It would be *worse*."

"Wrong. You'd be a fucking duchess, Eleanor. Short of the queen, you'd have more power than anyone else. My God, Lady Paget came from Massachusetts and keeps a cheetah as a pet. She doesn't give a fig about what anyone thinks of her."

"Good for her, but I know how they sneer at Americans over there. I know most of the girls who have married aristocrats are miserable, shunned and lonely while their husbands cavort all over Europe."

"That would not be us," he snapped. "Do you honestly believe I would abandon you to cavort?

That I wouldn't spend every single day of my life at your side, making you happy?" He put a hand on his sternum, like he was making a vow. "Love doesn't even come close to describing what I feel for you. I'm a wreck when we're apart, like I'm missing a limb. I bloody worship you, woman."

He waited for her to say it back, to confess what was in her heart, but she merely pressed her lips together. His chest began to cave in on itself, his hope deflating. "I know you feel something for me," he said softly. "I know this isn't one-sided."

"It doesn't matter. We are not suited for anything more than an affair."

"Wrong. We are completely suited, Eleanor. I've never felt this way about anyone else before."

She swallowed and pushed her shoulders back. "Then allow me to rephrase. I am not suited for anything more than an affair with you."

Though it hurt, he kept at it. "You might change your mind. Please, just give us a chance."

"I can't. I won't. You need to go."

The thin threads tethering them together began to snap, one by one, like broken strings on an instrument. She was slipping away from him—and there wasn't a damn thing he could do about it.

The weight of the estate, his legacy, his defective heart . . . It all felt like a thousand tons of pressure on his shoulders. He'd wanted just this one thing for himself, this one maddening woman who had turned his life upside down since the moment he saw her frolicking in the surf.

But the choice was never his. It had always

been hers—and she didn't love him enough to agree. He'd failed.

And he had to find a way to live with it.

His fingertips began to tingle, the numbness settling inside his limbs. He needed to leave before he grew light-headed and made a complete fool of himself. But he wouldn't go without sharing more of what was in his heart. She deserved to know.

Moving closer, he held his hands up as if to soothe a wild animal. Thankfully, she didn't pull away as he approached, or even when he gently brushed the hair away from her face. He just needed to touch her once more, however briefly. "Be happy, Eleanor. You are the most remarkable woman in the world. Do not allow these people and this city to make you feel small, and most importantly allow someone to love you." Leaning down, he pressed his lips to her forehead, breathing her in for the last time. "Thank you. For every moment you shared with me, for every smile you gifted me. I won't forget you."

Then he did the hardest thing of his life.

He left and didn't look back.

Chapter Twenty-One

❦

She was late.

Nellie arrived at the Meliora Club and went straight to the kitchen. The club was closed this morning, which meant the corridors were dark. She hurried, hating that the women were already here, waiting on her.

She had no excuse for tardiness, either. Other than a broken heart and a desire never to leave her bed.

Lockwood had walked out of her life two nights ago, and she hadn't any idea on how to bear it. She didn't regret her decision—deep in her heart, she knew it was the right one—but it *hurt*. God, did it hurt.

They never should have allowed it to reach this point, with feelings attached. She, for one, definitely knew better, well aware they had no future together. Her, a duchess? The notion was utterly ludicrous. He would be much happier with a plain and boring heiress, a woman who actually wanted to move there and pump out tiny aristocrats with sandy-blond hair and bright blue eyes.

Tiny slashes of misery widened in her chest, and she forced thoughts of the duke out of her head. It would take time, but she would recover. This suffering would ease, minute by minute, hour by hour, until it disappeared. Lockwood would eventually be a fond memory, one that would make her smile.

Right now, however, she'd be lucky to endure the next hour without crying.

Stop. I'm not one to pine over a man I cannot have.

She drew in a deep breath to compose herself before entering the kitchen. When she stepped in, thirty or so women were gathered there, and they all quieted, turning to look at her expectantly. "Hello," she said and put her carpetbag on the workbench. "My apologies for running late."

Mrs. Kimball appeared, her hands folded primly in front of her. "That's all right, Miss Young. We're awfully grateful you're here."

"It's my pleasure. I believe I have everything requested. Shall we set up like last time?"

"Yes, I've already made space for you." Mrs. Kimball led the way to the small office and gestured to the desk and chairs. As Nellie got herself settled, the older woman said, "I'll send in the ladies one at a time. May I bring you anything? Water or tea?"

"Tea would be lovely, thank you."

Mrs. Kimball didn't move, instead peering inquisitively at Nellie. "Is everything all right, Miss Young? You seem a bit down today."

That was an understatement.

But Mrs. Kimball had her own problems and

Nellie wasn't one to cry on anyone else's shoulder. "I'm fine. I haven't been sleeping well. Thank you for asking."

While the older woman didn't appear convinced, she was too polite to pursue it. She left Nellie alone, and soon the first lady came in, looking nervous. Nellie quickly tried to put her at ease as they discussed the shields the woman had ordered and how to properly use them.

On and on it went, the hours flying by, providing Nellie with a much-needed distraction from her own pathetic life. The women were grateful for her help, their appreciation a balm to her shattered heart. Another reason she was right to turn Lockwood down; this sort of endeavor would've been impossible for a duchess.

Love doesn't even come close to describing what I feel for you.

It didn't matter. Emotions weren't enough. *Love* wasn't enough. Though he claimed otherwise, he would eventually regret marrying a scandalous wife. She was doing him a favor by releasing him to find an appropriate bride.

And even if she didn't care about being snubbed or breeding ducal heirs, Lockwood wouldn't live to see old age. She would love him and then *lose* him in ten or fifteen years, except with a lot more tying them together. Better to cut it off now, before the loss completely gutted her.

She had suffered one devastating loss in her life already. She didn't need another.

After she finished with the last woman, Nellie noticed there was still one more brown parcel left in her carpetbag. It was marked for Mrs. Ingram.

She stood and stretched out her back. "You're sure there's no one left?"

Mrs. Kimball shook her head. "No one is waiting. Why?"

"I have a package left for Mrs. Ingram."

"I haven't seen her today," the older woman said. "Let's ask one of the other kitchen maids if they've seen her."

They walked out into the kitchen together, where a few of the kitchen maids were preparing for the afternoon tea. "Polly," Mrs. Kimball asked one of the maids. "Have you seen Mary today?"

"No, Mrs. Kimball. She hasn't shown up yet."

"Are you talking about Mary?" One of the other maids came over. "I heard from one of the girls next door that her husband worked her over real good. Said to tell us she wouldn't be back."

"This is Mary's husband we're talking about?" Mrs. Kimball's brows flew up. "Why didn't you say anything?"

"I figured you already knew."

Nellie put her hand up to stop the confusing conversation. "Wait, what does this mean? Has Mary—Mrs. Ingram—been hurt by her husband?"

"Yes, it appears so," Mrs. Kimball said with a fierce frown. "I wish I could say it was the first time."

"This one's different," the second maid said and pointed to Nellie's carpetbag. "It had to do with one of those brown packages. He told her she can't work here no more."

Nellie gasped. One of the brown packages? This was about contraception? As Nellie recalled,

Mrs. Ingram hadn't wanted her husband to find out she was using any sort of birth control device. *He won't like that I'm trying to prevent his seed from taking purchase.*

Nellie's skin grew hot and her hands began shaking in frustration. That monster. That ignorant clod. He must've discovered the sponge and taken his fists to that poor woman.

Something must be done. Nellie could not blithely go about the rest of her day, pretending Mrs. Ingram wasn't hurt. She felt partially responsible. She'd procured the items, after all. Had shown Mrs. Ingram how to use them and promised that her husband would be none the wiser.

Nellie's stomach twisted. She wouldn't be able to live with herself if she didn't help in some way. At the very least, she could pay for a doctor, if Mrs. Ingram needed medical attention.

"Do you know where she lives?" Nellie asked the second maid.

"No, but Ginny next door does. We could ask her."

"What are you thinking, Miss Young?" Mrs. Kimball's expression remained concerned. "I don't believe it would be proper to interfere."

No, it definitely was not proper, but when had Nellie ever let that stop her? This right here was why she and the duke never would've worked. Lockwood would not approve, and Nellie loved helping women too much to give this up.

"I wouldn't expect you to come," she told Mrs. Kimball. "I'm perfectly happy to handle this on my own."

"You cannot think to go to her residence alone," Mrs. Kimball whispered. "Her husband might very well be there."

"Yeah," the other kitchen maid said, "he lost his job a few months back and hasn't found nothing else."

Nellie wasn't scared of Mr. Ingram. In fact, she hoped he *was* there because the son of a bitch needed to be taught a lesson. It wasn't fair to punish women for preventing a child. Perhaps her cousin Finn wasn't busy today. "Don't worry about me. I'll bring a friend along."

"This feels very reckless." Mrs. Kimball was wringing her hands in her apron. "We should just leave it alone."

Absolutely not. Nellie could not leave Mrs. Ingram alone, suffering, when she was partially responsible. What if the young woman needed a hospital?

Besides, *reckless* was Nellie's middle name.

"I'll be fine." She picked up her carpetbag. "Let me go and see Ginny first. I must learn where to find Mrs. Ingram."

NELLIE TAPPED HER fingers on her carpetbag, trying to stay warm near a ground-level bakery as she waited. The Ingrams lived in a small four-story apartment building on the West Side, the kind that usually housed two families per floor. No one had gone in or out since she'd been standing here.

While she was reckless, she wasn't stupid. She'd sent a message to Finn and wouldn't go in until her cousin arrived. If Mr. Ingram thought to complain, Finn would take care of him. No one was dumb enough to challenge the leader of the Saints.

Except for Lockwood, of course.

The ache behind her sternum returned, even stronger this time. No. This wouldn't do. She had to put the duke out of her mind. This was what she needed instead. A purpose, a way to stay busy. If she were too preoccupied with other matters, then she wouldn't have time to think about him at all. Soon, he would be a distant memory.

A carriage pulled up on the wrong side of the street in front of the bakery. Nellie rolled her eyes. Only one man would dare park any which way in this neighborhood.

Sure enough, her cousin's long legs emerged from the inside as he hopped down to the walk. His right eye was still a tiny bit blue from where Lockwood—

Stop it. Just stop.

She strolled forward. "Hello, cousin. Thank you for coming."

"For you, caethrair? Anything." He kissed her cheek. "Now, who do I need to punch?"

"Settle down. I'm not certain it's necessary. I just need you with me, in case this woman's husband gets rough."

Finn slapped his derby on his head. "No problem. Where are we headed?"

"Over there." She pointed at the address she'd been given. "Third floor."

Nodding, Finn had a word with his driver, clearly one of the younger Saints. The boy looked no older than fourteen or fifteen, and gazed at Finn with hero worship in his eyes.

As they crossed the street, she asked him, "Is this your territory?"

"At present, this still belongs to the Gophers. But not for long."

"Are you making plans I should know about?"

"Nothing you should know about, Red. You keep that pretty little nose clean. After all, we can't have your duke associated with street toughs."

"He's not my duke anymore," she said quietly, almost under her breath as they stepped onto the walk.

Finn's hand landed on her shoulder. Her cousin's expression was suddenly very intense. "What happened? Because if he hurt you I will break both of his feckin' legs."

"It was my decision to end it. There's no need to give it another second's thought. I'm not."

Finn's voice was sincere and soft. "I'm sorry, Red. He seemed like a decent fellow. For an Englishman."

A lump lodged in her throat, but she forced it down. If this went on much longer, he was going to make her cry. She shoved at his shoulder. "Stop. We have more important things to do right now."

Finn cracked his knuckles one at a time. "I understand. Let's go rough some people up instead."

They entered the building and climbed the stairs to the third floor. She found the correct door and pointed to it. Finn nodded, then lifted his fist as if to bang on the wood. Nellie shook her head and grabbed his arm. "Let me," she whispered.

She gave a polite knock and they waited. After a long moment the door cracked open. Mrs. Ingram's swollen face filled the gap—and Nellie gasped. God, it was every bit as terrible as she'd feared.

Mrs. Ingram froze but quickly recovered. Fear replaced the surprise, and she glanced over her shoulder. "You have to go. Please." She started to close the door, but Nellie put a hand out.

"Wait, please. I need to know that you're all right."

"Who is that?" boomed a deep voice from inside the apartment.

"Go, please." Mrs. Ingram tried to shut the door again. "No one," she called out, but it was too late.

An older man with greasy hair and a drooping mustache appeared behind her. He jerked the door wide, his eyes raking Nellie from head to toe. "Who the fuck are you?"

"I'm here to check on your wife, Mr. Ingram."

"How do you know my name? And how do you know my wife?"

"That doesn't matter," Nellie snapped. "I want to make sure she's all right."

Ingram narrowed his gaze on his wife. "How do you know this woman, Mary?"

"I know her from the Meliora Club," Nellie said.

"I didn't ask you," Mr. Ingram snapped. "I asked her."

Finn stepped into the doorway. "I suggest you stay calm, boy-o."

Ingram studied Finn, then his mouth drew

tight as recognition dawned. "What the hell business is it of yours, O'Callaghan? This ain't your neighborhood."

"Be polite, or I'm making it my business."

"Please, Miss Young," Mrs. Ingram said. "Just go." The woman stepped back and that was when Nellie saw that her left arm was in a sling.

"What in God's name did you do to her?" she snarled at Mr. Ingram. "You goddamn animal."

Ingram closed in on his wife. "Tell me how you know this woman, Mary. Tell me right fucking now."

Skin gone pale, Mary began backing away. "She—she's the one who sold me the sponge."

Ingram whirled on Nellie. "*You.* You dared to peddle that *filth* to my wife, filling her head with the devil's work?"

Nellie didn't back down. Instead, she straightened her shoulders. "Allowing a woman to decide when to conceive is not the devil's work. If you ever had to grow and carry a baby in your body, you would understand."

"God wants us to procreate. It's our duty as husband and wife."

"No, it's not," Nellie said. "It should be a mutual decision between you both."

"Get this *whore* out of my house," he roared at his wife. "She is trying to make you a loose woman, just like her."

Finn stepped forward. "You'd better watch what you say in front of the ladies, or I'll knock all your teeth out."

Mrs. Ingram was crying now, trembling against the wall. "Please, just go."

"I won't leave," Nellie said, "not until I know you're all right, and he promises not to hurt you anymore."

Mr. Ingram went to the window, opened it up and yelled to the floor above. "Ho, Billy! Come down here."

"I wouldn't do that if I were you," Finn growled. "I can have ten men here in seconds who'll tear you limb from limb if I give the word."

"I'm not scared of you or your men," Ingram sneered. "My brother is a Metropolitan Police Officer."

"Good," Nellie said. "Because you should be arrested for mistreating your wife."

"This is a husband's duty, to discipline his wife," Ingram said, hitching his pants higher. "You have no right to interfere."

"You are twisting religion to suit your whims. You are supposed to love and cherish her, not—"

A man appeared at the bottom of the stairs. "What's going on here?"

Ingram pushed past Finn and Nellie until they were all in the corridor. "This one here"—he pointed at Nellie—"sold my wife a contraceptive. And gave her information on how to use it. She's also giving public talks at that fancy club Mary used to work at."

"Oh? Is that so?" The newcomer's mouth twisted, his dark eyes glittering. "Then you've broken the law."

Did he think Nellie a fool? She was aware distributing contraceptive information was illegal, but she wasn't about to admit it. Better to play dumb for now. "I know all about the ridiculous Comstock Laws, and I haven't sent anything through the mail."

"It's a bit broader than that," the officer said as he stepped forward. "Nowadays we're arresting anyone who's hand-selling these items or giving talks about them. Seems you've done both."

"This is absurd."

"Absurd or not, it's against the law. I'm putting you under arrest."

"The hell you are," Finn said, stepping between her and the officer.

The other man's smile grew wider. "Well, well. Finn O'Callaghan. It is my lucky day. Now I get to take both of you in. I'll be the hero of the Twenty-Second Ward."

"He's done nothing wrong," Nellie said. "You may take me, but you have no reason to charge Finn with any crime."

"Except assault and murder and theft," the officer said.

"You have no proof of any of that," Finn said. "It'll never hold up with a judge. I'll be out by nightfall."

The officer glared at Finn, likely realizing the truth of what Nellie's cousin had said. Arresting Finn was a waste of everyone's time. "Fine. Just her, then." The officer took out a pair of handcuffs. "Come along, miss. You're under arrest."

Chapter Twenty-Two

Wilkins," Lockwood bellowed to his valet. "Have you seen my pocket watch?" He searched through the wardrobe drawers for the second time.

Blast it. Why couldn't he find anything today?

"It is in the nightstand, Your Grace," Wilkins said from the threshold. "Precisely where you left it."

Lockwood stomped over and found his father's pocket watch in the drawer. "That's a preposterous place for it," he grumbled as he affixed the heavy timepiece to his waistcoat.

"Which is what I told Your Grace yesterday." Wilkins drifted back into the other room, so he didn't see Lockwood's frown.

It wasn't his fault. He hadn't been able to think straight for two days, not since he left the Youngs' conservatory. It was like he was in a fog.

I am not suited for anything more than an affair with you.

She hadn't lied, nor had she led him on. He had no one to blame but himself for his hopes and dreams, the plans he'd made without consulting her. God, he'd proposed to the woman and she'd turned him down. This was getting to be a regular habit here in America.

Which was why he'd instructed Wilkins to pack their things.

He couldn't stay here, not any longer. This was different than the broken engagement. Worse than losing Alice to Kit. Those experiences hadn't torn him to pieces. Only Nellie had absolutely destroyed him. Taken his heart and shredded it until he felt hollow inside.

So he had tickets on a steamer leaving the day after tomorrow. He wasn't telling his mother about his failure to find a bride here just yet. From experience, he knew it was better not to disappoint her until absolutely necessary. This was a conversation best had in person.

He rubbed his chest, wishing this ache would lessen even a fraction. Bloody nuisance, this heart of his. Not only did the thing beat incorrectly, it had also decided to fall in love with the wrong woman.

"How's the packing coming?" He slipped on his topcoat. There were matters to wrap up before he left the city, and he meant to see to all of them today. For example, he needed to visit the accountants and the hotel manager, and he'd scheduled a farewell call with Katherine Delafield, as well.

"Very good, Your Grace, but we should decide whether to keep some of the items you've acquired during your stay."

He strode into the other room. "Such as?"

"Like the bottles of champagne and the side-board liquor."

"Give it all to Lord Harkness. He's staying in the hotel." Potsie would definitely put the alcohol to good use.

A knock sounded. Wilkins started to put down the clothing he was folding, but Lockwood was already on his way to the door. "I'll see to it," he told his valet. "You keep packing."

He turned the knob and pulled. Finn O'Callaghan was there, looking annoyed. "Duke, let's go."

"Hold up." Lockwood glanced up and down the hall. Unfortunately, Finn was alone, and Lockwood's stomach fell. "What are you doing here, O'Callaghan?"

"I don't have time for questions. It took me a long feckin' time to find you. I'll explain on the way."

Lockwood didn't need to see her family and endure a reminder of the woman he'd lost. Not now, when the pain was too fresh. "If you don't mind, I'll take that explanation. I'm quite busy today."

"You're not too busy for this." Finn stepped closer. "She's been arrested. Now, get your god-damn walking stick or whatever it is you need to look fancy and follow me."

Arrested?

What the bloody hell?

Lockwood pushed the other man back, enough to let him out of the room, then closed the door behind him. Hurrying toward the lift, he said, "Next time lead with the arrest part, Irish."

"Next time trust me and don't ask so many damn questions. Do you think I'd be here otherwise?"

No, Lockwood supposed not.

"Let's take the stairs," he said, pointing in that direction. "It'll be faster."

As they descended, Finn began talking and Lockwood grew increasingly angrier. The absolute disregard for her safety . . . the recklessness . . . that foolish, stupid idiot. It was bad enough she was flouting the Comstock Laws and taunting the New York Society for the Suppression of Vice. Now she was confronting abusive husbands? "How in the hell," he growled, "did you condone such a dangerous and ill-advised outing?"

"You know Red. She gets something in her mind and it's impossible to talk her out of it. I figured I should go with her to make sure she didn't get hurt."

"No, you should've talked some sense into her. Or failing that, tied her up to prevent it."

Finn snorted. "You have a lot to learn about our family if you think that would ever work."

Once in the lobby Lockwood stopped by the front desk and quickly dashed off a cable. He slid some coins across the counter. "I need this sent as quickly as possible."

"Of course, Your Grace."

They continued outside, and Finn led him to a carriage with a young man waiting in the driver's seat. "Henry!" he called. "We're here. As fast as you can, yeah?"

The inside of the carriage smelled of whiskey and gunpowder, but Lockwood couldn't complain. Whatever got him to the Twenty-Second Police precinct expediently was all that mattered.

Finn stroked his jaw and regarded Lockwood thoughtfully. "Heard you two broke it off. Sorry about that. I was hoping you'd stick."

"So was I," he said sincerely. "But I'm still livid the two of you embarked on such an irresponsible outing today."

"How was I to know the brother was a police officer? And that he'd be one of these holier-than-thou types? Worse than the Catholics back in Galway, if you ask me."

"It doesn't matter. Eleanor had no business interfering at such a risk to her personal safety. That is what the authorities are for."

"Don't you know? We like a bit of danger, Your Grace."

Yes, he did know this about Nellie. It was what had made them such a good fit.

Except they hadn't been a good fit. He'd just been too stubborn to see it.

I am not suited for anything more than an affair with you.

He clenched his jaw and stared through the window. Thank God this hadn't happened after he left. He could still help her one last time. "At least you had the presence of mind to come and find me," he told her cousin.

"If anyone can help her fast, it has to be you. A duke's got to be good for something."

His name. Indeed, that was all Lockwood was good for. He had nothing else.

They pulled up to the police precinct. Lockwood got out, but when Finn started to descend he held up a hand. "You'll only make it worse. I have it from here, Finn."

"Are you sure?" Finn stared at the building like it was a case of head lice. "I'll come with you, if you need."

"I don't need. I'm a duke, remember? I will get her released."

"How?"

"I have it handled. Go home, O'Callaghan." Spinning, he hurried up the walk and bounded up the steps.

The station was busy but he quickly located the desk. A young officer glanced up from his paperwork. "Yes?"

"I understand a young woman has been brought in. A Miss Nellie Young?"

The officer checked his ledger. "Yeah, a few hours ago."

"I must wait on a friend of mine. May I?" He gestured to the wooden bench on the wall.

The officer snorted and went back to his work. "Suit yourself, Your Highness."

Lockwood didn't bother correcting the form of address—it was meant as an insult, anyway—and instead lowered himself onto the bench. He didn't believe this would take long.

Indeed, it was about half an hour before the precinct doors blew open and a small group entered. The man at the desk looked up—and his jaw dropped. "Commissioner. Sir." He flew to his feet and straightened his uniform.

A well-dressed man approached the desk, several officers at his side, and leaned against the desk. "Hello, son. I am looking for—" His head swung toward the bench. "Ah, there he is. Lockwood!"

"Commissioner Roosevelt." Lockwood rose and struck out a hand. "Nice to see you again."

Lockwood had met Theodore Roosevelt at a number of events over the past year, and he'd always liked the boisterous outdoorsman. They shook and Roosevelt thwacked Lockwood on the back a few times. "How have you been, duke? We never did set a date for you to come out to Sagamore for that fox hunt."

No, they hadn't—and now it was too late. "Perhaps when the weather improves. How are Mrs. Roosevelt and the children?"

"Fine, fine. Thank you for asking. I'm surprised to find you here."

"I am surprised myself, actually. But I find myself in need of your help. There's a woman who's been arrested—"

"Not here. Come with me." Roosevelt waved off the men trailing him and led Lockwood to a small interrogation room that wasn't being used at the moment. "Now, tell me what's happened."

"As I was saying, a woman's been arrested. A friend. Cornelius Young's daughter, Eleanor. Do you know her?"

"No, but I've met Young on a number of occasions. What's she been arrested for?"

"Violating Mr. Comstock's laws. Allegedly, she bought rubber goods and disseminated them, then instructed the ladies on how to use them."

"Contraceptives?" When Lockwood nodded, Roosevelt frowned, his gaze turning somber behind his spectacles. "Well, now. That is a serious offense. Is there any proof?"

"I couldn't say, but it's unseemly for her to be here. Surely, I may take her home and she may be questioned there later?"

"That depends. Let me talk to her. Then we can decide." He strode to the door and shouted into the corridor for someone to fetch a matron.

While they waited for Nellie to be brought from the female holding cells, Roosevelt asked after the officer who made the arrest. The officer came in not long after, wearing a smug expression that caused Lockwood to hate him on sight. The three of them waited in the tiny room, not speaking.

When the door opened, a matron led Nellie inside. A sharp pain went through the center of Lockwood's chest, the ache for her so palpable he could almost taste it. She looked tired and annoyed but incredibly beautiful, and he longed to bundle her in his arms and take her out of this place.

Her eyes widened when they landed on him, but she quickly recovered, her expression becoming a mask of indifference as she was helped into a chair. She didn't look at him again after that, and the matron removed her handcuffs.

"Miss Young, do you know who I am?"

Rubbing her wrists, Nellie quirked a brow at the man sitting across the table. "Indeed, I do, Mr. Roosevelt."

"Good. I realize we've never met, but I am acquainted with your father."

"I'm not surprised," she said, her voice cool. "Most men in this city are."

"Is he aware you are here?"

"No."

"Why haven't you asked to place a telephone call, then?"

"I have. They refused. Am I being charged with a crime, Mr. Roosevelt? Or do you plan on keeping me in a holding cell forever?"

NELLIE WAS FURIOUS. Boiling with rage, in fact. She hadn't been fingerprinted or photographed. Rather, she'd been stuck in a holding cell with a group of other women for hours, with no opportunity to plead her case with a judge. Instead, she had waited. And waited.

She knew the procedure—she'd been arrested once for public indecency after flashing her breasts at an officer—but they were in no hurry whatsoever to process her and let her post bail. It was as if they were content to let her languish in a cell. She was powerless, at the mercy of those who couldn't possibly understand what it was like to carry a child or risk death with each pregnancy. The officers blamed Nellie for acting inappropriately, when all she did was give a small number of women a tiny bit of control over their own lives. Now she was being punished for it.

Which told one all they needed to know about how men really felt about women.

And what on earth was Lockwood doing here? How had he learned of her arrest? Why wasn't he distancing himself from her and this impending scandal?

Those questions would need to wait. She had to deal with Mr. Roosevelt first. "I want a lawyer."

The police commissioner straightened his spectacles. "Before we discuss lawyers and such, we need to get to the bottom of these accusations. I'm told you were hand selling contraceptives, as well as giving talks on their benefits and uses. Is this true?"

"Don't answer that," Lockwood rushed to say. "Roosevelt, wouldn't it be best if Miss Young was returned home and then officers may question her there at a later time? This is hardly proper for a lady."

Ah, Lockwood was trying to save her, the poor, misguided man. Emotion clogged her throat, but she set it aside. There was no time for that, not when she had no intention of allowing him to do so.

"I'm happy to answer questions now," she said, and saw Lockwood flinch out of the corner of her eye.

"Excellent," Roosevelt said. "Because I'd like to hear those answers."

"Why? Are you opposed to the education of women, Mr. Roosevelt?"

"No, not when it stays within the bounds of the law."

"And if those laws are unjust and cruel?"

"They are still laws and must be obeyed. Even when we don't care for them, miss."

How nice that he'd never experienced oppression. That he'd always felt represented and supported by the systemic swaddling that made up the fabric of their society. But could he not understand the experiences of others?

She asked, "Then how will change ever occur,

sir? As a nation, are we not obligated to push back against tyranny? It's what our country was founded on, for heaven's sake."

"Tyranny!"

"Yes. When women are purposely kept ignorant and prevented from making choices that directly affect them, I call that tyranny."

"This is not tyranny," he said as if speaking to a small child. "This is a family matter—and a religious one, as well. Mr. Comstock is trying to prevent our public services from being used to intervene in delicate matters."

"Then why prevent hand selling? Why prevent anyone from speaking out or publishing books? There is no reason to keep women helpless and uneducated."

"We have a duty to uphold the laws, Miss Young. And we shouldn't interfere with what is between a man and his wife."

She sat back and folded her arms, irritated at his logic. "Then who will? Most of these women, they are married and either cannot afford or cannot handle any more children. But their husbands twist the words of the church to suit their whims. Who is left to suffer but the women?"

"This is not the time for a debate about procreation. I am here to uphold the law, nothing more. Did you break the law, Miss Young? Did you hand sell contraceptives and instruct women on how to use them?"

"Eleanor," Lockwood warned. "You should not—"

"Yes, I did." She would not back down. Let them burn her at the stake. At her trial she'd make such a public spectacle of herself that they would talk about it for decades to come. She would not be silent.

"I told you," the officer sneered. "High and mighty whore. That's all she is."

Lockwood lunged at the man, his face a mask of rage and violence. Nellie actually feared for the officer's life. "Lockwood!" she shouted.

Roosevelt was out of his chair and pushing the duke back to his corner. "Now, let's all settle down. Officer, we're finished with you. Please finish your report and see that it's filed."

"Wait," Lockwood said in his most ducal-like tone. "Does he have proof of the crime? I want to see the evidence."

"She just admitted it," the officer said, gesturing toward Nellie.

"She's under duress." Lockwood stared down the officer. "What evidence have you collected on this matter?"

Nellie kept quiet, too outraged by the word *duress*. Was he trying to humiliate her?

"That is a good point," Roosevelt allowed. "Is there evidence, Officer?"

"I have the word of Mrs. Ingram."

"Who, as I understand it," Lockwood said, "was severely beaten by her husband. He might've forced his wife to pin the blame on Miss Young. Again, where is your proof?"

"This is ridiculous," the officer snapped. "Who are you? Her lawyer?"

Lockwood drew himself up. "I am the eighth Duke of Lockwood, a peer of the British realm, and considering your country borrowed its entire judicial system from mine, I believe I know a thing or two about jurisprudence."

"Juris-what?" The officer looked to Roosevelt. "You aren't fixing to listen to him, are you, sir?"

The police commissioner appeared uncertain as he smoothed a hand over his jaw. "Officer, take a man with you and let's try to collect evidence of any crime. Miss Young, seeing as how you've admitted to breaking the law, I am going to hold you for now."

"Wait a moment." Lockwood pushed back the sides of his coat and thrust his hands on his hips. "I asked you here to help her, not throw her in chains."

"I don't mind doing a favor now and again, Your Grace, but I won't break the law. I've spent months rooting out the bad apples from my department. It would be the height of hypocrisy for me to not follow proper procedure."

Lockwood looked ready to argue further, so Nellie gave the police commissioner a bland smile. "Do what you must, sir."

"No. Dash it," Lockwood snapped, his face turning an alarming shade of red. Shit, his heart. He was getting worked up on her behalf and this was not good for his health.

"Mr. Roosevelt," she said without looking away from Lockwood. "I'd like a moment alone with the duke, if you please."

"I suppose it wouldn't hurt," Roosevelt said. "I'll give you a few minutes before I send the matron back in. In the meantime I'll see if we can't improve your accommodations while you're here."

"That's unnecessary."

"Miss Young, I may not be able to break the law, but I can do a kindness now and again." He strode from the room, leaving her alone with the duke.

Lockwood turned away from her, his hand rubbing his forehead.

"Breathe. You need to calm down," she said quietly. "I can't have you passing out."

Cocking his arm, he drove his fist into the wall with a mighty roar, cracking the plaster and rocking the entire room.

"I said to calm down!" she barked, then stood and hurried to his side.

"Goddamn it, I cannot believe this," he snarled and pressed the heels of his hands into his eyes. "All you had to do was say no. They have nothing, no proof whatsoever. You could have walked out with me."

"Breathe, Andrew." She moved to rest her cheek on his shoulder. "Thank you for coming. It was unnecessary but thoughtful of you."

He didn't move for a long second, his body vibrating. "You are not listening. This needn't happen, Eleanor."

"I won't pretend like I've done something wrong. I haven't." She stroked his back, greedy for the feel of him one last time. "Please, take a breath. I don't want you upset over this."

In a flash he spun and wrapped his arms around her, holding on to her tightly. The warmth from his body sank into her bones and flesh, and her heart reveled in the moment, his touch rejuvenating her better than any spa waters ever could. She clung to him, breathing into his throat as the seconds stretched.

Finally, he kissed the top of her head. "Why must you be so bloody difficult?"

"I told you I'd make a terrible duchess."

"Why didn't you tell me what you were doing with the contraceptives? Why keep it a secret?"

"Would you have approved, knowing I was breaking the law?"

"I thought my association with Roosevelt would get you released." Frustration colored his voice. "I cannot believe this backward country won't take a duke's request into consideration. If this were London—"

She couldn't help but laugh. "Lockwood, you know this isn't Scotland Yard. Things don't work like that here."

"I should've gone to your father. He would have you released already."

"My father pays for the best lawyers in the country to be at his beck and call. Money is what rules here, not titles."

"The one thing I don't have," he muttered.

She hadn't meant to hurt him, but it was true. Changing topics, she said, "You look terrible."

He exhaled a long breath. "I miss you, darling."

Those slashes around her heart opened once more, deep cuts that hadn't yet formed scars. The truth tumbled from her lips. "I miss you, too."

"Come with me."

"You know I cannot. Even if I weren't under arrest. You should go."

His arms squeezed around her. "I can't leave you here."

"You must."

"I cannot possibly do it, Eleanor. It's one thing to walk away in your conservatory. It's another altogether to leave you in a police station, where any number of things may happen."

"I'll be fine. When I am ready, I'll have my father notified."

"What does that mean, when you're ready?"

"After I've drawn attention to the cause."

"Oh, for Christ's sake." He groaned and shook his head. "You're planning a bloody crusade."

"I am, which is why you must distance yourself from me."

"I'd much prefer to marry you."

Though her heart leapt at the declaration, her brain remained full of common sense. Now more than ever, she would not saddle him with her reputation. "In another life, perhaps. One in which I'm not so scandalous and improper."

"You think I love you despite your recklessness." He pressed his face into her hair and spoke quietly. Solemnly. "I love you because of it, you daft woman."

Her throat closed, the pressure on her chest nearly unbearable. How was she supposed to ever replace him?

The answer was obvious: she couldn't. Lockwood had changed her forever. No other man could ever understand her so completely or send her heart fluttering like a girl with her first crush. She loved him with the stuff of poetry, all the flowery and sickening-sweet words that had ever been crafted.

And because she loved him, she wouldn't ruin his life.

"You should go," she forced out, though it emerged as a whisper. "Go, find your vanilla crème. She's ready to move to England and give you heirs. London society will love her."

"Please. Do not force me to walk away again. I cannot bear it."

"But you will—and deep down you know I'm right." She tried to edge away but his fingers clenched, holding her closer instead of releasing her. "You have to let me go, Andrew."

He shuddered and exhaled into her hair. Then his mouth found hers and they were kissing, and she could taste everything he felt, the frustration and the longing, all the emotions that were of no use between them. She thought about pulling away, truly she did, but instead, the moment stretched, her body arching into his one last time. The contact was both too much and not enough, and she never wanted it to end.

She was going to miss him terribly, so she'd take this kiss and store it away. Memorize his taste, his smell, every grunt and grasp, until it filled one of the trunks in her head. Then she'd lock all those thoughts away, long enough to dull the pain wrapped around her heart. At some point she would be able to remember this, but not anytime soon.

No, as soon as this kiss ended, she needed to forget. Except forgetting this, forgetting *him*, seemed impossible at the moment.

I'm fooling myself. I'm only making it worse.

Tearing her mouth away, she pressed her forehead against his cheek. "I'm sorry."

"For what?" His voice was rough, as if gravel lined his throat. "I kissed you."

"I'm sorry I cannot be who you need."

He gave a tiny shake of his head. "My darling, you are exactly who I need. You're merely too stubborn to admit it." His lips met her temple. "I'm leaving the day after tomorrow. If you change your mind, you know where to find me."

Nellie didn't say a word, not even after he left and she was taken back to her cell.

Chapter Twenty-Three

※

*E*ventually, the matron moved her to a private room that was clearly someone's office. Roosevelt's doing, no doubt. Though these were more comfortable accommodations, Nellie couldn't relax.

Lockwood was leaving.

Leaving New York . . . or leaving America?

Had he proposed to an heiress, then? He couldn't leave the country without a wealthy bride. So who had he chosen? The Twombly girl?

A sharp stab of jealousy robbed Nellie of breath and she had to put a hand on the wall to steady herself. It was going to be fine. *She* was going to be fine. It would just take time.

She'd been through a devastation before, the loss of the most important person in her life. She could withstand this. She and Lockwood hadn't even known one another that long. Not even a year.

The door opened and the captain appeared, a deep frown on his face. "We're letting you go, miss," he said without preamble.

"What? I don't understand."

"Reporters are swarming the entrance. We don't need this kind of commotion, so you're being released and we'll follow up with you at home. Roosevelt's orders."

Reporters? Excellent. She had a thing or two to say to them.

The captain hooked a thumb over his shoulder. "Let's go."

He didn't need to tell her twice. Nellie hurried through the door and followed him to the exit. As she passed by, the other officers glared at her, their animosity clouding the air like spoiled eggs. They obviously blamed her for causing trouble, but she hadn't asked to be arrested.

When she stepped onto the precinct's stoop, flash powder popped in the dying afternoon light. She tried not to react, instead merely waited as the photographers captured her image, and then the questions began.

"Miss Young, does your father know you are here?"

"Miss Young, what have you been arrested for?"

"Is it true you were sending immoral publications through the mail?"

Nellie held up her hand. "Gentlemen, please write this down and make sure to print it correctly. Women have the right to decide when to start or expand their family. These unjust laws would rather keep us ignorant, forbid us any control whatsoever on reproduction. I won't stop until Mr. Comstock's restrictive policies are revoked, and contraceptives are accepted as decent and necessary for all people. Thank you."

She pushed past the reporters on the stairs and ignored their shouts. When she reached the walk she glanced up and down the street for a hack, while the reporters trailed her and kept asking questions she had no intention of answering.

"Hey, gorgeous! Need a ride?"

Nellie's head turned toward the familiar voice. Katherine Delafield was on the opposite side of the street, leaning out from the door of a large closed carriage. "Oh, thank God," Nellie murmured and dashed across to the other walk. Eager to escape, she came around and pulled open the carriage door—and stopped short.

Three women stared out at her. Maddie, Alice and Katherine. Her friends.

"Get in already," Maddie said, beckoning with her hand. "It's cold out there."

Nellie shook off her surprise, climbed in next to Alice and shut the door. Alice threw a blanket over Nellie's lap, tucking it around her as the wheels began turning. Nellie looked at the three women. "What are you all doing here?"

"We're kidnapping you," Katie said.

"Kidnapping me? Why?"

Maddie reached over to briefly clasp Nellie's hand. "Because we love you and we haven't forgotten about you."

Nellie sighed at Katie. "You have a big mouth."

"I'm sorry," Katie said, though she didn't appear the least bit contrite. "But I'm worried about you. We're all worried about you."

"Yes," Alice said kindly. "We are concerned."

Nellie didn't know what to say. The weight of it all—her unhappiness, Lockwood's leaving, the frustrating arrest—sat in her stomach like a lead weight. She was touched her friends had come to the station, but there was nothing to be done for any of it.

But she didn't wish to talk about any of that. It was too depressing. So she went with practicalities instead. "How did you learn I was here?"

Katie answered, "Mrs. Kimball heard it from a woman who works next door to the Meliora."

Ginny, then.

Before Nellie could comment, Maddie said, "Can you believe they wouldn't let me post bail? The police were perfectly content to hold you without an arraignment, so I called some friends at the newspapers."

"Ah." Nellie smiled at her clever friends. "I wondered how the reporters found out."

Alice reached into a satchel and pulled out a square wrapped in brown paper. "Are you hungry? I made you something to eat."

"Starving. I haven't eaten all day." She took the parcel and began to unwrap it. "Thank you, Alice."

"You're welcome. It's your favorite, the chicken salad with walnuts and grapes."

The chicken salad was on bread to make it easier to eat. Nellie took a grateful bite. "You three are the very best."

Maddie nudged the toe of Nellie's boot with her own. "No, I'm not. I've been a terrible friend and I'm sorry. I had no idea what you've been going through."

"You haven't been a bad friend. You're busy with your life and your husband, as it should be.

Not one of you owes me an apology for that. I'm happy for each of you. And I'm fine."

"You're not fine," Maddie said. "We've been friends for far too long for you to hide anything from me, Eleanor."

Nellie shook her head. "I merely need time. Everything will work itself out."

"Will it?" Katie asked. "Because he's leaving, you know. Your chance for love and happiness is sailing back to England the day after tomorrow."

Pain bloomed behind Nellie's sternum again, like her ribs might crack open at any moment. She tried to school her features as Maddie blurted, "Wait, *he*? Love and happiness? I feel as though I'm behind."

Nellie quirked a brow at Katie. "Don't tell me you actually kept a secret for once."

Her friend lifted her chin. "Alice already knew, and I didn't think it was my place to share."

"My husband told me," Alice said quietly. "After you left the club the other night."

"Wait, Kit knows something about Nellie that I don't?" Maddie stared down at her hands. "I really have been a terrible friend, haven't I? I am informing Harrison tonight that I plan to cut back on the tournaments—"

"Stop." Nellie reached over to squeeze Maddie's knee. "You'll do no such thing. I was having an affair with the Duke of Lockwood, but that's over. It's for the best. He'll be happier with his debutante."

"Debutante?" Katie's brow creased. "Who are you talking about?"

"Whichever heiress he's decided on."

"There is no other heiress. No other woman at all, in fact. He's returning to London alone."

Nellie blinked. This made no sense whatsoever. What was the man going to do about his estate? The crumbling roof?

The buildings blurred outside the window as she considered this news. Was there a woman in England he hadn't told her about, a wealthy merchant's daughter who was eager to become a duchess? No, Nellie felt certain he would've mentioned it. More likely he was soured on American women for good—thanks to three of the four women in this carriage.

They were staring at her expectantly, so she took another bite of chicken salad. "He'll change his mind. Give it a few weeks and he'll end up in Paris, wooing debutantes as they travel through to order their Worth gowns."

"Do you honestly believe that?" Katie asked.

Nellie had to believe it. Because it would break her heart even more to think otherwise. "Let's discuss something else. How is the supper club, Alice? Maddie, how goes your lawn tennis?"

"We are not discussing anything other than you and Lockwood," Maddie said. "This is too important, Nellie. I want to know everything. Start at the beginning."

Nellie gave an abbreviated version of her affair with Lockwood, starting in the ocean the night before the house party began last summer.

"I'm astounded," Maddie said. "I had no idea any of this was happening."

"Are you angry with me?" Nellie asked. "Considering he was your fiancé not that long ago."

"Please. I would be thrilled if the two of you ended up together. He's a good and decent man."

Good and decent? Nellie smothered a snort. Lockwood might appear perfect on the outside, but the man was so much more underneath.

I'm going to cover you in bite marks, darling.

Mouth suddenly dry, she licked her lips. "Anyway, there's nothing to discuss. It was a lark and now it's over."

"Wrong. You love him." This was from Katie, Nellie's most unrelenting—and irritating—friend.

Nellie tried for nonchalance. "It doesn't matter. We didn't see eye to eye. I wanted an affair but he preferred something more permanent."

"He asked you to marry him?" Alice breathed.

Nellie picked at the chicken salad. "Yes, he mentioned the idea. But I shot it down straightaway."

"Why?" Maddie asked. "What am I missing?"

"Come, now. Me, a duchess in England? It's ludicrous."

Katie pointed at Nellie triumphantly. "I told you Lockwood asked for your father's blessing. I love it when I'm proven right."

"I don't understand," Alice said, deep lines forming on her brow. "If he asked, then why haven't you accepted? I think you would make a wonderful duchess."

Silence descended and Nellie struggled with how to put all her thoughts into words. When she didn't speak, Katie said, "It's because you are scared."

"No, it's because it's a terrible idea," Nellie snapped. "Move across an ocean and leave my father, only to be ridiculed by a bunch of snobs? No, thank you."

Katie didn't let up. "Your father will be fine, and since when do you care what anyone thinks of you?"

"I agree with Katherine," Maddie said. "You've thumbed your nose at society for years. What is this really about? Because I'm having a hard time believing facing down a little gossip is the problem."

"He's asking me to give up everything I am to become someone else."

"He's asked you to change?" Alice asked. "Well, that's not very nice of him. I wouldn't marry him, either."

"No, I don't believe he'd do that," Maddie said. "Anyone who meets you knows exactly who you are, Nellie Young. If Lockwood fell in love with that person, why on earth would he want you to change merely because you're on a different continent?"

"I agree. He knows you'll never pretend to be someone you're not," Katie put in.

You are exactly who I need. You're merely too stubborn to admit it.

He could say that now, but what about in the future?

And what happened when she was left all alone, grieving another tragic loss?

She considered telling her friends about the duke's heart condition, but she wasn't one to gossip. Furthermore, it was Lockwood's secret to tell. Though they were no longer sleeping together, it felt wrong to breach his trust.

Appetite forgotten, Nellie wrapped up the remainder of her sandwich. "He is still a duke, and that comes with a heap of responsibilities. I would be expected to toe the line, give him heirs and all that."

"Why is that a problem?" Maddie said. "You are clearly head over heels for this man. And don't deny it. I've known you a long time, Nellie. You wouldn't look so sad otherwise."

"None of you can possibly understand what this means! You each have your own lives here, husbands and fiancés who encourage your independence. You've forged your own paths. For God's sake, Maddie, you still use your maiden name on the lawn tennis circuit. So please don't tell me I should give up literally everything and move to a country I don't even like to be swallowed up by a husband's title. I would disappear in his shadow."

"Disappear!" Katie made a disparaging noise. "Can you not see the influence and power you could wield as a duchess? You're part of the establishment, the ruling class. You could make a real difference for people, Nels."

"But things are easier here," Alice said to the other two. "And I don't see Nellie thriving under such a restrictive society there."

"What about Jennie Jerome?" Maddie argued. "After she became Lady Randolph, she ran her husband's political career and founded the Primrose League. It's said she's very eccentric and holds tremendous influence."

Nellie groaned. "I don't want to do any of that. I just want to garden, fight the Comstock Laws and help women gain control over their repro-duction."

"And Lockwood?" Katie asked. "Are you will-ing to give him up?"

"I already have," Nellie said tightly. "You can't expect me to surrender my whole life, move to another country and leave everything I know be-hind." *Only to lose my husband in a few years.*

"I would do it," Alice said. "If it meant I got to keep Kit."

"Same," Maddie said. "I'd follow Harrison to the ends of the earth if he asked me to."

Katie didn't speak, so Nellie cocked an eye-brow in her friend's direction. "And? I suppose you'd follow Preston anywhere, too."

Scrunching up her nose, Katie exhaled. "I don't know. It wouldn't be easy. My father is here and all the memories of my mother. Leaving would cause me to feel, I don't know, disconnected from her. But we only get one life, Nellie, and so much of it is filled with tragedy. Shouldn't we try to hold on to whatever happiness we can?"

That was Aunt Riona's advice, but Nellie wasn't convinced. "Well, that may work for the three of you, but I can't uproot my entire life for a man. I wouldn't be able to live with myself afterward."

"So is it your fear or your pride holding you back?" Maddie asked. "Or maybe it's both."

The back of Nellie's neck turned hot. "You don't understand."

"What I understand," Katie said, "is that you're about to lose the love of your life. Is that truly what you want?"

Alice patted Nellie's knee. "Don't worry. There will be plenty of other men, plenty of other loves."

"Not like Lockwood," Katie said. "Not like this. And did you feel the same way about Kit, Alice? That he was replaceable?"

"No, but we shouldn't pressure Nellie into doing something she doesn't want to do. That's what my mother did to me my entire life. We have to let her choose."

"I understand, but this isn't the same." Maddie reached forward to grab Nellie's hand. "At some point you have to decide if you're willing to take a risk, if you're willing to trust in another person. I know it's scary. I've been there. But if you don't try, I fear you're going to regret it, Nels."

Nellie turned to stare through the carriage window. There was nothing to be done for it . . . even if she suspected that Maddie was right.

LONDON LOOKED THE same. Gray and dirty, somber and depressing. It was raining when Lockwood arrived and he thought the atmosphere was a fitting greeting, considering his mood.

She hadn't come to stop him from leaving.

Nellie had been perfectly content to let him walk out of her life, and Lockwood had to find a way to come to terms with it. Three weeks on a boat hadn't helped in the least. Each day had felt like an eternity, with nothing to do but think. The ache was just as sharp, just as raw, as if their exchange in the police precinct happened a moment ago.

Now he had to face his mother.

When he arrived in Grosvenor Square their

butler, Differts, opened the door. "A pleasure to have you returned, Your Grace."

Lockwood stepped inside and began handing over his things. "Thank you, Differts. My apologies for not providing notice."

"We are always ready to accommodate Your Grace."

"Is that my son I hear?"

Lockwood braced himself at the sound of his mother's voice. She was dressed for an afternoon of calls, every inch the duchess. "Good afternoon, Mother."

"Goodness, why didn't you send word you were coming?" She glanced over his shoulder as she came forward. "I don't understand. You have returned alone?"

He bent to kiss her cheek. "Come. Let's sit in the drawing room. I shall explain everything there."

"Tea, if you please, Differts," she told their butler. "And have Cook make His Grace a plate of food."

"That is not necessary," Lockwood said.

His mother's gaze did a sweep of him from head to foot. "Nonsense. You look terrible. Food, Differts."

When they were settled in the drawing room she didn't wait. "Where is your fiancée?"

"I haven't one."

She lowered herself slowly onto the sofa, as if her legs would no longer support her. His mother was nothing if not dramatic. "Tell me you are joking."

He strode to the window and stared out at the

dreary square, his hands resting behind his back. "I'm sorry, Mother."

"You are sorry?" Her voice rose. "We are going to lose everything and you are *sorry*?"

"Yes."

The silence stretched as he let her grapple with the news. Then she said, "We discussed this when you were here for the holiday. You were returning to New York to find a bride. What has changed between then and now?"

Everything had changed.

He'd loved the most amazing woman . . . and then lost her.

"I've changed my mind."

"No, this cannot be true. You had one task to accomplish in America and that was to find an heiress. I hear the place is practically dripping with them. So how have you allowed yourself to fail?"

"It is not important. I'll—"

"Not important! Tell me how this family and your title are no longer important. Our estate and this house. Centuries of Lockwood tradition and legacy. How are those things not important, Andrew?"

That she called him by his first name meant she was truly upset—and he couldn't blame her. He turned and gave her the grim news. "I plan to sell the Yorkshire estate."

She gasped, a high squeaking sound like she couldn't draw enough air. "Y-you cannot be serious. That house has been in the family since the sixteenth century."

He said nothing. Who cared about legacies and

estates when his heart was broken? Furthermore, he wouldn't live much longer, so let Tooter deal with the Lockwood legacy. Selling the estate would bring the duchy out of debt, and that was all Lockwood cared about at the moment. "You mostly reside here. Little will change for you if at all, Mother."

"Except all of London will hear about it. We shall be laughingstocks."

He continued as if she hadn't spoken. "I plan to begin the process immediately. I have a meeting this afternoon with my business managers, and the portraits have been shipped to New York for loan in a museum. We may discuss what to do with the rest of the furnishings and heirlooms when the place sells."

She rubbed her forehead slowly. "I am begging you to reconsider. Pick any young woman to marry. Any at all. Merely one with a dowry large enough to save us."

The thought of marrying another, of bedding her and producing heirs, turned his stomach. Perhaps someday, but not anytime soon. "I cannot."

"You selfish boy," she spat, her spine straightening. "I did not raise you to abandon your family and responsibilities like this."

"I am sorry to disappoint you."

"It's not only me, Andrew. Your father would be very disappointed in you, as well."

Lockwood's heart gave an awkward thump as his throat tightened. Yes, he would be recorded as the duke who'd lost it all. At the moment, however, he couldn't find it within himself to care.

Nothing mattered any longer.

A knock sounded, then two footmen and a maid entered with trays of provisions. His mother rose and strode toward the door. "Leave the tea and cakes for His Grace. He thinks of only himself, anyway. Refuse all callers. I must retire upstairs."

Confused, the servants looked to Lockwood. Clearing his throat, he said, "Please take it all downstairs and share with the staff. I have no need for any of it at the moment."

He turned back toward the window. He had no need for anything right now.

Chapter Twenty-Four

❧

$\mathcal{H}$er father found her in the conservatory.

Nellie wasn't gardening. Instead, she was staring through the glass and into the night sky, wondering about the duke. It had been a month since his departure, so he would've arrived in London by now. What was he doing? Who was he with?

"Hello, sweet pea."

Nellie looked over and attempted a smile. "Papa, hello. How was your dinner party?"

He kissed her cheek and sat down on the bench across from her. "Boring. I left early."

"Oh, that's a shame."

"I left early because I'm worried about you."

"Me? Whatever for?"

"You're not yourself. Ever since the arrest you've been different. Sadder. More withdrawn." He glanced around them. "The plants in here are starting to turn brown."

The darkness bubbled in her chest again, the pressure nearly unbearable. She was finding it harder and harder to get out of bed every day, and she hadn't touched the plants in at least two weeks. Food tasted like ashes in her mouth. "It's temporary, Papa. You know me. Eventually I'll be fine."

"The charges were dropped, so it cannot be your brush with the law that is bothering you."

Her father's lawyers, against Nellie's wishes, managed to get the charges against her dropped. It hadn't stopped her crusade, however. She was already scheming with the midwife on how to order more contraceptives and distribute them safely.

Her father continued, "I think it has to do with a certain someone going back to England, if you ask me."

There was no use pretending she didn't know who they were discussing. Lockwood's departure would've been discussed all over the island, gossiped about in every Fifth Avenue drawing room.

"I do miss him," she admitted. "But it was for the best."

"Best for whom?"

"For him. For both of us. I would make a terrible duchess and he would grow to resent me."

He shifted on the bench and crossed his legs. "Do you know what he said that morning we spoke? He said, 'I think she's perfect. I wouldn't change a thing about her.'"

The backs of her eyelids began to sting. Damn that duke. "No doubt he would come to feel differently."

"Why? Do you doubt his feelings?"

"No, but I would be ostracized and it would embarrass him."

"Do you think I gave a fig what New York society thought of your mother, an Irish barmaid?"

"You were a successful man by that point. Richer than most in the city."

His frown deepened. "So Lockwood's lack of financial resources means that he is weak, susceptible to gossip and public influence."

"I didn't say that." The idea of Lockwood as weak was laughable—if she felt at all like laughing.

"But that is what you said. That my money is why I didn't care about society's opinions of Siobhán."

She didn't appreciate the way he'd twisted her words, but there was no denying money provided a barrier from the unpleasant things in life. "It had to help that you could buy and sell nearly anyone in town."

He shook his head, like she didn't understand the way the world worked. "Money doesn't build character, sweet pea. People either have a sense of who they are or they don't. And if they don't, money only makes things worse. Not better."

"I suppose."

"You know it's true," her father said. "And when it comes to those we love, we are willing to make almost any sacrifice, any compromise, to keep them happy, because their happiness is our happiness. I suppose that means Lockwood isn't the right man for you." He watched her carefully, and she squirmed, trying to avoid those knowing eyes. "Incidentally, I hear he's put the ducal estate up for sale."

She inhaled sharply. The family seat? "But it's been in his family for hundreds of years."

Her father shrugged. "I'd say his priorities shifted in the last few months."

Disbelief cascaded through her. Had Lockwood lost his mind? He loved that property. He'd told her how he swam in the lake and tramped around on the land. In comparison, he hated London, with its cramped spaces and dirty air.

Moreover, what about his heart? With no lake, what would he do in London for proper exercise? Was he so keen on dying, then? The chasm in her chest split a fraction more, the distress causing her head to suddenly pound. That stupid man. Why not marry some fortunate young virgin instead?

"Jaysus, Mary and Joseph. Where in the hell are you?" A feminine voice echoed in the cavernous space. "I think I'm lost."

"We're back here, Riona," her father called.

Nellie perked up. Her aunt? She hadn't set foot in the Young mansion since Mama's wake all those years ago. Nellie jumped to her feet just as her aunt came around the corner. "Aunt Ri!"

"Damn, I never thought I'd find you." After putting her bag on the ground, she opened her arms and Nellie went in for a hug. "There's my girl," Aunt Riona said softly.

Nellie let her aunt hold her, the physical contact like a salve on her wounded soul. She didn't move, merely breathed in her aunt's familiar scent, peat and leather mixed with smoke.

"I'll leave her in your hands, Riona." Nellie's father kissed the top of Nellie's head. "See you later, sweet pea."

"Good night, Papa." She stayed close to Aunt

Riona for another minute, then pulled back. "What are you doing here?"

"Your da rang me, asked me to come and talk to you." Putting a finger under Nellie's chin, Aunt Riona tilted Nellie's face up to examine it. "It's a good thing he did, too. I've never seen you look so out of sorts. Let's sit down and you can tell me all about it."

They settled side by side on the bench and Nellie dropped her head onto her aunt's shoulder. "I'm happy to see you, but you didn't have to come all the way over here. Everything's fine."

"You don't look fine, and you haven't been by to see me in weeks. What's going on? Why are you sitting here in the dark?"

There was no use lying about it. Her aunt would get it out of Nellie eventually. "He's gone, Aunt Ri. I pushed him away and he left."

"They do that sometimes. Male pride and all. So what happened, then?"

"What do you mean? I let him go."

"Why'd you do a daft thing like that?"

Nellie shrugged with an ease she didn't feel. "Because he wanted to marry me and I can't see myself being happy living in England as a duchess."

"But you'll be happy here, without him?"

"Eventually, yes."

Her aunt made a noise in her throat and then reached for her satchel. "I can tell we need help for this conversation." She took out two glasses and a bottle of whiskey. "Let's get drunk and see if we can't solve this mess you've created."

Though she doubted spirits would help, Nellie

accepted a full glass from her aunt. "It's nothing time won't heal."

"Bollocks. Drink it," her aunt said, nudging Nellie's arm. When they finished those, Riona quickly refilled their glasses.

After their third drink, Nellie started to feel loose and uncoordinated. She kicked a rock with her boot. "This is ridiculous. I hate feeling this way over a man."

"I know it's hard, love. You've been independent for so long, just you and your da here in this big house. But it's all right to let yourself love someone."

Nellie's hands flopped uselessly in her lap. "Everything happened so quickly, and he pushed for an answer before I was ready to give it. And then he left."

"He's used to gettin' his way. He's a duke, after all."

"I don't care if he's a duke or a stable boy. No one is going to force me to do something before I'm ready. Really, all of this is his fault for being so bloody impatient!"

Aunt Riona chuckled. "There's that Irish temper. Have another drink. We've got to come around to the crying part."

"I don't cry, Aunt Ri. Not over men."

Sometime during the fourth drink, Nellie moved to the ground and leaned against her aunt's legs. Aunt Riona stroked her hair and said, "I know the idea of moving away is scary, especially when you don't know if it'll work out or not."

"It's not that. If I were unhappy, I'd just divorce

him and move back here. I don't give a damn about the stigma."

"So what is it, then?"

"I didn't think he'd actually leave," she admitted, her tongue heavy and awkward in her mouth.

"Do you know what I asked your ma when she was flip-flopping on whether to marry your da?"

Nellie pulled back and gaped up at her aunt. "Mama debated whether to marry him or not?"

"Of course! What, did you think your da swept her off her feet?"

"Yes, that's exactly what I thought."

Riona made a face. "No, she was too level-headed for that. She wanted him, but was worried about what would happen, whether his world would accept her or not."

"And what did you tell her?"

"That when you marry someone, it isn't your world and my world. It's *our* world. It's what you build together. And your parents made it work."

That made sense, Nellie supposed. "Do you think she'd want me to marry Lockwood?"

"She'd want you to be happy. She'd want to know if he makes you a better version of yourself or not. Some women, they end up with men who don't appreciate them or mistreat them. You want someone who lifts you up, not knocks you down."

I bloody worship you, woman.

By the time they finished their fifth drink, Nellie's head was in her aunt's lap, and sorrow had formed a lump in her throat. The truth finally tumbled out. "I love him, Aunt Ri. I love him and he's going to die and leave me alone."

"We all die, sweetheart."

"No, you don't understand." She did her drunken best to explain about the duke's heart condition. "It'll hurt less to let him go now, before I really get attached."

"Ah, I see. You think this is going to be like losing your mother and you're afraid."

Whether it was her aunt's patient words or the alcohol, Nellie felt the black cloud overtake her and she broke down into tears. All the heartache and grief came out then, her eyes leaking onto her aunt's skirts as her aunt stroked her hair. It was for Lockwood, but also for her mother. For Mrs. Ingram and the unfairness of the universe. Nellie couldn't catch her breath from the force of her sobs, and a handkerchief somehow made its way into her fist.

When she quieted, Aunt Riona said, "You've been holding that in a long time, love."

Yes, Nellie had. Too long.

"I miss her," she confessed. "Why did she have to die so soon?" Nellie's memories of her mother were scant. Little moments in time here and there, like picnics and swimming, but she remembered how Mama made everything better and more exciting.

"No one has the answer to that question. But I miss her, too. She was a gem, your mother."

"I wish I'd had more time with her."

"I know, love. I feel the same. But no one said life was easy."

"Is it strange that I feel closer to her in the house, surrounded by her plants? If I leave, it's like a part of me will stay here with her."

"These are only things," her aunt said. "Our loved ones live in our hearts and mind, not in plants and places. She is a part of you. Always. No matter where you go."

After a few minutes of silence Nellie said, "And yes, I miss him. I miss him and I hate it. It's awful. I can barely get out of bed."

"Love isn't pretty. It's a terrible, terrible thing that tears you up inside. But it can also be wonderful. It's the source of life's greatest happiness, to have that one person who understands you better than anyone else. And your duke, he loves you."

"Sometimes love isn't enough, though."

"That's not true. If two people love each other, that's a bond that can withstand anything life throws at you."

"I don't want to lose anyone else," Nellie whispered, her voice ragged.

"Do you think I expected to lose my Colin so soon? But even cut short, I wouldn't change a thing about my time with that man. And no doubt your da feels the same way about your ma. Some love burns bright and hot for a short time, but it's no less meaningful."

"It makes me sad to even contemplate Lockwood's death. How did you bear it?"

"You remember, you cry. I have my boys, so I always have a part of Colin with me. But I live with the regrets, too. If I'd known, I would've done more to appreciate every single moment while he was still here. I regret all the times I went to bed mad, pushing him away instead of letting him have me. I'd give anything for just one more time with him."

"Are you saying it's better to know that Lockwood won't live long?"

"Maybe. Then you'll make the most of what you have. Nothing is guaranteed in this life, love. Know what your mother said to me when she was dying?"

Every muscle in Nellie's body tensed. Did she wish to hear this? Swallowing, she croaked, "No."

Aunt Riona smoothed Nellie's hair. "She said, 'Make sure she remembers where she comes from.' And you come from a long line of strong Irish women, love. We Flanagan women live hard and love hard. We fight tooth and nail for those we care about. Most importantly, we never give up."

The message twisted through Nellie's veins, clogging her throat and twisting her stomach. "You think I'm giving up. With the duke, I mean."

"I think you're letting the fear of more grief hold you back. But you're strong, Nellie, stronger than you even know. Go out there and live and lose, fight and love. We could all die tomorrow, whether it's a fever or a fall under a streetcar. Don't miss out on life because you're scared."

"I won't see you or Papa as much if I leave."

Her aunt snorted. "Your father will buy a neighboring estate just to be close to you. And he'll likely build a big steamship to carry us all back and forth to one another whenever we fancy."

"He would, wouldn't he?"

"In a snap. He wants you to be happy, even if that means visiting you in dreary England and putting up with all those snobs. And you won't be able to stop me from visiting. A Flanagan woman, a duchess? I need to see them all bowing and scraping for your favor with my own eyes."

Nellie smiled—and it felt good. Her head was clear, lighter, even though she was definitely drunk. "My duke beat up on Finn, didn't he?"

"He certainly did. Stuff of legend, it was."

"Hmm. Aunt Ri, the room is spinning."

"That means it's time for bed." Aunt Riona helped Nellie to her feet. "Tomorrow you can decide what to do about your duke."

"What do you think I should do?"

"I can't answer that for you, love. But let me ask you. What's worse—loving him and being deliriously happy together for a short time, or never having that at all?"

After the past few weeks, Nellie instantly knew the answer. Her legs weren't working right, so she wrapped her arm around her aunt's shoulders. "I love him. So very much. I'm miserable without him."

Aunt Riona took Nellie's weight and started walking them toward the path. "And?"

"And I'm going to have to go to dreary England, aren't I?"

"God help you, but I think you might."

Chapter Twenty-Five

❧

Bridgewater Towers
Yorkshire, England

Lockwood stared up at the soaring Elizabe-
than architecture, the high chimneys and Italian-
influenced facade. Thirty-five main rooms, with
seventy-five lesser rooms throughout the four-
story structure. The first Duke of Lockwood,
Walter Talbot, a favorite of Queen Elizabeth, designed the manor, after he'd established himself
by making a fortune in wool. The fourth duke
had then improved upon the place, putting in the
arched windows and enclosing the loggias. The
duchess of the sixth duke had created the exten-
sive gardens in the back, including a hedge maze
that Lockwood remembered playing in as a boy.

And he, Andrew Talbot, the eighth Duke of
Lockwood, would be remembered as the one
who lost it.

Bridgewater had been sold.

Indeed, it was a relief to have it bought so
quickly. If the property had languished on the

market, it would've been considerably more heartbreaking. The good news was they were out of debt and Lockwood was able to leave a nice sum for his mother, too.

His hope was that whoever had purchased Bridgewater would enjoy the place as much as he had.

Rubbing his chest, he tried to not think of all that might've been here. It was too painful, and he could not endure it any longer. The past seven weeks had been torture.

Did she miss him? Or, was she back to attending her scandalous events with another fencing teacher?

I am not suited for anything more than an affair with you.

Those words. They were talons inside his lungs, his heart. He wished he could forget them and forget her. Forget ever going to America at all. But there were too many reminders, too many memories.

"Your Grace." Thatcher, his secretary, came through the front door and onto the drive. Lockwood's dog, a brown pointer named Rufus, followed. "I've just received word that the new owners are on their way here to tour the property."

Bending to pet Rufus, Lockwood forced a small nod, though his chest threatened to cave in at any moment. "Very well. I suppose that is their right. You'll alert the staff?"

"Yes, Your Grace. They've been informed."

"We need to begin a list, Thatcher. An inventory of everything in the house, so that we may decide what to do with it all."

"I've already begun, Your Grace." This wasn't surprising. The fourth son of an earl, Thatcher was young and extremely competent.

Lockwood straightened and put his hands behind his back. "Good. I'll let you handle the tour, if you don't mind. I'd prefer to wander through the hedge maze one last time." He planned to move to London permanently tomorrow. Thatcher and the Bridgewater staff could handle the packing. Lockwood was too depressed to be of any help.

"Very good, Your Grace. What if they wish to speak with you regarding the house?"

He shook his head, pulled up the collar of his greatcoat and started toward the side of the manor. "Tell them I am not in residence. Come on, boy." Rufus trotted after him, happy to be outside.

The sound of carriage wheels reached Lockwood's ears as he stepped inside the maze. *Let Thatcher deal with them.* Lockwood purposely hadn't asked anything about the buyers. It was beyond strange to think of others living here, raising children on the property. Already he could feel the weighty stares of his ancestors as he passed their paintings.

You failed us, they seemed to be saying.

Yes, he had. All because he fell in love with a woman who had no interest in marriage. His mother still wasn't speaking to him, which should make for interesting dinner conversations when he returned to Mayfair tomorrow.

Rufus ran on ahead, knowing the maze every bit as well as his owner, and Lockwood followed at a slower pace, the hedges surrounding him to block the late February wind. He was already short of breath from the walk. His interest in exercise had waned significantly since returning, but he couldn't bring himself to care. At least Tooter was in fine health, so there was no need to worry over the future of the title.

It's merely a house.

That was what he kept telling himself. None of this mattered, not really. It was a big empty pile of stone, and if he had no one to share it with, then why bother keeping it?

Rufus was already in the center of the maze, sniffing the ice that had settled into the bottom of the fountain. Lockwood sat on the bench to rest, content to watch his dog explore the frozen ground. "You'd best enjoy it now, boy," he said. "You won't have nearly as much room in London."

Minutes later Rufus perked up, his ears twitching. The dog darted off into the maze, probably scenting a rabbit or other small animal. Lockwood checked his timepiece and wondered how long he would need to sit here. Would Thatcher retrieve him after the new owners had departed?

Soon, an overly excited Rufus bounded back into the center and headed straight for Lockwood. He scratched his dog behind the ears. "Catch whatever you were chasing, boy?"

Then he heard footsteps on the gravel. Had Thatcher come to get him already? It seemed impossible that the new owners had finished this quickly.

Eleanor stepped into the clearing.

Lockwood froze, his limbs numb while his brain tried to make sense of it. She was here. In England. At his estate. No, former estate.

Good God. Why?

She seemed to sense the riot inside his head, because her mouth curved into a small smile. "Hello, Lockwood."

There were a hundred things he wanted to say, but what came out of his mouth was, "What are you doing here?"

"I heard there was a crumbling pile of rocks that needed saving."

"What?"

She drifted closer and he forced himself to his feet. Christ, she looked gorgeous, her nose pink from the cold, strands of red hair blowing in the soft breeze. He could hardly believe she was here. It seemed like a fever dream, the kind he had as a boy during his illness.

When she stood before him she reached up to stroke the beard he'd grown since returning to England. "Very nice. You look like one of those rough outdoorsmen who chops wood and builds things."

He shivered as her gentle fingers smoothed along his jaw. "Do I?"

"Yes. I quite like it."

Then he would never shave it. "I don't understand why you're here."

"I told you. There was a beautiful English estate for sale and I happened to be in the market."

"You . . . bought Bridgewater? How?"

"Cold hard American cash, Lockwood. You know, the green stuff. Bread, bucks. Though it lacks a heated swimming pool. I am planning to rectify that first."

Hands trembling with the need to touch her, he shoved them into the pockets of his greatcoat. "But why?"

"Because I can. Because this place is important to you." She patted his lapel, smoothing it and avoiding his eye. "Because you are important to me."

Hope sparked in his heart, a tiny flame that brought the organ back to life with an awkward thump. But he'd been wrong before, so he strove to remain calm instead. "Am I?"

"Yes." The word was soft but loaded with meaning. As if she were nervous, she edged away to examine the fountain. "Though I hear a handsome duke comes with the property, as well. It's what really sold me."

"He might be persuaded to stay on, but you'll need to convince him."

"I plan to try. Tell me, is he terribly fussy? I can be a bit stubborn at times, especially when I'm backed into a corner."

"He can be stubborn, too, but something tells me he'll be very forgiving with you."

She cast him a quick glance from under her lashes. "Even if I cause trouble?"

"Even if you cause trouble."

"Because I will be difficult. I'm nothing like these meek women he's used to, the polite ladies who do as they are told."

"Precisely what he needs, if you ask me."

"He might change his mind." She looked over her shoulder, her green eyes like vibrant gems in the gray surroundings. They were eyes he could drown in.

Christ, he loved her so bloody much.

His voice was strong and certain. "Not a chance in hell."

"Still, I will give him ample time to consider his options before any long-term arrangement is finalized."

"Absolutely not. A long-term arrangement is a condition on which the duke will not bend."

She faced him now, her chin set at a determined angle. "Andrew—"

"It's all or nothing, Eleanor. If you thought I'd be satisfied with anything less, then you've wasted your time in coming here."

Though he was dying for her, he would not give in on this point. He wanted her by his side for every moment he had left on this earth, blessed before the eyes of God and man. Nothing less would do.

She closed the distance between them and slid her palms over his chest. He stared down at her lips, dying for a small taste of her once more, as she whispered, "Wouldn't you rather live in sin with me, my love?"

The long-awaited words sent goose bumps along his skin, but this was too important. He forced himself to step away. "I want to marry you. I want the world to know that I've pledged myself to you, that you've honored me by becoming my wife. And it will happen very publicly or not at all."

Their gazes locked for a long moment, the world distilled down to just the two of them.

"I thought you would be happier to see me," she finally said.

In other words, she thought he would give in on everything she wanted. "I am very pleased you're here. Indeed, it feels as though my chest is going to crack open and spill out onto the dirt at your feet. But you knew what I was asking for when I left New York. If you weren't ready to agree, why are you here?"

"I love you," she said quietly. "I'm terrified of what may come, but I cannot do any of this without you. I'm sorry I pushed you away and I hope you can forgive me."

The words soaked into his bones, his heart, creating a bond that would never break, never crumble. He would meet her nerves with calm resolve, her doubt with infinite certainty every single time. "What changed your mind?"

"I think I needed time to wrap my head around it. I let my fear hold me back. Then my aunt asked what was better—to have you for a short amount of time or not at all. I immediately knew the answer. I want you for however long I'm able."

In a few steps he was pulling her into his arms, his mouth meeting hers. He kissed her roughly, with hardly any finesse. He was too greedy, too desperate but she seemed to understand, kissing him back with just as much intensity. When he opened his mouth she did the same, and their tongues met in a frenetic tangle, flicking and twisting as their breath billowed into the cold air. There were too many blasted layers between them but he still ran his hands over her, needing to feel every part he could reach. He would never tire of her, never stop wanting her with every beat of his heart.

When they finally eased apart, he pressed tiny kisses along her cheekbones and eyelids, across her eyebrows and nose. She sighed and rested her forehead against his jaw, and they stood there, just breathing each other in. The terrible knot in his stomach plaguing him for almost two months finally eased, and he slid his palms along her spine. Then over her back and shoulders. Down her arms and elbows, until he threaded their hands together. "I realize I am asking you to give up quite a lot to move here and become an aristocrat, but I vow to make up for it every single day we are together, Eleanor."

"Indeed you will—and I am keeping the estate in my name."

He brought her hand to his mouth and kissed it, clutching her close. "I would expect nothing less. It's yours, after all. But you will marry me."

"I'll marry you under one condition."

His lips twisted at her words. "That I tie you to my bed and have my wicked way with you?"

"That's a forgone conclusion. No, I'll marry you if you go to Austria or Germany this summer to see the heart doctors." Good mood diminished, he released her and started to move away—but she grabbed his lapels, stopping him. "Andrew, please. Not every year, just once."

He hated to see the hope in her gaze, because it was for naught. Doctors couldn't fix him and hearing the news would devastate them both. He didn't want to go, but perhaps it would help her come to terms with his condition, help her prepare for the eventual loss. "If I go this summer, you'll marry me in St. Paul's Cathedral?"

"Yes."

"Fine. I shall go."

"Then I shall marry you in St. Paul's bloody Cathedral. But fair warning. I will divorce you if you do anything I don't like."

As if he'd ever let her go. "Dukes don't divorce."

"This duchess will—and I vow to embark on several public affairs afterward merely to humiliate you."

"If I am stupid enough to lose you, then I deserve no less, darling. But I won't lose you, because I plan to spend every day of my short life making you happy. I love you, beyond titles and estates, and beyond all sense and reason. I am nothing without you by my side."

He heard her breath hitch. "I love you, too."

"Good. And you promise to talk to me whenever you're afraid? You promise not to push me away again?"

"Yes, I promise. You're stuck with me."

He kissed her once more, this time slowly and sweetly. "I'll never let you go. Whatever comes, we'll face it together. That is what it means to love someone."

"And here I thought it meant exemplary orgasms."

His lips curved into his first smile in weeks. "It definitely means those, as well." His gaze slid to the bench. It was a decent height for what he had in mind. "Perhaps you need a demonstration as a gesture of good faith."

"A demonstration of what?"

"Exemplary orgasms. Lean over and put your hands on the side of that iron bench."

"You can't be serious. It's freezing, Andrew."

"Yes, but my mouth is very warm. Please, darling. I'm dying to taste you."

She dragged a finger over his throat and bit her lip. "So polite. What's happened to my crude and rough duke?"

God almighty, this perfect woman. Wrapping his hand around the nape of her neck, he squeezed gently and put his lips near her ear. "Bend over and lift your skirts, Eleanor. I want to lick your pussy and make you scream out my name."

She swayed on her feet, her hand landing on his shoulder to steady herself. "Jaysus, Lockwood."

"Move." He swatted her backside. "After your climax, I'll take you inside and show you the house you have purchased."

Epilogue

❧

Paris, 1897

Eleanor loved Paris, and Paris definitely loved Eleanor.

From his vantage point against the wall, Lockwood happily watched his wife hold court in their drawing room. She knew everyone, was well received in all the various circles, no matter how low or high.

A deep British voice cut through the noise in the drawing room. "Her Grace is a marvel."

A smile tugged at Lockwood's mouth as he addressed the Prince of Wales. "She is, isn't she?"

Bertie lifted his glass in tribute, a lit cigarette in his fingers. "A true bohemian. Say, have the two of you an understanding?"

For other partners. "Absolutely not," Lockwood said with cold finality. No other man would touch her while Lockwood's heart still beat in his chest.

"Now, no need to get prickly, duke. You cannot blame a man for asking."

No, Lockwood didn't blame others for coveting

his wife. He'd covet her, too, if she wasn't already his. "While I do not blame you, I feel it's only fair to warn you that you'll not live to succeed your mother as king if you try it."

Bertie chuckled in response. "Will you both return to London for the jubilee? The Devonshires are hosting a ball, you know."

"Eleanor wishes to travel to New York this summer. We shall likely stay through September." He and his wife split their time between Yorkshire, Paris and New York. It was hectic, but the lifestyle suited them.

Here in Paris, her avant-garde beliefs and exuberance made her nearly a celebrity. She hosted frequent gatherings with a wide variety of artists, writers, thinkers and dancers. On any given night they would host the likes of Loie Fuller and Auguste Lumière, or Isadora Duncan and Pierre Bonnard.

No matter where they were, however, she never missed an opportunity to speak out for women's equality and contraceptives. Her writings had been featured in newspapers and magazines, with her position proving too powerful for repercussions. Even Anthony Comstock himself would not dare to arrest America's favorite duchess.

His wife looked up and caught him staring. Her lips curved into a knowing smile and she excused herself, coming toward him. The emerald green dress she wore was tight, with a neckline that bordered on the indecent. He couldn't wait to peel it off her in a few hours.

When she was close enough, he reached for her

and tucked her into his side. He never tired of touching her. "Hello, darling."

"What are you two discussing over here so seriously?" Her gaze shifted between Lockwood and the prince.

Bertie took a drag off his cigarette. "You, if you must know."

"I am flattered, Your Highness. Incidentally, you must bring Ms. Bernhardt by this week. I saw *La Princesse Lointaine* the other night and I am dying to discuss her part in it."

How quickly Eleanor had turned focus onto Bertie's famous occasional mistress. The prince nodded once. "I'm seeing her tomorrow. I'm sure she'd be thrilled. Though I know the two of you will merely badger me about politics."

"Women's politics, Your Highness. And as a lover of women yourself I would think you'd wish for us all to have the same rights."

Bertie pushed off the wall and tugged on his vest, straightening it. "I know better than to argue with you, Nellie. If you'll excuse me."

"Coward," Eleanor muttered when the prince made his way over to a dancer.

"You'll bring him around on the issue of suffrage yet, love." He kissed her head. "Tonight is another smashing success."

She turned toward him and rested her hand on his chest. "Did he bring up the jubilee? He's asked me twice already."

"Yes, but I said we'd be in America this summer."

Biting her lip, she studied his eyes. "You may change your mind about the trip, you know."

"We made a deal. I will stick to my half of the bargain."

A German doctor had performed a successful cardiac repair last year, and Eleanor had begged Lockwood to go for a consultation. Then it had been his turn to negotiate, to press for something he wanted in exchange.

To his ever-loving shock, she'd agreed.

They would start trying for a child after Eleanor returned from New York next year. Lockwood could hardly bloody wait.

"And I will stick to my half," she said, drawing her hand through the beard he kept for her. "I must admit, I am looking forward to the trying. No shields, no womb veils . . . just your seed shooting inside me."

He inhaled a short breath, the words igniting an inferno in his gut. "If you do not wish to end this dinner party prematurely so that I may fuck you in that dress, then you need to cease speaking."

Eleanor threw her head back and laughed, drawing eyes from across the room. "You're too predictable."

"And you are too gorgeous and utterly desirable."

"Seeing as how you are already excited, I suppose I shouldn't tell you about my surprise, then."

"Surprise?"

"Your heart, love." She patted his chest. "I'm not certain you can take it."

He drew his finger along her décolletage, pleased when she shivered. "Now I'm even more curious."

"You know when I disappeared this afternoon?"

The devilish sparkle in her eyes gave him pause. The last time he saw that expression on her face was when she talked him into buying a pet boa constrictor. She now adored the snake, though Lockwood couldn't for the life of him understand why.

"You said you were going shopping."

"I did. Sort of. You see, Lady Randolph gave me the name of a tattoo parlor here in Paris . . ."

His fingers tightened on her hips, the air disappearing from the room. "You had your body tattooed?"

The tip of her tongue, pink and perfect, emerged to wet her lips. Her voice was low and husky. "I had your name tattooed in a place where no one but you will see it."

His heart skipped then began to race, a staccato in his chest. Fucking hell, this woman.

Desire flooded his body and he made a swift decision. Raising his head, he announced in flawless French, "Pardonnez-moi, but Her Grace is not feeling well tonight. Our staff will show you out."

His wife did a poor job of smothering her laughter. "Andrew, it's still too red and sore."

He didn't care. Taking her hand, he began leading her from the drawing room. Their guests were finishing their drinks, trying to hide their smiles, as the duke dragged the duchess upstairs, fooling not a soul.

"Say, if you change your mind, Lockwood, do let me know." Bertie's voice carried up the steps and Eleanor's eyes narrowed as they entered their chambers.

"Change your mind about what?" she asked as he locked the door.

"Nothing you need worry about." He shrugged out of his evening coat and tossed it onto a chair. "All you need to know is that you're mine . . . and I'm never giving you up."

Acknowledgments

❦

Well, we did it! *high five*

I had so much fun writing Nellie's book, which has been rolling around in my head for a few years now. And Lockwood is just . . . sigh. I love him so much.

A few historical notes and explanations. Settle in!

The Gilded Age saw an unprecedented reversal of women's reproductive rights. Until the middle of the 19th century, abortion was legal and viewed as a private medical procedure. Madame Restell, a "female physician," was the premier abortionist in NYC. She offered up preventative powders, female monthly pills, and other abortifacients. She performed surgical abortions, and also opened up a boardinghouse where clients with unwanted pregnancies could give birth in anonymity. She facilitated the adoption of infants. And she was popular enough to afford to live in a Fifth Avenue mansion.

Enter Anthony Comstock. An anti-vice crusader,

US Postal Inspector, and founder of the New York Society for the Suppression of Vice, Comstock lobbied Congress to make it illegal to distribute "obscene, lewd and lascivious" material through the US mail. The incredibly broad and subjective Comstock Law was quickly used to prohibit the mailing out of any birth control, marriage manuals, anatomy textbooks, or information about abortion. This was eventually widened to make it illegal to directly provide, discuss, or hand out information on birth control. Even for doctors. Comstock made it his personal mission to take down Madame Restell, and he was successful.

Many politicians, scholars, scientists and wealthy folks were in favor of the Comstock laws. Immigrants were flooding the country, and xenophobia was at a fever pitch. In 1883, the theory of eugenics (later referred to as "scientific racism") emerged, claiming that some people and groups were inherently better than others and should reproduce. White women were called upon to do their "duty" to the race by having more white children. I couldn't resist putting Theodore Roosevelt, a supporter of eugenic measures, into a scene with Nellie, but Roosevelt was far from alone in his views.

The movement became "Social Darwinism," and bled out into all areas of US policies, from immigration law to imperialism. It led to laissez-faire capitalism, and the belief that the government should not help the poor, because this interfered with the survival of the "fittest."

(Which they applied to mean only rich white people.)

Blatant racism followed as politicians targeted non-whites. The anti-Chinese movement gathered enough steam for the US government to pass the Chinese Exclusion Act, which prevented Chinese men from bringing Chinese women into the country. In addition, if they left to go back to visit their families in China, they were unable to reenter the US. Laws in the South reversed Reconstruction voting and civil rights, and we saw the beginnings of Jim Crow. By 1900 separation of the races was sanctified by the Supreme Court in *Plessy v. Ferguson*.

The eugenics movement would go on to sweep through Europe. By the 1930s it was a full-blown political movement and we all know what happened then. (At least, you should. If you don't, please look at ushmm.org.)

History doesn't happen in a vacuum. The parallels to what we are experiencing now compared to the late 19th century are truly terrifying. Please support abortionfunds.org, arc-southeast.org, yellowhammerfund.org and other organizations that are fighting for reproductive rights across the county.

Hat tip to Tessa Dare for giving me the idea of having Lockwood jilted in the first three books in the series!

Hat tip to Sarah MacLean for giving me the idea of starting with the moonlight swim!

Hat tip to Diana Quincy for reading an early version and giving me great feedback, as always!

Much thanks to Tessa Woodward, Madelyn

Blaney, Naureen Nashid, Amanda Lara, Guido Caroti and the entire team at HarperCollins/ Avon for all their guidance and support.

Lastly, thanks to all the readers who like to fall in love as much as I do. You're the BEST.

*G*ive in to your Impulses!

**These unforgettable stories only take a second
to buy and give you hours of reading pleasure!**

Go to *www.AvonImpulse.com* and see what we
have to offer.
Available wherever e-books are sold.

AVONIMPULSE

IMP 0811